Maud Jean Franc

Marian

Or, The Light of someone's Home

Maud Jean Franc

Marian
Or, The Light of someone's Home

ISBN/EAN: 9783337082406

Printed in Europe, USA, Canada, Australia, Japan

Cover: Foto ©Andreas Hilbeck / pixelio.de

More available books at **www.hansebooks.com**

MARIAN;

OR,

THE LIGHT OF SOME ONE'S HOME.

A Tale of Australian Bush Life,

BY MAUD JEAN FRANC,

NEW AND CHEAPER EDITION

LONDON

SAMPSON LOW, MARSTON & COMPANY
Limited

CONTENTS.

MARIAN;

OR,

THE LIGHT OF SOME ONE'S HOME.

———◆———

CHAPTER I.

WHEREIN "SWEET WOMAN HAS HER OWN WAY."

"She told her purpose, and her will express'd;
He, listening, yielded—for he thought it best."

"'It does not matter,' Mr. Burton? but I say it *does* matter. I am sure it's a burning shame, that a man of your wealth and position in the colony should have so little care for the education of his children!"

"I don't know, I'm sure, what you're driving at, missus," was the measured retort of her husband, as very quietly, very leisurely, very unconcernedly, he reached forward for the tongs, and lifted one of the glowing embers to ignite the tobacco in his black pipe. He generally took refuge from his wife's attacks in its soothing influence.

B

"You do, Burton—you know as well as I do. Haven't I been worrying and worrying these last six months and more, about one and the same thing?"

"Truly so! You may well say that!" was the dry response; and the pipe was quietly re-admitted into the lips that had parted to utter the sarcasm.

Mrs. Burton felt too indignant to reply. Her indignation only betrayed itself in the energetic manner in which she continued her operation: she was churning, and the splash of the coming butter, and dash of the barrel, formed an apt interlude to the dialogue. But it was not in her nature to be silent long when she had an end in view—a point she had determined to gain; and in a sarcastic tone she resumed, "I can't forget old England and its advantages, if others can."

"Old England!—advantages!—who forgets? Not I," responded her husband, this time rather hastily, for his pipe went out, and he had to raise another ember from the hearth to re-light it. "I know this very well though, old woman," he resumed: "if we had stopped in the 'old country,' your bread would not have been so well buttered, nor your pockets so well lined."

"Well, I know that. 'Old woman,' indeed; you are getting colonial, Burton."

"Pooh! 'what's in a name?'" was the laughing response. The farmer had an old attachment to Shakespeare, and quoted him on all important occa-

sions. " But I say, Bess, my darling, after all, can't
you civilly tell a fellow what you want, without
wasting such a lot of breath.   I am willing and waiting
to hear reason."

" And to attend to it when you hear it ? "

" That's as may be.   But as to education, for that's
the point you are argufying, I suppose, what more do
you want?   Have I not in the busiest time of the
season consented to send two of the boys off to school,
and have they not been gone right off these six months
past ? "

" The boys! yes, that's all right enough ; and badly
till now have they come off, poor fellows !   But the
girls ? "

" That's your look-out; you can do as you like
with them.   Send them too.   Come here, Bessie, you
gipsy ! " he exclaimed, as a little thing of eight years
old went flying through the room with a garland of
wild scarlet pea-flowers wreathed round her slender
little figure.   " Come here, pet, and tell me, would you
like to go to school? "

" To school?   Oh, no, father.   I love making hay,
and feeding the calf, and milking Jenny, and getting
flowers too well."   And the blue eyes were lifted
roguishly to those so fondly looking into them, and the
little figure wriggled up and down to get free from
the clasping hands—the rosy mouth just upturned a
minute to kiss the lips that smiled upon her, and she
was off.

" So much says our Bessie for the school scheme,"

said the father, looking after the little flying figure, and laughing.

"You spoil that child, Burton. What matters it what she says on the subject? However, as it happens, I never dreamt of the school for them. All well enough for the boys; but Julie and Bessie are rough enough already, and it's not likely I should want to send them to a mixed school, and they shall not go if I can help it. No, I had no such idea; my thoughts were quite different."

"I'd like to know them," said her husband, laconically.

"Indeed; I intend you shall. In short, the poor girls are running wild. I'm getting quite ashamed of them when strangers come. They must have a governess."

"We—we—whew! That's the English of it, is it? And where is your governess to be put, pray, missus? We've barely room as it is."

"I suppose you're not so busy that you could not add a couple more rooms, nor so short of timber either," she added triumphantly; "'where there's a will there's a way,' Mr. Burton."

"S'pose there is, wife, but any way will work hard agen this. I thought you were so anxious to get up to the new house, that this very day I sent the men off carting stone. If I stop to build you two more rooms to the old place, you'll have to be contented with it another year. We shall have harvest at our backs before we can turn ourselves. My hay is looking fine

already. I warn you, not a stone will be touched if I
set to building more rooms here, so you can take your
choice."

His wife was silent for a little, weighing the advantages. She knew her husband's tone of voice too
well to feel for a moment she could urge the accomplishment of both her wishes with any chance of
success. The erection of a handsome house, in the
most beautiful and richest part of their home section, had long been the desire of her heart. Indeed,
a garden of four years' luxuriant growth had long
pointed out where the future " Hall " was to rise;
and fruit and vegetables were there in abundant
variety. Yet time had passed on, and substantial
stone barns and outhouses had multiplied, but the
family still lived on in their old slab hut, with its
grey thatched roof, a room being added here and
there as increased accommodation was required, till
it had grown of no inconsiderable size—a thorough
colonial monstrosity. And yet there was a certain
degree of the picturesque lingering around it—slab
hut as it was—that a little redeemed it from the title
of " monstrosity " in its widest sense. Trees had
been left standing at intervals, uncircled by the
fatal ring. The blackwood, with its rich foliage and
dark slight trunk ; the luxuriant cherry-tree, so beautiful in proportion and hue ; the airy, feathery she-
oak, so singular and weird, amidst whose branches
the breezes of heaven whispered their secrets ; and
here and there a lordly gum, evidently permitted to

remain for its majestic breadth of trunk and deep fulness of leafy branches. There was something, too, in the style of the building that betrayed a little native taste; something in the deep setting of the windows, which were unusually large—in the wide spread of the verandah encircling the house—in the very door-step inviting your entrance, that redeemed the whole character of the dwelling. Within, too, there had been an attention to plaster and flooring which was very comfortable and respectable. The furniture was good and substantial, though in many cases rough; and when Mrs. Burton glanced around her broad kitchen—well, though colonially appointed—the gleam of her eye, as well as the exclamation of her tongue, expressed her satisfaction, as she said,—

"We can afford to wait for the new house, Burton."

He drew a long breath, and rose from his seat with a yawn of relief. "Very well, Bess, as you are satisfied, I am. I'm not in such a hurry to quit the old place, I'm sure. There's enough timber felled I suppose for your purpose. We'll set to, right away."

"Yes," said his wife, looking up eagerly from her butter-mould, "now do, for if you and Alf go to Adelaide next week, I'd like you to bring back a governess with you."

"We—we—whew!" replied her husband, with a long, low whistle, "that's not much in my line. However," he added to himself, as he threw an axe upon his shoulder, "I suppose for the sake of peace it will have to be done."

CHAPTER II.

> "A perfect woman—nobly plann'd
> To warn, to comfort, and command;
> And yet a spirit still, and bright,
> With something of an angel light."

VERY bare of furniture, and very desolate in appearance, was a certain little room in a mean, detached cottage in the vicinity of Adelaide. Indeed, there was little but a superfluity of boxes and cases, evidently bearing the impress of a recent voyage, and these had been heaped up and spread out in every available posture and position to supply the place of chairs and couches, and even tables. Feminine hands had done their best to render the articles in question as much like reality as cushions and coverlets and drapery could make them. A few flowers had been gathered somewhere, and stood smiling from a tiny vase at the very barrenness of the place they smiled upon. But no—they had something else to smile upon; some things were in keeping with the flowers, at any rate, in that poor dwelling.

By the rude mockery of a table, two ladies were seated at needlework. Before one of them stood an open work-box, of Indian manufacture—evidently a relic of days of luxury. Both were *petite* in height and figure—there the resemblance ceased—excepting in that proof of gentle blood which was visible in each alike at a single glance. The one was very fair —pale and fair as a snowdrop—and with soft, silky hair of almost golden hue, rolled over a plait of velvet away from her brow and checks. The beauty of her complexion was, however, her chief charm; she was pretty, nothing else—no particular expression—nothing but complexion and a rather good set of features to attract the many glances of admiration that were levelled beneath her broad hat, when she first passed through the streets of our busy metropolis. A lovely child of three summers played at her feet. The same dazzling complexion—the same blue eyes—the same silky hair in one as the other. It needed not the often-reiterated exclamation, "Mamma! Mamma!" to testify the relationship between them.

The other lady, the owner of the elegant work box, seemed to have monopolized all the character in her countenance; though a very pretty feminine countenance, it was constantly *prononcé;*—pretty as small and delicate features, full curling rosy lips, sweet hazel eyes, and rich brown natural ringlets could make it. The complexion was rather dark, but enlivened by the rich blood which softly tinted her check. The eyes in repose were almost voluptuously languid; excited, they glowed with very intensity, and the full, broad, noble brow was so tastefully sheltered by the soft, dark curls in their natural wave, that it had not a whit of the masculine in it. A little graceful figure she was, reclining on her box-seat against the rough plastered wall, with eyes bent down on her work so that their deep fringe almost kissed her cheek. She was in a thoughtful mood, and the expression of her face was very grave.

For a long time the little Emmeline had all the prattle to herself; but at length the last lady gave an upward glance, and, as though by the touch of a magic wand, the expression of her countenance entirely changed—the lips parted, the cheek lighted, the eyes danced with the sweet smile that sprang forth at her words.

"Well, Isabel, is William to be successful to-day, or not? A penny for your thoughts!"

"Oh, I don't know," sighed her companion, wearily; "I wish we had never left England."

"But as we are here, dear Isabel, would it not be better to hope for the best, and make the best of things, as we have already done with our boxes?"

"As *you* have done."

"Well, dear, as *I* have done, if you refuse any copartnership in the matter. However, I am quite hopeful to-night. It may be those beautiful hills tinted with rose-colour—dear Isabel, do look at them! are they not lovely?—it may be those that have touched my day-dreams with the same rosy hue;

I cannot say, but assuredly I believe William will return successful to-night."

"And you are a true prophetess, Maid Marian, this time, at any rate!" exclaimed a cheerful voice in the entry, and with the voice entered the gentleman in question, all life and spirit, whose first mad action was to snatch up the child from the floor, and toss her high to the ceiling in triumph, while the young mother looked up in absolute terror, forgetting in the midst of her expostulations to ask a question, which deficiency Marian immediately supplied.

"Be serious, William, can't you?" she exclaimed. "Don't you think we are dying to know all about your success? Come, sit down, do—there's a kind cousin!"

"I declare," he exclaimed, at length yielding to her entreaties, and sinking into her seat, "I declare I could hug every one of you for very joy. Here have I been toiling about, day after day, for more than a fortnight, with the precious remembrance of a sinking capital, and not an atom of success in any quarter, and to-day I have lighted on the very thing—a situation that will make us independent again, little pale one! Think of that!"

Isabel did think, and tears of joy came with the thought, but she wept them out on her husband's bosom. After all the anxiety of their first fortnight in the colony, it was so very sweet to look forward to comfortable certainty again. The husband and wife were too much engrossed for a time to think of any thing but each other, and Marian quietly resumed her work, though the flush of excitement and disappointment had deepened on her cheek; for *she* had a stake in the lottery of life;—*she* had also been anxiously looking, all those weary days, for a letter—an answer, only a single one, to her advertisement, and none had arrived, notwithstanding all her weary waiting.

"Wait—trust still," she thought to herself; "the answer will come, 'if it tarry, wait for it.' Oh! it is hard work this waiting, and when the purse is so nearly empty. But the promise is accompanied by the injunction 'Be of good courage.' What faith it requires!—and yet I will not despond."

"Here, Marian! bless me, what a fool I am! look up a moment, dear Isabel," exclaimed William Grenville, impetuously rising: " the answer's come at last, so don't look so grave. There's a pair of them to choose from!" and diving into his pocket, he threw two letters into her lap.

"At last!" she exclaimed, the colour mounting to her brow. "And I have doubted!" was her mental exclamation.

She tore open the first, and quietly perused it, the colour mounting every moment higher and higher, even to the roots of her hair. It was from a bachelor, requiring not a governess, but a housekeeper, or rather, a wife. She tossed it aside to her cousin, simply saying,—

"You can do anything you like with this."

"I should like to chastise the fellow for his impertinence then!" was the excited reply, as he read the letter in company with his wife; and then tearing it passionately in pieces, threw it into the stove.

"I fancy the best answer will be none at all," replied Marian, with slightly curling lip. Turning again to the other letter, "O William," she exclaimed at last, with a brilliant smile, "this will do—the very thing! two little girls to instruct—with light domestic employment—to be treated as one of the family—at a farmstead fifty miles up the country. This will do, and I shall do for it."

"Dear, brave little Marian!" and William Grenville caught her round her waist, and gave her a hearty kiss. "I don't know what we shall do without you. Fifty miles away! No, child, I think you had better wait."

"Wait for what?" replied Marian laughing and blushing. Then pushing back his arm, "I must wait to-night, so says the note; to-morrow I shall certainly *wait on* Mr. Burton. As to the distance, Isabel has you to take care of her, and we can write to each other, and you will know I am safe."

"Not so sure of that," teazingly replied William. "I don't seem to like your going. We shall have some of those rough bushmen running off with you, perhaps, and never see you again."

"Rest secure on that score," said Marian, making an abrupt rise, and darting from him just as he seemed inclined to repeat his offence.

CHAPTER III.

FIRST IMPRESSIONS OFTEN HAPPY ONES.

"The open brow, the softly boaming eye,
The happy smile,—what else could they require?"

" I TELL you, Alf, I don't like the job. I wish we could have got your mother down. I know well enough how to set about hiring men-folk; but women-kind are a different thing—governesses of all others! I am afraid I shall never remember half the questions to ask her."

" I should not ask her many, father," replied Alf, laughing; " I think if I liked her looks and manners, I should be satisfied without any more."

The father turned a full, clear, half-quizzing eye on the youth opposite him, and slightly shook his head. " No doubt that would be enough for *you*," he replied, " but how would it do with the mother ? "

Alf only laughed, and went carelessly on with his breakfast, and his father musingly continued—" Yes, it must be something beyond good looks, if Julie and Bessie are to get any good from their governess."

" But good looks don't hinder good teaching, father," urged the youth.

"Maybe not.   I wish you could have done the business; but I see that would never do though— you are only seventeen, Alf.   Besides, the lady herself wouldn't like it.   Well, it's time I was off, or I shan't have done that stroke of business I mentioned to you about the wheat, in time for this other appointment."   And he jumped up, took his hat, and left the room.

"Don't forget, father, the servant mother wanted," shouted Alf mischievously after him, as he walked down the passage.

"Confound the petticoats!" was the reply, deep and low.

If he had only a lady-friend to do the business for him!   But he had not; for the lady at whose house the appointment was made, he learned, had been suddenly called away a few miles from Adelaide, and his time was too limited to allow him to wait her return.   He had only, therefore, the alternative of meeting the governess in person; and with many uneasy, awkward feelings, the wealthy landowner, with his pockets lined with gold, turned his steps to the house in question.   He reached it, and a moment after was shown into a little parlour, half dark it appeared to him, for the blinds were let down to exclude the sun, and everything appeared black as he entered.

When sight was restored to him, he became conscious that a little figure had risen from an adjacent couch, and stood waiting his pleasure—and such a little figure—such a sweet, fresh face—that the worthy farmer, scarcely knowing what he did, seized the little hand, and shook it warmly.

"I am here in compliance with the request of your letter," said a soft voice. But Mr. Burton interrupted—"Oh, yes. Do you think it will suit you though, miss? You have never been in the country, have you?"

"I have only arrived a fortnight in the colony," said Marian, with a smile. "I want a home—I cannot stay with my friends; I wish to be useful and independent."

"I think you'll do us well enough," returned the farmer, entirely forgetting the string of questions, and as much taken as Alf would have been by the pretty little face and figure. "I guess you'll do us —that is, the missus—well enough. But the thing is, miss, I'm afraid you won't like our country ways and life."

"I think I shall, very much," replied Marian, laughing. "Will you try me?" she added, quietly.

"With all my heart! and if you should not like up home, I'll engage to bring you back to your friends. That's all fair."

"Or if Mrs. Burton should not like me," put in Marian, rather archly.

"No fear of that," said the farmer, laughing; "my good wife has a kind heart in her, and nags no one but me, and I don't care, so you will be safe. Now don't you want to know something about us?"

"My cousin came with me. He has learned from the gentleman of the house all that is necessary. He will be happy to see you, sir. He is waiting below. Do you leave town soon?"

"By six to-morrow morning at latest," returned the farmer. "Can you be ready?"

"The notice is short; but I can be ready as you wish. My cousin, Mr. Grenville, will bring me and my luggage."

"Then till that time, good-bye;" and he heartily shook her hand. "I will see your cousin, and arrange matters with him;" and with another glance at Marian, he turned away, well satisfied with the business he had accomplished.

"Well, father, is this irksome matter settled?" was the laughing exclamation of Alf, as, about two hours after, Mr. Burton sauntered into the room in time for dinner.

"Settled, signed, and sealed, boy. What's for dinner?"

"I don't know. But, father, have you seen her? Is she good-looking, this governess?"

"Yes. A regular stunner. A great deal too pretty and too good for the bush, Alf; that's all I'm afraid of. But she thinks not, though I told her as much. She thinks she shall like the bush."

"So say I," said Alf, "if she's any sense. Who would not prefer the bush to dusty old Adelaide? My throat won't get clear till I've had a good drink of water from our spring. It never does."

"Well, I'm afraid she won't like to stop. I have a very good opinion of her, poor young thing—an orphan too. Her friends speak highly of her. I don't think the bush will suit her; she's too pretty."

"Why?" asked Alf, half piqued for his favourite home.

"Why—if you were a little older, Alf; but then there is Allen. Well, I have my own thoughts; but I am afraid, after all, it won't do."

Alf waited with no little curiosity the approach of *six* the next morning. The Irish servant was already in the dray, with her own and the young lady's luggage, besides a whole host of home-purchases, from hats for the girls to tobacco for the men. Alf and his father were riding, and on a horse close by was a new side-saddle; and when, within the time, Marian Herbert appeared in her riding-dress and broad hat, her soft brown ringlets playing over her flushed cheeks, her hand clasped in that of her cousin, Alf felt she was almost too good for them.

"She will be the light of some one's home," thought Grenville, as, having assisted her to the saddle, and received her half tearful, half gay adieu, he stood moodily watching her as they cantered off. She turned once and waved her hand to him. He raised his hat from his brow, and the next moment she was gone.

Left alone with her new companions, very naturally Marian's first inclination was to look at them more closely. She could do this very well beneath her broad hat without being observed. She took her fill of observation. The farmer rode at her side. A fine, tall, stout man he was. So strong he looked, as though he could have lifted her in his arms, and carried her all the way without fatigue. There was a free, frank, open expression in his countenance that greatly pleased her. The lines of the mouth were relaxed very often to smile, and his laugh was genuine and hearty.

Mr. Burton, or Squire Burton, as he was often called in his own neighbourhood, was by no means a bad-looking man; and Alf, who rode slightly in advance, had all the glorious promise of his father's manhood. He was truly the *son of his father;* the same clear brow, the same laughing blue eye, the same tall figure, only it was fair hair that curled up from his sunburnt brow and peeped beneath the brim of his cabbage-tree hat.

" If these are only samples of the rest of the family, I shall do very well," thought Marian, as she finished her observations; and by the time they reached the end of their day's journey, the three were on the best possible terms with each other, and Alf had so far forgotten his shyness as to leap from his horse when they stopped at the little inn where they were to pass the night, make a stirrup with his hand, and receive the little governess, as she dismounted from her steed, in his arms.

" Yes," he murmured to himself, before he closed his eyes that night, " I am afraid she is too pretty, too gentle to manage Julie and Bessie, the wild gipsies, however she may succeed with Allen and me."

CHAPTER IV.

A SLY PEEP IN THE MOONLIGHT.

"In full-orb'd glory, yonder moon divine,
Rolls through the dark blue depths."

IT was October; and though the days were warm, the
evenings were generally chilly. Now and then, to
be sure, would come a suffocating night, close and
sultry, when open doors and windows became very
desirable, just to remind one of what might be
expected later in the season. But in general, particularly in the October of our tale, closed doors
and blazing logs were still considered pleasant and
requisite.

The dew had fallen heavily after sunset, and the
evening consequently proved cold and comfortless
without, but a glowing log breathed a warm welcome
on the wide hearth of the homestead sitting-room,
and the rich light danced and gleamed over the
plentifully set tea-table, glittering on the bright
spoons and shining blue ware, and immense can-like
tea-pot. Mr. Burton and Alf were expected home—
two who were always missed from the homestead
when away, and warmly welcomed on their return

On counting the cups, too, that stood in readiness on the board, it was easy to discern that one more than the family was expected, without the evidence of slight nervousness that Mrs. Burton occasionally exhibited, or the flushed cheeks that the girls turned towards the door at every slight sound that rose without.

It was a very pleasant room, that sitting-room—very; in spite of that colonial look of homeliness that was strongly visible everywhere. The tables—there were two of them—one back against the wall, the other, stretching its huge length down the centre of the room—were, like the chairs and settles, of roughly hewn gum and cedar, with the exception of two large easy-chairs, occupying either side of the hearth, whose luxurious cushions of maroon leather and good workmanship made them look a little out of place with the rest of the furniture, only the leather had lost its pristine purity, and bore evidence of being often in requisition. They were for the use of the heads of the family, but little enough Mrs. Burton used hers. The seat she slighted was by common consent usually occupied by her eldest-born, Allen, her favourite son, if indeed she had any favourites.

We have said it was a difficult matter for Mrs. Burton to keep quiet long. It was not her forte, perpetual motion suited her better. At the present moment, as she considered it unbecoming her dignity to appear engaged in any domestic employment on the first entrance of the stranger, she had taken a seat near the table, and was knitting away with an energy which promised the speedy completion of the stocking in hand. She was a little woman—big men usually take little wives—a plump little woman, with a pleasant, brisk, motherly air and soft motherly eyes, albeit eyes that could flash and sparkle when they liked, and that saw into everything that was going on. The hair that swept from the brow in soft bands was very light, a kind of hair that is unknown to silver; and a very pretty tasteful black cap, with a running wreath of forget-me-nots on either side behind the ear, completed the pleasant picture. She had been very pretty, that was evident in the good features remaining, and by no means vulgar; for, amidst all her colonial experience there was a sort of *gentility* (we will use the hateful word, for we have no better to express our meaning) remaining. And notwithstanding a decided love for her own way, and attachment to the last word, as her husband always said, she was a devoted wife, a careful, industrious housekeeper, and a most loving mother—in her turn tenderly beloved.

Bessie, the pet, the romp, the plaything of the family, was seated on a low stool at her mother's feet, mischievously engaged in tying a handkerchief round the head and face of a black kitten, and then making it run, and merry was her pealing laughter as, in its fright and blindness, it knocked first against one thing and then against another, mewing aloud in its terror.

In the depth of one large chair—her father's chair—sat Julie, a tall, fair girl of thirteen, with languid blue eyes, and a very pale, delicate complexion, tinted only with the faintest rose. Her long silken hair was parted smoothly behind her ears, but hung over her shoulders in profusion in a state of nature. One little hand supported the pretty rounded chin, the other lay listlessly upon her lap. Very pensively was the little maiden gazing into the fire ; and had she been a year or two older, the tinge on her cheek, deepening with every passing sound, the quiver of the red lips, the trembling of her hands, would have warranted other conclusions. As it was, she was only expecting the governess, and not a lover.

In the opposite chair, his accustomed seat, reclined in perfect ease the eldest son, Allen, with a book in his hand, from which he now and then threw a very amused look at his mother and Julie. He noted well the rapid, restless movement of the knitting-needles, and the quick flushing of his sister's cheek.

"How frightened they are at this unknown woman!" he thought, with a smile curling his slightly moustachioed lip; "frightened at the very fulfilment of their wishes. I wonder myself rather what she is like ; it does not follow necessarily that she must be either old or ugly."

A fine-looking young fellow Allen was, but not so stout as Alf. His eyes were of a deeper blue,—more his mother's eyes, more like Julie's,—and his waving hair, sweeping far back from a very good forehead, was much darker, and carefully attended to, while his brother's was often in disorder. Even the dress he wore had somewhat a gentlemanly appearance; the dark stuff jumper descending lower than ordinary, and open at the bosom to display a clean shirt and carefully tied silk neckcloth; and his boots, though strongly, were neatly made, showing that appearance was studied almost equally with strength; they were clean, too, these latter appendages, for he liked clear boots, though he very often had to clean them himself. But somehow or other, all the lighter—the less rough—portion of the farm-work fell to Allen by common consent. He in general transacted business in Adelaide, rode to the neighbouring township for letters, or, stock-whip in hand, brought in cattle from the run, or drove them out, as might be. He undertook the buying or selling of stock, the overlooking of the men, sometimes the payment of wages. In all these things he was his father's right hand—the pride of his mother's heart. But he never touched the handle of a plough, never drove a dray, never held a sickle; Alf was the master here, and as skilful in his departments as his brother in those peculiar to him. There was several years' difference between the brothers, though Alf looked much older than he really was.

Two other boys there were, Frank and Charlie, the one between Alf and Julie, the next between Julie and Bessie. These, as our first chapter intimated, were at the distant township, *getting education*, and had been doing so *right off* for six months. Poor boys! in common with other bush children, they had had little enough previously, except that which the farm afforded, and of that they had had a pretty good share. We need not say how culpable is the conduct of many parents in our adopted country, who, awarding to the schoolmaster a quarter now and a quarter then, are pleased to term this *educating their children.* Surely no better fate awaits the unfortunate tutor of these very wild *young ideas* than that inflicted, according to the heathen fable, as a severe punishment—the filling with water of a tub full of holes. O love of the filthy lucre, how dost thou worm into the very heart of our people! Gold, gold! what a canker thou leavest in the soul!

But why should we say all this at the present moment, when, too, *Education* was very pleasantly cantering along the beaten road to the homestead in Squire Burton's company. Forgive us, gentle reader, that even for a moment we should have forgotten it.

"Your father is late," at length said Mrs. Burton, addressing Allen, and giving vent to her growing weariness.

"A sure proof he has some one with him not accustomed to long journeys on horseback, mother," replied Allen, smiling.

"Hark!—yes! Here they are. There is Alf's signal." And clear and musical, though still distant, rose the well-known cooey on the quiet breeze.

Allen rose quickly from his seat, and took his hat.

"Where are you going, Allen?" asked his mother, anxiously.

"To the slip-panel, mother; it's not worth while for father or Alf to dismount to let it down." Then, turning laughing to his sister, who had sprung to her feet, and stood shivering with excitement before the fire, he put his arm caressingly round her, exclaiming, "You little goose, how you tremble! What have you to be frightened about? Don't you think your big brother will be able to protect you from all the governesses in the colony?"

"O Allen!" and the tears came quickly with the sigh, but they were hid on his arm: "O Allen, I can't stay in the room."

He took hold of the pale little face in both his hands and kissed the trembling lips. "You shan't then," he exclaimed, firmly. "Go, put on your hat and shawl, and come with me. We'll have a sly peep at this formidable governess together in the moonlight."

"Where are you off to, Julie?" inquired her mother, as, wrapt in shawl and hood, she joyfully but timidly followed Allen to the door.

"She is off with me, mother. I want her." And knowing *that* explanation was conclusive, they set off together.

"O Allen," said Julie, with a sigh of relief, "I am so glad you let me come with you."

"You are trembling yet, little puss;" and he passed his arm firmly round her waist.

"Oh, I don't care now," said Julie; "I don't know why I am so frightened, either."

"Nor I. After all, perhaps you may frighten the lady more than she will frighten you, Julie."

She laughed merrily. "I! How could I, Allen?"

"How? Why with this long hair of yours. I should not wonder if she take you for a mermaid. I hope she reckons hair-dressing among her other accomplishments, and will make my little sister a young lady in appearance; as lady-like as she is good and pretty."

"There is Alf's cooey again," said Julie, after a moment's pause. "Won't you cooey an answer, Allen?"

"I never cooey, Julie, but I will answer;" and ne turned up the end of the whip he held in his hand, and blew a series of clear, shrill blasts. The moment after they stood at the slip-panel, and Allen leisurely let down the rails one after the other, and then, taking his sister again round the waist, drew her into the shadow of a she-oak, a little on one side of the entrance.

"There now, Julie, we can satisfy our curiosity as much as wo like. We can see them clearly in the bright moonlight, but they cannot tell us till we show ourselves. Ah, there they come, helter skelter! No. Well, I never! Bravo, Alf! Do you see them

Julie?   Alf is not overawed at any rate; he is leading her horse."

"Where, Allen, where?" whispered Julie.

"Coming down the hill.   Don't you see?"

"Oh, yes.   She wears a large hat.   Allen, hark!" For a clear sweet laugh, in answer to a speech from Alf, came echoing down the hill.

"What do you think of that, Julie?" exclaimed her brother.   "Nothing very frightful there, I should say."

"The slip-panel is down, father," cried Alf, "and Allen is somewhere about, I know.   That was his whistle, I'm sure."

Allen and Julie laughed in their retreat.   They could not be seen, and at the same moment the whole party rode into sight.

"The homestead is close at hand now, Miss Herbert," cried Alf, laughing.   "This is father's home section."

"I am very glad, for I really am tired now," returned Marian's musical voice.   "Do we dismount here?"

"If Allen was only here," cried Alf, "he could help me in with the horses, and then you could walk up to the house with father."

"Allen is here," said his brother, coming forward with Julie.   He had whispered that an introduction in that pale moonlight would be better than in the full blaze of the log-fire at home.   "Allen is here, at your service, Alf;" and raising his hat from his brow, he approached the lady's horse.

"If the young lady would allow me to lead her horse, I should suggest that plan as the best. The grass is very damp. I think my sister's feet are already wet."

"My son, my eldest son Allen," said the squire, riding up. "And well, I declare, there is one of your pupils, Miss Herbert. Why, Julie! is that you?"

"Could not stop in the house till you came, father! so I brought her along," said Allen, laughing.

Julie was thankful he had spoken for her, though she was very much reassured by a sight of the face beaming beneath the hat, and by the kind pressure of the little hand that bent over the saddle to take hers, as well as by the easy manners of her father and Alf.

"Lift her up to me, Allen; she is not more glad to see me, than I her," said the squire. And Allen took his sister in his arms, and placing her before his father, returned to his self-constituted post.

"Two more of the family," thought Marian—"all well yet;" and she gave a satisfied glance at the tall, not ungraceful figure in the belted jumper, who walked before with such perfect *nonchalance*, the bridle on his arm, and his hand upon the neck of the horse.

"All right, Julie?" he whispered, as he lifted her down from her father's horse, when they stopped at the door.

A low satisfied "Yes" rewarded him for his trouble, and he turned away to assist the young governess to alight. As he did so, the full light of the sitting-room poured through the open door, and the sweet face beneath the hat was fully revealed to him.

CHAPTER V.

THE NEW HOME.

"No home is by the wanderer found—
'Tis not in place : it hath no bound.
It is a circling atmosphere
Investing all the heart holds dear."

VERY timidly the morning sun stole in and gilded one end of the pillow on which Marian's head rested. It did not wake her; she had been awake from the first peep of day, not dreaming, but reflecting upon her novel situation. She had been successful, very successful; she thought of this with clasped hands and closed eyes. He, the "Father of the fatherless," had not forsaken her, she could trust Him still, trust Him with all her perplexities, all her troubles, all her trials, and she would do so, for in no safer hands, in no safer friend could she confide.

She sat up a moment, leaning back against her pillow, to survey her room ; for the night previous she was too tired, too glad to jump into bed, too thankful to fall asleep, to notice anything about it ; and now, refreshed with a quiet, undisturbed night, she enjoyed looking round her and taking notes accordingly.

And a very neat little room it was for a bush residence; but Marian had too recently arrived from England not to be greatly amused with what she saw. The rough, plastered, whitewashed walls, the calico ceiling, the uneven, loose-boarded floor, diverted her highly, and the quaint little window, in its wooden framework, unpainted, unpolished, seemed so strange to her. And yet in how many houses, instead of that calico ceiling, she would have looked up to the rafters, and seen the stars shining above her head; instead of that rough-boarded floor, her little feet, as she sprang from her bed, would have encountered the bare earth.

But was there a repining thought in the depths of Marian's heart? No, not one. Only pleasure—thankfulness; yes, absolute pleasure. The reception had been so kind, so warm, that she felt in reality she should "be treated as one of the family." And this prepared her to be pleased with all she saw. It was so pleasant, in this strange land, to find a home—the very thing of all others her soul craved after. Her eyes soon formed an inventory of her accommodation. A large packing-case, neatly curtained with chintz, and covered with a snowy cloth, did duty as a toilette table; on this a large and rather handsome looking-glass swung in its polished frame; a washstand of unpainted wood, the work of some country carpenter, supplied with ample earthenware accommodation, and plenty of fresh, clear water and towels, occupied another corner. Two chairs, and her little iron bedstead, white and snowy in its arrangement, completed the list. She walked to the window, and drawing aside the little white curtain, looked out. Ah! that was a sight worthy of long regard, for the additional rooms had certainly been built at the best side of the house. What a slope—green and grassy! down from the very house it went, ending in a little creek, the murmur of whose waters she could hear even there. There they came, rushing and tumbling wildly down a little broken declivity. She could see the miniature cascade, the white foam, the troubled waters, as they rushed on and on, hiding themselves at length from her view amidst a cluster of tea-tree bushes. Then across that creek, spanned by a fallen tree, how pleasant to look! up and up the eye must go. Grass, and huge blocks of rock, and flowers showing their blue heads, and trees—golden-tipped, light, feathery trees, new to her eye—the mystic she-oak, with its strange whispering leaves, in clusters they stood, here and there interspersed by an old gum or a young cherry tree; and above all these was the sky, fair, rose-tinted in its first young beauty, blushing at her regard.

Marian crept back to her bed with her lashes positively gemmed with happy tears; she threw her arms round her pillow, and hid her face upon it, and in utter gratitude of heart she breathed forth her morning prayer—a prayer that she might not have come vainly to this lovely spot; that her life might be one of usefulness, of devotedness to Him who had given it; and as she prayed, she slept, and her sleep was sweet.

When she again awoke, it was with the very audible sounds of active life around her. The inmates of the homestead had long been up, and were all employed in their usual avocations. The lowing of cows, the cackling of hens, the neighing of horses, and the rumbling of the dray-wheels all burst upon her astonished ear together, and presently a strange, sharp, cracking noise without, followed by a rush of trampling hoofs, completed her consternation. In a moment she had leaped to the floor, and was once more at the window. Peeping this time more cautiously between the curtains, she was just in time to hear a repetition of the strange sounds, and to discover its cause. A mob of cattle rushed passed the window, cows fresh and wild from the run, with tiny calves lowing at their sides, and behind and round them, here and there, exhibiting no little skill in his horsemanship, Allen himself, stock-whip in hand, the immense lash of which he flourished to the no little disturbance of Marian's nerves. She flinched with every crack.

And there, as she stood with her dishevelled curls resting on the delicate, frilled collar of her white night-robe, scarcely recovered from her startled awakening, the door of her room was softly opened, and Mrs. Burton peeped in. She had expected to find the inmate of the room still sleeping, but as this was not the case, she advanced boldly in with a kind "Good-morning."

Marian was peeping yet through the window, and, more startled than ever, turned hurriedly round to see who had entered. A bright blush and a sweet smile stole over her face as she recognized the intruder, and took the offered hand, exclaiming, " I fear I am very late. Am I not ? "

" I intended you should be, after your long journey," replied Mrs. Burton ; " I tried to keep the house as quiet as I could, but I expect Allen's whip has done the mischief."

" Oh, thank you ; but I am quite rested now ; I ought to be up. That whip startled me much ; I could not imagine what it was."

" Have you never heard a stock-whip before, my dear ? " said Mrs. Burton, laughing.

" Never. I was never even at a farm-house in England ; I have always been accustomed to London."

" And do you think you shall like a country life ? " asked Mrs. Burton, rather doubtfully.

" Oh, very much ! " said Marian, warmly, " I am sure I shall."

Mrs. Burton looked very pleased. " We shall have something to teach you, as well as you us," she replied, smiling. " There's a deal of difference between town and bush life."

" I shall like of all things to learn."

Had she said this as a mere stroke of diplomacy, which was far from the case, it would have been impossible for her to have uttered anything that would have gained her a place so quickly in the heart of the mistress of the homestead. She was rewarded by a very loving look, a pressure of the hand, and finally a very motherly kiss ; and then assuring her that a nice little breakfast would be awaiting her in the sitting-room, the kind-hearted woman bustled away, and left her to dress in peace.

She very soon accomplished that task, and stood in the sitting-room once more. How pleasant it looked in the morning light, with the bright bar of sunshine all across its floor, and breakfast nicely arranged for two, at one end of the long table. For two ? Yes, for the family had long since taken their morning meal ; and Allen, who had just returned from his early ride in the scrub, was hungry,—she heard him exclaim, laughing, to his mother, as she entered, "hungry as a hunter." He stopped short, not a little confused, as he caught sight of Marian in the entrance ; then mastering his bashfulness, with an effort he came forward, throwing aside his hat on his way to receive her, and wheeling the large chair he usually occupied, to the place assigned her at the table.

"Mother tells me my whip startled you very much this morning," he exclaimed, after rather an awkward pause. There was a look of merriment in his eyes as he said it.

" I was a little frightened," replied Marian, smiling. " The sound was new to me. Had you far to go for those cattle ? "

"Not far—twelve miles—I started at four this morning."

"Do you call twelve miles not far?" asked Marian, in surprise.

He laughed. "A mere trifle; our next-door neighbour is four miles distant. We have twelve miles to go for our letters."

"You cannot go very often for them, then." The tone was rather a concerned one.

"Every week, Miss Herbert," put in Mrs. Burton; "no one thinks much of such a ride in these parts."

Marian was glad to hear of it. The thought of her letters lying twelve miles distant for weeks would have been very intolerable.

"Oh," said Allen, "after you have been here a little time you will think nothing of such a ride. Here is part of my morning's work," and rising, he drew to her feet a string of wild pigeons—bronze-winged pigeons—beautiful even in death.

"Oh, what lovely creatures! What a pity to kill them!" and Marian took them in her hand and smoothed the ruffled plumage.

"I fancy you will not say that at dinner, Miss Herbert," was the amused reply. "By the bye, mother, don't stew them, put them in a pie, they are much nicer so."

CHAPTER VI.

"Fresh as the month, and as the morning fair,
Adown her shoulders fell her length of hair."

A few days passed on, and Marian Herbert and the homestead inmates were thoroughly at home with each other. Besides her morning occupation of instruction, she had taken many lessons. She had tried her hand at milking, with Julie, to the very great amusement of the brothers, who contrived to be by on these occasions. She had churned and made up butter with Mrs. Burton; sliced tobacco for the Squire's pipe; hunted for eggs with Bessie; practised leaping her horse over a log with Allen, and spoilt a beautifully crowned furrow with Alf, who insisted she should make a trial of the plough, because she told him "Ploughing looked easy enough, though very awkward;" and so she had been scarcely a week with them when she was as much domesticated as though she had been a year. Her natural, free, frank way and manner, and ready aptitude in adapting herself to the habits of those around her, were the principal cause of this, but scarcely more so than the careless, independent feeling engendered in the bush, yielding equality to all. Besides, hospitality is one of the household virtues of an Australian homestead, and in her case it was fully exercised.

Julie and Bessie were not long in discovering they had nothing to fear from their new governess; the roguish blue eyes of the romp took but a five minutes' consideration of the subject, and then the little hand stole into that extended to her, and with a sly upward glance she exclaimed,—

"I don't think you will beat me."

"Beat you, Bessie?—no. How could you think of such a thing?" returned Marian, laughing. "I am here to teach, and not to beat you. Do you not know, Bessie, it is one of the most delightful things to learn?"

"Shall I be able to feed Jenny's calf, and play with Watch, and hunt eggs, if I learn?" asked Bessie, rather wistfully.

"Assuredly you will, and I will help you," though the last clause in the conditions rather puzzled Marian.

"Are eggs gifted with the power of locomotion in the bush?" she asked of Alf, who was present at Bessie's examination.

He looked up from the spurs he was brightening with rather a puzzled expression, and she repeated the question in a simpler form.

"Bessie talks of 'hunting eggs;' do eggs in the bush run off as soon as laid, like the hens that lay them?"

"Ha! ha! ha! Ha! ha! ha!" Alf laughed most heartily.

"Why, Alf, what is the matter?" cried his mother, peeping in at the sitting-room door in surprise.

"He is only laughing at my ignorance, Mrs. Burton. I did not quite understand what Bessie meant by 'hunting eggs.'"

"Bessie, you will show Miss Herbert how you hunt eggs, won't you?" said her brother, a little recovered from his laughter.

The little girl looked from one to the other with a grave kind of scrutinizing glance. She was not quite satisfied as to the subject of their laughter, but she answered "Yes," half bashfully, and then added, with a look up at Marian,—

"Shall I?"

And that being conceded, Miss Herbert was soon instructed in the egg-hunting business, and Bessie's little wild heart from that day forth was entirely won. The daily lessons went on well and rapidly, and so did the amusements too, a trifle less boisterously, perhaps, excepting when her father or Alf took a share in the fun, and they loved to see her in her wildest moods. On the part of the latter, Marian suspected a little mischievous intention; but she left it to time to tame the little gipsy (for a work of time she knew it must be), and never hinted her suspicions.

In Julie she had a more tractable pupil. The materials were of a different character altogether. Not simply because she was older, but constitutionally, habitually different. Much might be ascribed to her attachment to her eldest brother, much to his affection for her. When he was at home she was always near him. He often chose her for his companion when he went to shoot in the neighbouring scrub; and, seated together under some shady tree, he had taught her to read. He read with her and to her from a volume of fugitive poems, that softened her nature, refined her spirit, subdued her style. To Allen, who had no little romance in his inner nature, it was a great pleasure to see his pet sister rapidly improving in loveliness as she increased in years. He had been the secret instigator at his mother's elbow, broaching the question of a governess, for he knew that his sisters would have a handsome dower, and he longed to see them occupy a good position in the land of their birth. Education, he knew, was the first step on the ladder of life.

To give pleasure to Allen was a joy to Julie's heart. She had not forgotten what he had called her,—"a mermaid," with her long, loose, flowing hair; and after that she stole many times to the glass, to see if she could possibly devise any way more becoming; for it was yet a stretch beyond her courage to appeal to Miss Herbert on the subject. But it was all in vain. Her inventive powers had flown.

At length, about three or four days after her arrival, Miss Herbert, as she was passing quietly through the room adjoining her own, which had been set apart for the school-room, and simply, though neatly, furnished for the purpose, was suddenly arrested by an unexpected sight. There was an antique glass in one corner of the room, placed there for no particular purpose, excepting that of adding to the furnished appearance of the place. It had been made use of that evening though, evidently, for before it was brush and comb, and tangled ribbon; and seated on a chair, with her long, fair arms extended on the table beneath, and her face hidden on them, while in wilder disorder than ever, the beautiful hair fell over her shoulders, was Julie, in despair and tears.

What could it mean? Marian stopped a moment to ask herself the question—just a moment—and then softly tiptoed to Julie's side, and lifted her up, exclaiming with a half-merry, half-sympathizing face, "Why, Julie!"

Julie half struggled to get away, in her sudden surprise; then glancing into the kind face looking down at her, she as suddenly twined her arms round Marian's waist, and hid her tearful eyes on her bosom.

"In trouble, Julie, and not tell me!" said Marian, half reproachfully. "Come, come, that is scarcely fair."

"But it is such a little—such a silly trouble, you will think," said Julie, half smiling.

"Not so little, Julie, if it can bring all these tears, surely!"

"Oh, but the thing itself is! It is not for myself I care."

" Whom for, then, Julie ? "

"For Allen. You see, Miss Herbert," continued Julie, gathering courage, " Allen does not like to see me with my hair like this; and I have been trying, oh, so many times, to alter it, but cannot." The tears were fast flowing again.

" You are very fond of Allen, Julie."

" Oh, yes. He does everything for me."

" And you would do *everything* for him? I understand, Julie." And Marian kissed the white brow from which she was parting the soft abundant hair.

" Why did you not tell me all this before? I do not like your hair in its present state either, love ; and unlike your brother, have been busy devising a plan to make it more presentable. Come into my room; we will see what can be done, and whether it is possible to please this anxious brother of yours."

Allen had been, since morning, at a distant station. But after the evening meal had been taken, his cup and carefully prepared tea remained in waiting. It was almost dark when at last he was seen crossing the creek with his hot and dusty horse; and leaping from his saddle, he threw the reins across the animal's neck, leaving it to take its own way to the stable, and entered the house. It was all quiet in the sitting-room—dark and silent. The family was all dispersed about the house and yards around; and quietly taking his accustomed seat, he leant back at his ease, and looked musingly into the fire. But he had not been seated there very long before there was a gentle footstep behind his chair, and his eyes were suddenly covered by two little hands.

"Julie! Ah! puss, it's a poor game to try and deceive me," he laughed, taking hold of her hand, and lifting her round the chair on to his knee. But he suddenly stopped then. Was it Julie? and half relinquishing his hold, and wholly withholding the kiss, he exclaimed, "Why, what young lady are you?" for in the murky light, the gracefully rolled silken hair, the pretty Madonna-like face, were unknown to him.

The low laugh of unutterable pleasure reassured him.

"Why, *it is* Julie!" he exclaimed in astonishment, "after all. You sly puss! Is this how you treat your brother? Come, let me have a good look at you. I shall want a dozen kisses for this, mind." And he again pulled her on his knee, and a very good look he took—a very satisfied look indeed.

"Ah, Julie—that's it; you beat Ellen Graham all to nothing. Dear me, what a difference it makes in you! You are transformed. I don't know you. I shall have to take care now that some one don't run off with my little sister. Run, puss, and get a candle, and then give me my tea. Here, give me another kiss—now—quick."

She soon came flying back again, laughing and blushing, with the light in her hand, followed by her mother.

"Yes, hasn't it made a difference in Julie?" said

the latter, in reply to the look of delighted astonishment Allen cast at his sister.

"I couldn't have believed it," he returned. "It makes quite a young lady of her." Then pulling off his cap, he threw it to the other end of the room. "Beg pardon, Miss Julie, for wearing my cap in your presence," he continued, half teasingly.

"Oh, don't, Allen!" and Julie drew up close to him, and hid her face on his shoulders. "Shall you not love me as well with my hair like this?"

"A great deal better, little silly, if that is possible. Look up, darling, and tell me, is this Miss Herbert's doings?"

Julie did tell him; and Marian, when she came in shortly after, was surprised by his warm thanks.

CHAPTER VII.

> " There is a lesson in each flower,
>   A story in each stream and bower ;
>   On every herb on which you tread
>   Are written words which, rightly read,
>   Will lead you from earth's fragrant sod
>   To hope, to holiness, and God."

THE first Sabbath in the bush! and what would it be like? Marian went to sleep with that thought upon her mind, and her dreams conveyed her back to her English home and the quiet house of prayer. The soft, mellow chime of bells was mingled with the breeze in her happy sleep. But the morning light dispelled the illusion. She awoke—and with a half sigh remembered how far distant she was from all most precious to her. But then came sweet Bible words to relieve her sadness, and " I will be with thee in all places whithersoever thou goest," was a promise that soothed her sorrowing spirit, and chid her for her sadness.

" Can I want more? " she asked herself; " can I have more? Having Christ, have I not all things? What can it signify *where* I am, *He* being there? Oh, it cannot, it cannot. I will trust in Him, and be not afraid." It was yet early, but she arose, and tying on her large hat, Bible in hand, found her way quietly out of the house, and sauntered across the little creek that glistened from her window in the morning sun, and up, up among the she-oaks and blackwoods and rocky masses of stone, till she had gained the top of the ascent. And then how well was she repaid! Far down below her was the homestead—quiet—undisturbed—wrapped in deep slumber. How far below it looked, embosomed by the distance in trees, with the little creek, as a silver thread, twining in and out, till it was lost among the bushes at the bend of the hill. The old gums—those gums upon which she had gazed so contemptuously when first she saw them after her voyage, comparing them with the gracefully timbered trees of Old England,—even they excited an interest—even they looked beautiful in the morning sunlight. And between those trees, how beautiful were the glimpses of the hay! some waving, some already mown, sending through the air a sweet, sweet fragrance. And yet another tint of green was there in the graceful ears of corn—not yet "white unto harvest," but bearing ample promise of abundant future.

Behind her rose other hills, thick with foliage, in dark relief against the sky; others still green with the unseared grass and herbage, swelled and undulated without a single tree upon them, and yet their very indentations rendered them beautiful. To her right hand, meeting the clear horizon, the glassy waters

of a lake were visible. The morning sun had left
a portion of his radiance on its smooth unruffled
bosom. Between her and the lake there seemed a
continuation of scrubby plains, though more immediately near there was an abundance of fenced land,
rife with the reward of the husbandman's labour.
The left looked towards Adelaide. She could see the
slip-panel at which she had been first introduced to
Allen and Julie, and the long, narrow, fenced-in road
up which she and Alf had so gaily cantered on approaching it. How pleasant it looked—delightful for
a ride: the young wattles on either side, yellow with
profusion of blossom, and pouring their perfume on
the early breeze. How glad she felt that she had
quitted her room betimes, and explored this dear
hill, whence all the most beautiful points of the land-
scape could be seen at once, and where her retirement was so complete. She started, for at that
moment a strange wild " Ha-ha-ha-ha ! " was poured
contemptuously into her ear, and half frightened she
sprang to her feet, for she had seated herself on the
trunk of a fallen tree, to enjoy her view at leisure.
But who was her rude disturber ? One of the farm
men, perhaps ? She began to descend the hill fast,
as she remembered how far distant the homestead
was beneath her, not wishing for such a companion.
But she had not proceeded many yards when the
same defiant laugh of derision was repeated—this time
quite close to her; and the next moment there flew
out of an adjacent tree a strange-looking bird, with

enormous bill, who, perching upon a huge block of stone some little distance off, again repeated his ridiculous laugh.

This time Marian joined it heartily, blushing at her fears.

"How silly I was to be sure!" she exclaimed. "I had forgotten all about this singular bird; for this must be the 'laughing jackass.' I shall ask Allen, for I shall only get laughter and quizzing from Alf; he never will give me a straightforward answer to a question." And still laughing, she retraced her steps, and again took her seat on the fallen tree.

But now that merry triumphant laugh had swelled to a complete chorus, and at once the inmates of every nest responded. Some with sharp, shrill, single cries; some with strange twittering; some with a note or two sounding like the commencement of melodious bird-song, but no more than commencement; yet, above all—soft, clear, rippling, gushing— was poured forth the exquisite song of the native magpie, gurgling joyously; inexpressibly sweet and touching were some of the notes. It seemed as though that little throat throbbed with ecstasy. Marian's heart throbbed in sympathy; and burying her face in her hands, and bending low upon a projecting branch of the fallen tree, she poured out her soul in Sabbath prayer and praise.

"Where's Miss Herbert, Alf? Do you know?" asked his mother, walking into the sitting-room, where the cloth had just been spread for breakfast.

"I, mother !—how should I ?" answered Alf, merrily; "in her room, I suppose."

"No, she isn't; her window was open when your father first got up. Breakfast's ready."

"I haven't seen her. She's off exploring somewhere, I dare say. Where's Bess and Julie ?"

"Bessie's feeding the calf, and Julie's not very well. She's not up yet."

"Ah, well! I'll try what a cooey will do. I'll look for her." And Alf left the room.

He carelessly drew to the edge of the creek. Allen was there, watching the deep, cool draught his favourite horse was imbibing, and enjoying as usual the quiet charm of the running rippling water.

"Well, Alf!"

"Well, Allen! what am I after? says the look of your face, as clear as looks can speak."

"Since you read the question so well, what is the answer? I'm not so clever. Is it breakfast?"

"Not exactly; there's no cooey yet. I'm after a missing heifer."

"What! Red Poley again? Why, I thought I fastened her in securely last night."

Alf laughed a low chuckling laugh. "No, it's not Red Poley, never fear! It's Brown Poley, if you like to call it so."

"Have done with your enigmas, Alf, and say clearly what you mean," said Allen, impatiently. "Am I wanted?"

"Some one else is," said Alf, with a double meaning

in his tone. "Well then," he exclaimed, seeing there was no time to trifle any longer, for he caught a glimpse of his mother at the door, "do you know where Miss Herbert is? Breakfast is waiting."

"It would have waited less time had you told me what you wanted before," replied Allen, coolly pointing up the hill, where, just peeping through the trees, a fold or two of Marian's dress, and the large drooping hat, were visible.

Alf laughed again, his teazing, tantalizing laugh, and glanced archly at his brother. "I thought you were over-particular with Prince Charlie's breakfast," he mischievously exclaimed, springing over the creek, and up the hill beyond hearing; but Allen had not answered—he had only turned disdainfully away and walked slowly towards the house. He stood a moment at the door before entering, and gave one upward glance. Alf, with Marian's hand fast in his own, was half-leading, half-compelling her footsteps down the steepest portion of the hill, saucily laughing at her fears.

Not very well pleased by the sight, evidenced by the knitted brow, the compressed lip, and under-breathed "Pshaw," Allen did not look again, but quietly took his seat at the breakfast-table, and engrossed himself so entirely with attention to his pale little sister Julie, that he never even raised his eyes, when a moment or two after, his brother entered with Marian leaning on his arm, and a most provoking smile on his lips, as he took away her hat and book, and placed her in her seat, drawing his own chair close to hers, and as far from Allen's as agreeable to his mischievous humour.

"And what are you going to do with yourself to-day, Julie?" asked Allen, affectionately, as he carefully selected a tempting morsel of ham for his delicate sister. "Will you take a ride on Dapple? You want something to relieve those poor pale cheeks."

Julie threw one arm round her brother, and lifting her lips to his ear, whispered something that rather oddly brought the blood to his brow, for the whisper was a very audible one. "Take us to chapel, dear Allen. I know very well Miss Herbert would rather go there than anywhere; and it would be a famous ride, too."

"Miss Herbert again," thought Allen; but he felt he must say something. "Speak for yourself, little one; how do you know Miss Herbert wishes to ride?"

"Oh," said Julie, blushing, "I heard her asking mother how far it was to chapel, and I knew you would take us."

Alf laughed. "Well done, Julie! And so I'm to be left out of the question it seems? or perhaps you think *my* escort will not be acceptable."

Julie looked doubtfully at her brother, but did not reply. Allen coloured highly, and looked down, and Alf merrily continued,—

"You see, Miss Herbert, Julie places the affections

of everybody where her own are, and I am of course no sort of a companion ; but you will bear witness to the contrary, will you not ? ”

Marian laughed. “ What is the question ? If it is whether I should like to ride to chapel or not to-day, I can speedily answer that,—I should, very much indeed.”

“ With *me* for an escort ? ”

“ Be quiet, Alf! you will offend Miss Herbert.” It was his mother who spoke ; for she had seen the upward glance and flash of Allen's eyes, and was fearful of something worse. A laugh from Alf ended the discussion, and breakfast went quietly on, and then the party separated. Marian stole off to her own little room, and sat, book in hand, at the open window waiting till her pupils should come to her as she had requested them. But the wild little Bessie was off after the calves, and Julie was nowhere to be seen ; Alf, too, had left the house on some mission, and the other inmates had each their employment, although it was the Sabbath.

Hearing a low tap at the door, Marian looked up, and thinking it was Julie, replied, “ Come in, dear.” But it was entirely out of her calculation that Julie's brother should accept the invitation ; he did, however, though he scarcely entered the door.

“ Was Julie right, Miss Herbert ? ” he asked hesitatingly. “ Would you really like a ride to this chapel ? ”

“ I should indeed, Mr. Allen,” said Marian, with

animation. "That is," she continued, rather subdued by the thought, "if it will not make too much trouble. Is it very far?"

"Ten miles—a mere nothing. You would like it. That is sufficient," said Allen, quietly leaving the room. "Can you be ready in an hour, Miss Herbert, —you and Julie? I'll have the horses round by that time," he exclaimed, returning.

"Oh, yes, and thank you," said Marian, really gratified. "How kind of him," she thought, as she busied herself with preparations, in which Julie soon shared, radiant with pleasure.

"Alf is going too," she exclaimed, "and he has not been for such a while. We none of us go very often. Allen sometimes takes me, because he does almost anything I ask."

"He has done what you asked to-day, Julie."

"No, Miss Herbert, to-day it is for you, not for me only."

"He is very kind to us both, then, Julie," was the reply; and Marian renewed her preparations.

The hour passed away, and the horses stood ready saddled at the door. Hymn-books and Bibles were carefully stowed away in the pockets of the saddles, and Marian and Julie were lifted to their seats by the attentive brothers. In a few moments all four were pleasantly cantering along a rather narrow track round the base of the she-oak hill; the delicious breeze uplifting hats and curls and veils in very wantonness, as they gracefully passed along. How delightful that breeze was to Marian! What a sacred Sabbath stillness was there in the country around! As yet the grass was unseared, and flowers fair and lovely to the eye bent beneath the feet of their horses. The whole air was rife with the perfume of the wattle, and in and out its fragrant boughs twittered its little familiar, the wattle-bird, a wee brownie, with a beak the hue of the flowers whose name it bears. The Blue-Mountain parrot frequently flew across their path, and flocks of small green paroquets were scattered at intervals among the grass, almost invisible till close approach, so exactly did their plumage resemble the colour of the herbage.

"Is not this a little better than dusty Adelaide, Miss Herbert?" asked Alf, archly, reining his horse to her side, after they had cantered on some distance in silence, and the widening of the track permitted them to ride abreast.

"It is not comparable with Adelaide at all, Mr. Alf. My real thoughts of Australia were rather gloomy on entering her port and city," replied the lady addressed. "Your country, or bush, is really delightful."

"But after all, not English," said Allen "Alf cannot appreciate that distinction, for he is a native of the colony, born and reared on the same soil. I, to be sure, was a mere urchin when we left the mother-country; but for all that, memory and feeling and liking are pretty strong. I should like once more to tread on English ground."

"That of course is very natural to any one who claims it for a birth-place," replied Marian; "and there are many things in England that one must regret, many things that can never be the same here. Yet I am quite of your brother's opinion, it is the fault of the discontented if they do not make themselves happy in such a land as this."

"Hurrah for Australia!" shouted Alf, in boyish enthusiasm, tossing up his hat, and catching it again as he passed.

"Your love for your country, Mr. Alf, is making you forgetful of the day," suggested Marian, gently.

" The day—oh! Sunday—yes, I did forget. But, Miss Herbert, it is easy to see you have not been long in the bush; we do not think much of such things as these out here. Sunday is not kept among the wattles."

" You are giving Miss Herbert a very bad impression of our character, Alf," interposed Allen, gravely.

"Not a false one, though," said Alf, merrily ; " not one in fifty miles round would think of playing the game we are to-day. No, indeed! they saddle their horses fast enough ; the men to cattle-hunt, the women to visit and gossip with their neighbours. Little time or inclination for chapel-going, I fancy ! "

"One then would almost imagine that the universal feeling in the bush is, that this is a country unsanctified by the presence of a God, in which His precepts are not to be regarded, His word not read, His throne unaddressed ; a country over which He exercises no rule, where man's natural passions and feelings and inclinations are to be left unrestrained," and Marian's cheek glowed with the indignant expression of her thoughts.

"It is rather a highly-coloured picture," replied Allen, sadly, " nevertheless, too true; and I am afraid the inmates of the homestead too closely adhere to the outward semblance of sentiments which I do not believe any of them in reality have in their hearts."

"'A people who forget God,'—'God is not in all their thoughts,'" said Marian, slowly, solemnly, thoughtfully, urging her horse forward as she spoke.

Julie bent down towards her horse's neck, and a bright tear glistened on the pummel of her saddle. Allen looked very grave, and rode on in silence. Even Alf showed some evidence of thoughtfulness, though he lingered behind to cut a twig from an overhanging branch, and whistled in an undertone, as he slowly followed. He did not, however, again forget himself, or resume his boisterous air, for the rest of the ride.

It was a little chapel, built of roughly hewn stone, and seated with plain benches, but Marian felt as she approached it a kindred warmth of feeling arise. Here, at least, were some who loved to keep holyday; here, at least, were some whose homes were consecrated to God; and as she gathered up her long habit, and followed with Julie into the lowly temple, her heart arose in thankfulness at this proof that God was present, even there. Nor did the primitive character of the service, the unlettered address, the rude singing, or repeated " Amen " responses to the prayer, dispel the fervent reverence with which her whole soul bowed before Him who condescendeth to " men of low estate."

Alf glanced vainly many times for a response to the ridicule that curled his lip; but Julie sat silent and pale by the side of her governess, many times turning a timid, half-inquiring gaze upon her; and Allen, with his head resting on his hand, was looking very grave. Those words were following him, " God is not in all their thoughts," and for the first time there seemed something almost fearful in their import. And thus it ever is. We may again and again read the word of God as applicable to the case of others; but it is only when brought home to our own hearts that it proves as a " sharp two-edged sword, dividing asunder the joints and marrow."

CHAPTER VIII.

HARVEST.

WEEK after week passed, bringing with them the busy harvest months, and there was little time for excursion or recreation then for Allen or Alf, or, indeed, any of the household. It was a strange spectacle to Marian, though familiar enough to farmers of any breadth in Australia,—the large kitchen, fitted up with groaning tables, surrounded by sun-embrowned men, all well qualified, in spite of heat and fatigue, to do credit to the abundant fare. In those days there was not much time devoted to lessons; even Julie and Bessie were employed; and, as a matter of course, poor Charlie and Frank had to throw aside their books and slates for the sickle or the reaping-machine. Morning after morning Marian emerged from her room, enveloped in a large apron, with sleeves tucked up above the elbow, ready to thrust hands and arms into the depths of the flour bag. Many a charming little nicknack of cookery from her busy fingers found its way into the lunch-bag of the father and brothers, neatly stowed there by the pleased mistress of the house; and as bushmen are by no means insensible to the attractions of the table, it was no wonder there were eager inquiries as to the source from whence the unusual luxuries came.

"Well, father," said Alf, archly, one morning, as he drew from his wallet a novel species of pastry, with which his plate immediately fraternized, and saw the same result follow the opening of the other bags, " well, father, after all, were not our fears groundless? and is not our governess a stunner?"

"Won't do always to go by appearance, Alf, that's what it shows;" and Mr. Burton went on composedly and very satisfactorily eating his luncheon.

"Who'd have thought of those bits of white hands turning out such first-rate bread as we have had this week?" persisted Alf; "mother says she insists upon making all that we use."

"She beats Margery out and out—my word!" chimed in Frank, eating his morsel with evident gusto, and plunging his hand into his bag for more.

Allen ate his in silence.

"This is Cherry's milk. Miss Herbert milked Cherry this morning," whispered Julie in her favourite brother's ear, as she brought her bright can of rich milk to his side.

Her answer was a kiss, and he accepted a draught as though very thirsty, and then stealing away her can, pulled her to the ground by his side, and taking off her broad hat, fanned the heated brow, gently saying, "I wish Miss Herbert would do another thing, dear Julie, and forbid your coming out in the heat; you will be ill, pet,—your head is burning."

"She did not know I was coming, Allen," said Julie, resting the burning head wearily against her brother's shoulder.

"Well, you must promise me not to come out again in the hot sun. Mind, I shall take nothing more you bring. As to Bessie, the little gipsy will take no harm. Come, pet—do you think I want to lose my little sister?—What! tears?"

And thus Marian was fast stealing into the hearts of the homestead people, and was already writing pleasant, cheerful letters to her cousins, who, now comfortably situated, sent her many invitations to come to them.

"I have got what I wanted, dear Isabel," she wrote, "a pleasant home. Mrs. Burton is almost like a mother to me, and Mr. Burton is one of the kindest of men. I am getting very much attached to my pupils, to Julie especially; and really, my dear cousin, much as I like to be with you, I cannot help feeling that my little glimmering light is destined to yield its tremulous flicker in this very spot. It is a very pleasant thought to me, that I may become the instrument of good here; you know, God sometimes works by very feeble instruments, and by very meagre talents. Tell William I am both well and happy, and very sanguine."

It was really a pleasant sight to see the loaded wagons, moving heavily along the tracks, groaning beneath the precious grain; and Marian liked the deep, drowsy hum of the machine, as it came from the old barn, where the winnowing was gaily going forward. Once, when short of hands, she went and gave her assistance, filling and refilling the tin dish to Alf's rapid turning. The noise was not quite so agreeable on close vicinity as at a distance, but she endured it the whole of one afternoon most bravely, heeding neither aching arms nor aching head, and rendering real assistance. As to Alf, it was really too pleasant to see those little hands working for him; he never thought of her possible fatigue; and towards the end of the long afternoon, when Allen, who had been away on business, entered the barn, she was wearied, heated, and with a severe head-ache.

"Why, Alf, how's this? I'm surprised at you! Miss Herbert is not used to such work."

The machine was stopped at a look from him, and Marian's dish fell from her hands, as for a moment she leant against the machine-handle, the colour fading from her lips. Allen caught her as she was falling, and carrying her to the door, laid her on a heap of chaff at its entrance, while snatching off his hat, he fanned her vigorously with its broad brim.

"I am sure, Miss Herbert, you must think me a very thoughtless fellow," said Alf, in a tone of vexation, as he held a glass of water towards her,

Allen took it impatiently from him, and held it to her lips.

"Certainly, you manifest great consideration," he replied.

"It was entirely my own fault," replied Marian, as revived by the air and cold water, she attempted to rise; "I tried my strength too far. I should have given over before."

"You should not have been here at all, Miss Herbert," said Allen, "if I had been at home."

Alf laughed, and turned again to his machine, and Marian suffered herself to be led to the house.

And so an abundant harvest was gathered in; and gradually the men not connected with the farm passed away. The hum of the winnowing machine was still heard, but there were hands sufficient at the homestead for that, and Allen returned to his usual duties.

"You are going to Adelaide to-morrow, are you not, Allen?" The soft voice and twining arms were Julie's. Her brother was seated at one corner of the veranda, near the sitting-room, smoking a little ebony pipe, and quietly musing. He laid down his pipe, and put his arm round her. "Well, Julie, and what then? What am I to bring you?"

"Oh, I want something so much. Do you know, Allen," she continued, as usual approaching his ear, "Do you know Miss Herbert can play---on---on the piano? Would you like me to learn?"

"I should like you to learn every nice accomplishment, my little sis. What then?" He thought, but he did not say, how often he had looked at the little hands, and concluded that they were familiar with the piano-keys; and if so, how much a piano must be missed.

"I should like very much to learn if I could." And Julie hid her face on her brother's shoulder.

"And what is there wanting to prevent your commencing at once?" asked Allen, teasingly.

"O Allen, a piano! If I only had a piano! I know the notes already, and my time-table."

"Hey-day! you have made progress. Well, well, we will see what can be done;" and he rose as he spoke. "Mind, Julie," he continued, detaining her, "if I buy a piano it will be mine, and I shall only lend it to you and Miss Herbert."

"Oh, yes; oh, yes;" and Julie's blue eyes swam with happy tears.

"Can you keep the secret, then? You must not breathe a word of it till I come back from Adelaide."

"Oh, I won't, I won't!"

"How about the music-books, though, Julie?"

"Oh, Miss Herbert has heaps and heaps. That large brown trunk that was so heavy, you remember, Allen,—well, that has only books and music and drawings in it."

Allen walked slowly away. There was a burning thought at his heart; if delicate fingers like Marian's, familiar as they were with ivory keys and crayons, could descend to the humble requirements of life, could make a pudding or a cake, or even household bread, and do all attempted so well, why should he, because he was a farmer, throw aside his Euclid or his algebra, his German or Latin, those cherished studies of former days? Why should he not in his wallet of provisions for the outward man, place a little mental aliment when bound for a distant station? Nay, why should he not keep up the natural talent for drawing he knew he possessed, when spare moments intervened? If a bushman, he would not be an uncultivated one. And in addition to the piano, there was a reserve of drawing materials and classics for himself, jotted down in his memorandum-book, which, could Alf have seen, would have called forth again and again his tantalizing laugh.

A little later in the evening, Allen asked Marian for her commands in Adelaide, and she brought from her desk a letter to her cousin, which he promised to deliver into her own hands. It contained a little commission for some kind of fancy work for Isabel to procure, and the parcel was to be consigned to Allen's keeping on his return. So he particularly requested, and Marian was glad to yield to his entreaties.

The sun had not stolen over the top of the she-oak hill, when Allen's horse stood at the door ready caparisoned for the journey. He was seated at his early breakfast, which one of the maids had prepared for him. His hat and whip and gloves lay near him, and his last cup of coffee was nearly finished, when the door of the sitting-room leading to the bed-rooms was lightly pushed open, and Julie, wrapped in her dressing-gown, appeared.

"Why, Julie! out of bed at this time in the morning? It's too early for you, pet; you are as pale as a snowdrop, if you know what that is. Now, tell me what other commission you have for me."

"I only came to say good-bye, Allen. You will be away a whole week, you know."

"A whole week! Is it possible, Julie? Well, so I shall; but I think the memory of my pale little sister at home will survive it."

"And will you remember something else?" Julie asked rather bashfully; "something we talked of last night, Allen."

He laughed, and pulled her to him, taking his pocket-book at the same time from his coat. "Look here, pet :—Mem.—a piano—Marshall's. There, will that satisfy you?"

"Oh yes! I'm so glad!" and Julie kissed him again and again. He returned with affection her caresses; but at length arose, saying, "This won't do, pet; I must be off; the drays started hours ago. There; you may stand at the door and see me start, and then run to bed again."

To bed and to sleep; but her sleep was full of dreams: Allen formed a considerable portion of them; her governess and the beloved piano came in frequently enough. But she slept and dreamt on to a rather late hour that morning. Her secret burned within her, but she did not betray it.

CHAPTER IX.

LOST IN THE GULLY.

DAYS and nights must pass away, many and long, before the arrival of Allen and his treasures, thought Julie with a sigh as she awoke next morning; but that they *would* pass, however slowly, was an unspeakable comfort. Then the joy of anticipation was something: the surprise that would await the homestead folks when the first notes of the piano sounded; Miss Herbert's glow of pleasure as her fingers again renewed acquaintance with the keys of the instrument; Bessie's wild delight; Alf's teasing laugh, —all this formed a portion of Julie's anticipations, and many a time she was obliged to run out of the room to conceal the gladness which would otherwise have betrayed itself.

"What is the matter with that girl?" exclaimed Mrs. Burton, after one of those joyous paroxysms had compelled her exit.

"You may depend Allen has something to do with

it, mother," said Alf. "I never knew him go to Adelaide without a commission of some sort from Julie. He's wild about that girl!"

"I do not wonder at it," said Marian; "a very sweet girl I think she is. She is very fond of him besides."

"Bess is more to my taste. There is no nonsense in her. She's as wild as a young horse; wants a pretty good hard bit, too—not very tender-mouthed."

"Bessie is a dear little girl, but not to be compared with her sister," said Marian, warmly. "Bessie is all nature—lovely nature, certainly—but there is something *spiritual* in Julie."

Alf dropped the axe-head to which he was neatly affixing a new handle. With a bang it fell to the floor, and he suddenly faced round upon the young lady. "That's it—that's it; that's the very thing, I suppose. My coarser nature can find no fellowship with the finer texture of spirit. Come to think of it," he exclaimed, affecting to muse, "there is a very spiritual look about that fair, thin, white face."

"With its blue veins, Alf," returned Marian, gravely, as she saw Mrs. Burton pass out of hearing. "That term you are quizzing may have more meanings than one. I often fear our Julie will in reality be only spirit ere long."

"Ha! ha! now, Miss Herbert, I did not think you were so romantic."

"I am perfectly serious, I can assure you, on such a subject I do not like to say so to your mother, but I am sure Julie ought to go to Adelaide and have medical advice."

"You don't say so!" said Alf, beginning to look grave; "why, I don't see much the matter with her. She's not over-strong, and rather thin,—spiritual as you call it," he replied, relapsing into merriment. "Now, Miss Herbert," he exclaimed, "confess for or.ce that you are encouraging fear." And he coolly lifted the axe-head from the floor, and gave a succession of such deafening blows, as though purposely to preclude the possibility of answering. But Marian saw, beneath all, a deep under-current of feeling he was doing his best to conceal.

Marian and the two girls were seated at lessons in the school-room very diligently one lovely afternoon nearly a week after Allen's departure, when Mrs. Burton came, and opening the door, looked good-humouredly in upon them.

"Are you for a walk this afternoon, Miss Herbert?" she asked, smilingly. "I have been putting up a few little niceties for the poor man who was so badly hurt with the dray-wheel the other day; I hear he is still very weak and ill, and he might fancy something coming unexpectedly. Sick folk usually do."

"Oh, I should like it very much, dear Mrs. Burton," said Marian, springing up, "but I am afraid I shall never find the way. He is on Alex. Turner's section, is he not?"

"Yes; he and his wife work for Turner, and live in one of his huts. Poor fellow, I am very doubtfu whether he will ever work again.   But I did not mean you to go alone, Miss Herbert—Julie knows the way—don't you, darling?"

"Yes, mother.   I have been twice to Turner's; once round the road, and once across sections."

"Well, you had better go round the road, then, for creeping under fences will shake all the jelly to shivers. You can't miss your way—it's as clear as daylight; and you will be back before sunset."

"Then come, Julie, let us get on our hats at once. Is Bessie to go, Mrs. Burton?"

"No; I want Bessie.   Donald Melrose's wife has just come in, and brought her little Maggie; besides, you'll have plenty of trouble with the basket, without her."

Neither Marian nor Julie seemed to think much of the trouble.   It was just one of those pleasant days which often occur in the very middle of an Australian summer, after the floodgates of heaven have been opened, causing the arid soil to sing in gladness, and little timid flowers, here and there, to put forth their modest blossoms.   Here and there, too, a green patch of herbage caused an uplifting of joy in Marian's heart.   To her spiritual perception it spoke of the revivification of love and hope and faith in the soul, after the gentle dew from on high had descended; of those sweet fruits of the Spirit which modestly peep into view when Jesus has been near with His loving influence, as "dew on the tender herb."   Marian remembered the beautiful words of Scripture as the grass was lightly pressed by her feet.

But the promise was not for a temporal, but a spiritual blessing. How she rejoiced that it was so, and
how often in her own experience had she found the
promise fulfilled!

Their way led them round the road; but the road
was little more than a dray-track, on one side of which
a continuation of hilly ranges abruptly rose, and on
the other, scrub and wattles and massive gums falling
back from the wheel tracks for many a weary mile.
The sun came not too hotly upon them as they walked,
for the hill and branches sent forth the cool shadow,
and the soft breeze wandered up and down through
the wattles, and whispered mysteriously in the weird
she-oak leaves, and in and out among the tea-tree
bushes. Through a bed of the very greenest, freshest
water-cresses, a slender creek ran murmuring along
their pathway, now and then widening, and over-
shadowed by branches, sending forth from its dark
water the bul-bul of the great bull-frog, as a bass to
its own silver treble.

"How much I like those deep-mouthed notes issuing from the dark, weedy waters," said Marian, pausing
on a little rude bridge of logs which had been thrown
across the creek for the convenience of drays. They
were on the borders of Turner's section. They knelt
down together on the rough logs, and looked into the
quiet waters. The fresh cress grew on either side
luxuriantly, but wilder herbage was mingled with it
beneath the bridge, and thither the frogs took refuge,
and croaked at pleasure.

"Hark! one—two—three—four of those full bell-like notes," said Marian, "all in time, regular, and musical. Have you ever thought of that before, Julie? music in the croak of a frog?"

Julie laughed a glad little laugh, for the word music brought back the recollection of Allen's near return and its consequences, but she had never associated the croak of a frog and melody together in all her life before.

"You do not think it musical?" said Marian, returning the laugh. "Nay, Julie, only listen, Bul! bul! bul! bul! like deep-toned bells; and that murmuring, rippling water is whispering another quiet song. Oh, it is very sweet; do listen!"

"I have never thought of it before," said Julie.

"I once read that a 'heart in right tune can find music everywhere,'" said Marian, thoughtfully. "What should you imagine was meant by a heart in right tune, Julie?"

Julie thought a moment, and then half-hesitatingly replied, "Is it a contented, happy heart, a heart pleased with everything, that is meant?"

"By no means a bad definition, dear Julie, though I believe the author of the sentiment went even farther than this. He was comparing the heart of man to a harp. The strings of that instrument are extremely liable to become out of tune. Weather has great influence upon them; a slight accident may jar and produce discord; but rightly tuned and skilfully played, the melody is very sweet. Very much like the heart, dear Julie, and its feelings and thoughts and actions; those delicate strings which yield little but discord till a heavenly influence has passed over them."

Julie turned her soft, blue eyes wistfully to the face of her young governess. She was quick of apprehension; she began to understand the comparison.

"I think I have read something like this in a little hymn-book you lent me," she at last said—

> "Strange, that a harp of thousand strings
> Should keep in tune so long."

"Yes; that is Dr. Watts's. There he refers to the heart as the seat of life and health. The heart has innumerable vessels connected with it from which the blood flows to every part of the body: these vessels he compares to the strings of a harp. He is taking it in a more literal sense than the other author, Julie. It is of the mind—the understanding —the soul, the first is thinking, when he talks of the heart being rightly attuned; and it is the soul under the influence of God's Spirit he alone considers so. Naturally you know, Julie, every heart is out of tune, for the Bible tells us that the 'heart is deceitful above all things, and desperately wicked.' Have you not read this, Julie?"

It was a faintly whispered "Yes," in reply, and her blue eyes were now swimming with tears.

"'Deceitful and desperately wicked,'" repeated

Marian, half musingly, "but little harmony there—discord, terrible discord! and this to arise to the ear of a great and holy God! Have you never thought of this, Julie dearest?"

"Sometimes—lately," was the half-choked whisper.

Marian tightened her clasp of her young companion's hand, and they walked on some way in silence. She could scarcely command her own voice, and the little hand she held quivered and trembled sadly. "Ah! full of discord, indeed!" she continued with a sigh, after the silent interval. "All discordant, but not past tuning, dearest, not past tuning. 'The blood of Christ cleanseth from all sin.' It is the application of that blood which restores the harmony. When the soul feels that *that* blood has been applied, then steal forth the notes of melody. All is melodious then; nature has new charms, there is a new fountain of happiness opened—' the love of Christ that passeth all understanding.' Do you understand anything of this, Julie?"

"I think I do," was the softly spoken reply.

They were almost in sight of the house to which they were going, a bush-fence alone divided them from it; but Marian was earnestly interested and hopeful in her pupil. She put her arms round her, and kissing her fondly, exclaimed, "And what is the state of my dear Julie's heart, discord or harmony? Is love to God attuning its strings, or is it still discordant with hatred? Harmony or discord, dearest

Julie? There is no *middle state*—one or the other must exist."

The slight frame shook and quivered with excitement, the eyes filled more and more with tears, the voice was almost choked with sobs as she answered, " O Miss Herbert, it seems to me all discord. But I want, oh I do want to love God. I do want to feel that He loves me !"

Marian's own tears welled up from her earnest, loving eyes. She clasped her little pupil closer to her. " Thoughts and wishes and prayers of harmony, my darling; sweet tokens of the breath of the Holy Spirit upon the strings; for, never from the desperately wicked heart alone could even a *wish* for the love of Christ arise."

They stood a little while quietly recovering themselves before entering the house, and then creeping through a hole in the bush-fence, walked slowly towards the hut where the sick man lay; such a hut as no one in the home country would think of consigning his horse to, but in which a whole family contrived to live very much to their own satisfaction, in plenty, if not in comfort. It made no kind of difference that a rude stable closely adjoined the sleeping apartment, spreading its aroma powerfully through the place; that the walls were of rough slabs, with their crevices stopped by a mixture of clay and chopped straw; that the apertures intended for windows, were covered with calico, instead of glass; and that even at the open door two or three pigs wandered at will, and a whole bevy of barn-door fowls had to be chased away before Marian and Julie could enter. But when they had entered, in spite of the rude exterior, things wore a little better aspect. The settles were chiefly of home manufacture, but there were one or two very good cedar chairs and a polished table of large dimensions. In one corner of the room, near a large gaping chimney, stood an easy-chair, a recent purchase, covered with chintz, which at least told of no lack of means. In this chair the invalid was seated. Had he been in health, he would certainly have looked out of place in it; but now sickness had given a pallor to his cheek and a languor to his athletic frame, that made it a little more in keeping with the luxury; and his clothes, though rough, were scrupulously clean, for he possessed a truly industrious and cleanly wife, who came forward to meet the visitors with a very gratified countenance, and gave them a profusion of thanks.

Fresh home-brewed beer foaming from the bottle, and home-made bread and butter were instantly placed before them, and regardless of all they could say, they were obliged to sit down and partake of the hospitality and chat a while, though Marian from time to time cast many anxious glances at the fading sunbeams.

"Now we really must go," she at last exclaimed, jumping up. "We shall scarcely get back by dark if we go round the road."

"Did you come round the road, miss?" said the

woman in a tone of surprise; "it's only half the distance cross sections."

" Is it easy to find the way ? " asked Marian, rather concernedly.

" Oh law ! yes, ma'am ! Why, Miss Burton knows the way, I think."

" Yes," said Julie, " I know the way. I came once before, you know. Besides, we have nothing in the basket now, and you do not mind creeping under the fences, do you, Miss Herbert ? "

" I am not very fond of it, Julie ; but as you say, I don't mind particularly when the way is shortened by it, and it is late already, that is an object."

" I'll see you across the paddock, miss ; I would come farther, only for my man, he's no one just now to stay with him."

" Oh pray do not come at all," said Marian ; but that was not to be thought of, and the three started across the paddock.

" Now, miss," said the woman, leaning on the fence at the other side, and pointing to a narrow foot-track in the grass, winding through a vista of trees, " keep right away along this here track, till you come to the next fence; you must then leave it and go past the fallen gum to your left to the next fence ; then you will come to three or four tracks all leading dif-ferent ways : just take the middle one, and that'll bring you right home."

" Oh yes !—I know the way, Mrs. Payton," said Julie, confidently. And with renewed farewells, and thanks, and professions of hope for the invalid's speedy recovery, they parted; Marian and Julie briskly pursuing the slender pathway, and cheerfully chatting as they went.

"Now we are to leave this track," said Marian, as they crept under the first fence with some little difficulty, for crinoline and muslin were never contemplated when the fence was made. They then stood a moment, looking round them, rather puzzled.

"Ah! there it is!—all right, Miss Herbert!" cried Julie, triumphantly, "this is the fallen gum, and this is the track. We are right again;" and on they went, swinging the empty glasses. Julie talking of next spring flowers, and Marian pleasantly joining with words or smiles, as they carelessly traced the path and arrived at the second fence, creeping under as before.

"The middle path," said Marian, looking very mystified; "Mrs. Payton said there was three, but here are *four* paths, Julie. How shall we know the right one now? Can we have come wrong?"

"Oh no! I remember the way exactly. I am sure we have come right so far!" said Julie, earnestly. She looked searchingly round her.

"There used only to be *three* paths, I know," she continued half to herself; "this must be *a new one* and this one must lead home."

"They are all so alike to me, I can scarcely see any difference," said Marian, rather uneasily; "certainly that dray-track is rather fresh-looking."

"Yes," said Julie, eagerly; "and I think this broad one must be the right. Oh, it is, I know—I remember that tree with its strange, white, crooked trunk. Oh yes! all right, Miss Herbert, come on!" and she went a few steps forward in her haste to see further proofs of her assertion, for her mind a little misgave her.

"We must indeed make haste," said Marian; "see, the sun is leaving the tree tops. We stayed too long at Mrs. Payton's. What now, Julie! are we not right?" For the poor girl had stopped suddenly and looked round in distress.

"I've quite forgotten the way. It don't seem right a bit, Miss Herbert! What shall we do?"

"I do not know, I'm sure, dear. We should have gone round the road; but now we are here we must do our best to find the way," replied Marian cheerfully. "What makes you think this is the wrong track?"

"We ought to have crossed part of the creek by this. Oh dear! oh dear! let us go back."

"Why, Julie! I thought you were a braver bushwoman," said Marian. "We will go back and try another path. I dare say the next will be right."

They hurried back and turned into the next most promising, and pursued it some distance as fast as they could, for the sun had set and the shadows were deepening every moment.

"Are you sure about the creek, Julie?" said Marian, after a little while, and no appearance of it,

"Yes, quite sure," said Julie, turning her eyes, now fast filling with tears, on her companion. "This cannot be the right way."

"Oh well, never mind; we will go back and try the next path," replied Marian, affecting a cheerfulness, for Julie's sake, which was in reality very foreign to her feelings. To spend a night amongst the opossums and wattles was beyond the very utmost stretch of her romance, and the dread of encountering wandering cattle was uppermost in her mind. So she placed one arm round the already trembling girl and hurried back once more.

They reached the first spot again in safety, but the darkness was coming on rapidly and there was no moon. They had to stoop down to find the track at all, and it was with a beating heart that Marian again turned for the new adventure.

"If Allen was only at home," she thought, "or even Alf," and Julie expressed the thought in words, "Oh how I wish I could hear Allen's whistle or even Alf's coocy!"

"I wish so too. Perhaps Alf will be home by this time."

"And mother will send him out!" said Julie, almost joyfully; and in the strength of that hope they hurried on and on, but no creek passed across their way. Marian felt sick and weary; on every side among the bushes were the, to her, terrible cattle-bells —and once or twice, peering through the trees close to her, were the glaring eyeballs of the startled animals.

Her breath came rapidly, and the voice with which she attempted to cheer the terrified Julie was low and husky.

"We are wrong, quite wrong, dear Miss Herbert, I am sure about the creek, even if Mrs. Payton had not said so. This is not the way. We must go back again," she whispered beneath her breath.

"We shall never find the way back, I fear," said Marian, in a low, desponding tone. But they turned again.

"Ah, we are off the track!" she exclaimed, as they suddenly came in contact with a brush-fence that stopped their way.

"We cannot be far off a house then! Oh I wish I could cooey!" and she tried, but failed.

"I will try," said Marian, and she made an attempt—then another—growing louder as she continued; and Julie gathering courage, alternated the cooey.

"Hark! What is that, Julie?"

"A *more-pork*, I think."

"There—there it is again! Did you hear? *That* is not a *more-pork*."

"No; it's Allen's whistle. Oh, I am so glad. Oh, I'll cooey again." And with a wild gladness she forgot fatigue, fright, and all, in the certainty that he would find them; and her sweet full cooey rang out on the quiet night air. It was immediately answered by the same prolonged whistle, only much nearer, and at the same time by a loud cooey and a shout in another direction.

"That's Alf," said Julie; and she threw her arms round Marian, and cried for very joy, looking up in her tears again to cooey once more. A moment after, and a horse was heard making his way through the scrub, and the next instant Allen was at their side, exclaiming as his sister sprang to his arms,—

"Why, Julie, darling! Miss Herbert! how you have frightened us! Thank God you are safe!"

"Halloo! Here you are. Where in the world were you going? into the waterhole?" and Alf sprang towards them with a shout and laugh.

CHAPTER X.

FIRESIDE CHAT.

"Happy the fireside student—happier still
The social circle round the blazing hearth."

WHETHER to laugh or to cry at the exquisite sense of safety, succeeding so much tension of feeling, Marian scarcely knew more than her pupil. Her feelings had been of a deeper and more highly wrought nature, and the exertion of concealment had been with difficulty sustained, and now the revulsion was almost beyond her strength. She leaned heavily against a tree that stood close by, faint and almost breathless; while Allen was busily engaged in placing Julie before Alf, who had now mounted Prince Charlie, intending first to deposit his sister at the sitting-room door, and then to take the horse to the stable.

"And now," said Allen, after cautioning his boisterous brother to ride slowly with his burden," if Miss Herbert will accept my arm, I think I can promise to lead her with perfect safety." He turned round hastily in alarm, for she did not answer, and for the first time he perceived her situation.

"Miss Herbert! Miss Marian! you are not well;

you have been very much frightened. Dear me! how very thoughtless! Here, Alf, come back!" But Alf had no such intention, he was half-way home already. His laugh came ringing back to his brother's ears.

Marian's slight faintness, however, soon gave way to an hysterical burst of tears, which even more alarmed her companion for the moment, though it restored her.

"I am very foolish," she said after a little, "but you must bear with me. You know it is only a few months since I came from London, and totally unacquainted with country life."

"Bear with you!" said Allen, earnestly; "I'm afraid you'll never forgive me for being so selfish in my love to my sister as to forget you, or rather, seem to forget you. I had no idea how fatigued and alarmed you were; and now I have sent off the horse, —at least, Alf has chosen to ride off."

"Oh, I am better; I can walk well. Those foolish tears have relieved me; they are the safety-valves of a woman's feelings, you know, Mr. Allen. I shall be quite recovered after a cup of your dear mother's tea. I am afraid our misadventure must have occasioned you a great deal of fatigue. When did you return?"

"Just in time to find the whole household disturbed about you," replied Allen. "Alf was off already exploring, so I never dismounted till I saw you."

"How kind of you! I am sure I am very much obliged."

"I am afraid I should have very much disobliged myself if I had not come, supremely selfish as the admission is," returned Allen. "Do not be afraid to tire me; pray lean on my arm. I cannot feel you at present, and keep fancying I have left you behind me."

Marian laughed, and complied partly with his request, for she was really tired.

"I don't exactly know—I can't understand where you have been, or how you were lost," continued Allen. "My mother seemed to imagine herself in fault, as being the moving agent in the business. I did not wait long to hear particulars; I guessed at your probable destination from Bessie's exclamation about Turner's, but what in the name of fortune should take you there was beyond my power of comprehension."

"Many things happen in a week, Mr. Allen," said Marian, archly. "There's no knowing what might happen; during the last few days, I might have gone altogether, instead of only losing myself."

"I should hope not that," replied Allen, rather gravely. "I hoped—that is, we all hoped—you were becoming attached to the old homestead."

"I only stated what might have occurred, not a probability, you know," said Marian. But Allen's gravity increasing, she changed the subject, and began to recount the afternoon's chapter of accidents in full, rousing herself with some little difficulty, but with perfect success; and they had reached home before either was aware of it.

There the welcome was unanimous, though Marian had much quizzing to undergo at the expense of her bush experience.

"My poor child," said Mrs. Burton, affectionately taking off her hat as she leaned back in the large chair to which Allen had led her, and kissing the pale cheeks with a tenderness which soon brought a bright bloom into them, "My poor child, we have been in sad trouble about you, both you and Julie; and it was my fault, too, for sending you."

"Oh, no, Mrs. Burton; it was my presumption in crossing sections," laughed Marian.

"It was only my fault," cried Julie, earnestly; "I ought to have known better than to go a way I knew so little of," and the tears were coming into the blue eyes once more.

"Your fault, pet!" said her brother, coming behind her chair, and stroking down the soft hair from her brow; "well, never mind it now. Have you nothing to say to me after this whole week of absence?"

"O Allen, yes, a hundred things; I am so glad you are back, for one."

"Then suppose, Julie, we defer hearing the ninety and nine till after tea. Have you any idea, darling, how hungry it is possible for a day's ride to make one?"

No one had had tea, late as it was, for no one dreamt of sitting down until the wanderers were restored; and now the bright fire on the hearth—for the evening was chilly—the well-spread table, the refreshing tea, and cheerful circle of faces, were doubly sweet. There was not one clouded conntenance. To the mother, Allen's return was sufficiently pleasant; to the squire, the fact of some very excellent sales of wheat having been effected, was quite agreeable enough to pour the sunshine on his broad brow; and for Allen, Marian, and Julie, a sweet home-feeling was enjoyed by each to the full. Alf and Bessie carried sunshine with them wherever they went, each to be sure in their own way; so laughter and merriment were nothing new to them.

A very pleasant evening it was to all parties, and passed rapidly away. Julie soon found time to whisper her question—that which of all others she was longing to ask—and she was made happy for the rest of the evening by the reply—

"Yes, pet; coming on the dray, so prepare your fingers."

"How soon will it be here, dear Allen?"

"Not soon enough to be unpacked to-night. Can you wait till to-morrow?"

Julie laughed, and hid her face on her brother's shoulder, but her joy was full that evening.

"What is it you promised to bring for Julie?" asked his mother, after the excitable girl had gone to bed. "She has been wild, I think, since you have been gone; laughing to herself, and skipping about, and telling none of us the reason."

Allen smiled. "Forgive me, mother; it is a little exclusive secret between Julie and me—time will unravel the mystery."

"That's a comfort. I'm afraid you'll spoil the child though, and Miss Herbert is almost as bad," she continued, smiling at Marian. "Between you, Julie is a perfect pet."

Allen coloured, but appeared pleased with the union of their names. He said nothing, however, but simply turned and looked at Marian.

Alf laughed. "What say you to the declaration of *partnership*, Miss Herbert?" he asked, mischievously. "Do you plead guilty of the offence?"

"No," replied Marian, smiling and blushing; "certainly not guilty of spoiling."

"Only of the *partnership?*"

Marian made no answer.

"Pray to what do you plead guilty, Mr. Alf?" asked his brother.

"To a little *second sight*, that's all, Allen," was the provoking rejoinder: "you know *coming events cast their shadows before*," and with a loud laugh he sprang up and left the room.

There was an uncomfortable silence for a few minutes. Allen sat biting his lips and casting covert glances at the drooping head in his neighbourhood. There was a broad smile on Mr. Burton's face, which he strove to hide behind his newspaper; and his wife's knitting needles rattled again. At length, taking compassion on the mutual embarrassment, which for a time he exceedingly enjoyed, he addressed a business question to Allen, and the conversation resumed its usual flow.

"The dray's coming, father," said Alf, re-entering the room about an hour after, just as Marian had risen to take her candle and retire.

"Happy to hear it;—proof that Black Jack has not fallen sick on the road, and needed his favourite remedy, *brandy*," said the farmer drily. "Now are you not dying to know what's in your parcel, Miss Herbert?" he asked, placing his broad hand on her shoulder, and looking merrily into her face, for she had put down her candle when Alf brought in the news. "Is it not a little too bad to have to wait till the morning for the news and the ribands?" he inquired teasingly.

"You will not have to do that, Miss Herbert, if you wait here a few minutes; I have put your parcels where I can get them immediately;" and Allen went out, followed by his father, whose face was most unmistakable in its merriment.

"Alf," said his father, after the unloading of part of the dray, while Allen had gone with the precious parcels into the sitting-room; "Alf, when do you think the ploughing will be done?"

Alf knew very well by the tone of voice that there was more in the question than met his ear. He replied in the same sort of tone, "Another week will finish it. Why?"

"Only that I think of revoking my former determination. The stone carting may go on. It's high time we got the new house up."

"Oh, oh! *The shadow of the coming event!*" laughed Alf; "well *I* think so too."

"It's rather reversing the bee-colonizing system for the *old* bees to turn out to make room for the young ones, but your mother has set her heart upon the new place."

"But I say, father, I think you are getting on a little too fast," said Alf, laughing. "Whatever we may think of Allen, we are by no means sure of the lady's inclinations. For instance, how do you know that she does not prefer *me?*"

"*You—you!* Well, these colonial lads! No—no; wait till your *whiskers* grow before you talk of preferences. Humph! for the matter of that, I was no older myself, and *more* of a stripling, when I first fell over head and ears in love."

CHAPTER XI.

MUSIC IN THE BUSH.

"Like some wild air
Of distant music, when we know not where
Or whence the sounds are brought from."

"Morning sleep is sweetest," says one; "morning dreams always come true," another proverbially exclaims. And certainly Marian enjoyed a very pleasant sleep, and a great deal of reality stole into her dreams, even after the sun had risen, and her usual hour for repose had passed. She had read a long, diamond-crossed letter from her cousin Isabella, and a short, brief, pithy note from William, before closing her eyes; each had something of importance to say, the former a great deal about Allen; and as the remarks were highly favourable, it was no wonder that the young farmer occupied a considerable portion of her dreams. Reality and fiction entangled themselves together in interminable confusion. We are no dream-tellers, and by no means intend to inflict upon our gentle reader the various phases assumed their entanglement, only *par parenthèse*, premisthat there was a happy termination to all; also, that towards the end of that dreamy sleep there were sweet sounds mingling with the dream, stealing softly over her senses, and one by one unlocking them. She awoke at length, with a smile upon her lips, and the music still trembling in her ear and memory. And yet, was it a dream? No. She was awake now, seated on her bed. The sounds were real then, and had woven themselves in her dream. But whence could they come? There was no regular strain; and as she listened, combinations of harmony, evidently accidental, came now and then from the keys of a piano.

"A piano! Oh," thought Marian, "Julie's joy is interpreted now. The sly little puss; I believe half her pleasure consisted in the thought of the gratification it would afford me. How quietly, too, Mr. Burton has managed to elude suspicion, and keep his secret."

Mr. Burton indeed! But it was Mr. Burton, junior, whose secret it was.

Marian opened the door of her room, and Julie sprang in and ran towards her, flushed with excitement and joy.

"O Miss Herbert, did you hear it? Oh, do come and look; isn't it a beauty?"

"It is indeed, dear Julie," said Marian, advancing into the little study, one side of which was occupied by a pretty cottage piano, "quite an addition to the furniture of the room." She ran her fingers across the keys to Julie's intense delight.

The sweetness and fulness of its tone pleased her much.

"Well, Julie, it is a beautiful instrument!" she exclaimed, sounding several chords in succession, and testing its full powers and depth of tone. "I am sure you ought to show your sense of your father's kindness by taking great pains to learn."

"Oh, but father has nothing to do with this. It is only Allen. He bought it with his own money. It is his, Miss Herbert; but he says he has lent it to you and to me as long as ever you like."

"Your brother, is it?" said Marian, colouring with surprise. "He certainly shows both taste and kindness."

"Oh, he is always kind. If I had asked father, he would only have laughed at me, and said the *churn* was the best music, as he always does. But Allen— there, I had only to tell him how fond of music you were, and what lots of music you had"——

"Not lots, dear Julie; have you no better word?" interrupted Marian, glad to shelter herself behind her profession at the moment.

"How much music you had," said Julie, correcting herself, "and he said he would get a piano directly."

"You have a kind brother, Julie; he is very anxious for your improvement," Marian managed to say, still running over the keys. "Where is he now?"

"Oh, he's gone to the township after the other

drays. Black Jack and Tom helped him to take the piano out of its case, and bring it here before any one was up, for he had to go early."

In truth he had made a special errand to the township in order to be out of the way of his father's and brother's bantering; an errand which he knew very well would detain him all the day, and he hoped a little of the novelty would be worn off before his return. He was also a little nervous respecting Marian's opinion of his purchase, and had resolved to hear it first from Julie, for which purpose he had commissioned her to watch for his return towards tea-time, at the slip-panel.

Mrs. Burton was both proud and pleased with the addition to the homestead. It was almost difficult to say which feeling predominated. Certainly it added not a little to her pride, that the action belonged so entirely to the son after her own heart, her own English-born, partly English-educated, Allen. Allen and Julie were to her the connecting links between refinement and that coarse vulgarity which *had been* in the homestead, and which *was* in her colonial associations. The first sounds from the keys of the new piano sent thrilling home-memories to her heart— memories long buried, yet surviving still. She was a girl again—a merry, light-hearted girl, dancing to her sister's music, or singing low, soft songs to its sweet accompaniment. What years had passed since then, and how changed was she who then sang! She turned away to hide the tears that came with the memory, and yet that memory was not bitter.

As to Allen's dread of banter from his father and brother, it was by no means exaggerated. It was well he was not there to witness the first explosion. As it was, the peal after peal of laughter that burst from the tormentors, very much disconcerted poor Marian. She thought it a very novel way of welcoming the pretty plaintive air she played, and she rose from the piano with somewhat heightened colour.

Alf, notwithstanding his merriment at the brother's expense, was not a whit less pleased. He was fond of music, and could with difficulty tear himself away from its sounds.

"I wonder what put it into his head! I don't believe I could have dreamt of such a thing as bringing a piano up into the bush, if I had tried ever so much," thought Alf.

"Well, missus, the new house may go up now," exclaimed Mr. Burton after one *more* prolonged laugh than usual.

"I'm very glad to hear it," said Mrs. Burton, a little sarcastically, for she felt rather scandalized by the excessive, and to her, unaccountable mirth of her husband and Alf. "I'm happy to hear it; if all your laughs prove as productive, you may laugh on, though what you find to laugh about this morning goodness knows."

'.You know, missus, as Alf says, 'Coming events

cast their shadows before,'" and with another burst of laughter they went off to their work.

The day wore away as usual, the customary studies were pursued, the various little domestic duties attended to with precision, no particular extravagances were perpetrated, for Julie testified her joyous feeling very quietly by an occasional smile, and now and then a clasp of Marian's hand. But the day wore away on the whole very pleasantly. There was one little half-hour of intense excitement for Julie, when the music-book was brought out from Marian's store, and she received her *first* lesson. Her hands trembled so excessively that they in reality *fluttered* over the keys, and the first sound following the pressure of her fingers absolutely made her start from her seat.

But, as we have said, the day wore away, and the evening's shadow came on ; and mindful of her promise, Julie noiselessly took her bonnet, crept unobserved from the house, running swiftly along the dray-track to the slip-panel, stopping every now and then to recover breath and listen for Prince Charlie's footsteps. Having reached it, she stood leaning on the fence, peering eagerly into the growing dusk for her expected brother.

The night was still and dark, yet there was enough of murky light to render the surrounding objects dimly visible, and to invest them with a fantastic and sometimes startling appearance. The over-wrought feelings of Julie, bush-maiden though she was, caused her to feel a certain degree of timidity ; and she gave an involuntary start at beholding a tall white figure, stretching its arms towards her; but she smiled as she remembered it was but an old and time-bleached tree. Now, of course, her feelings were very different from those of the previous night—here she was at home, and had so often waited and watched by the old slip-panel that she could have easily found her way to it blindfolded. Still she could not help thinking of the troubles of that dark wandering in the bush, of the pleasant afternoon's walk, of the conversation—and Julie sighed deeply as she wished her heart might breathe only melody, like a well-tuned instrument.

She little knew how engrossing her thoughts had proved, or how audibly her sigh had been expressed, and she uttered a slight scream and started violently as she felt her face suddenly covered by her brother's well-known hands, while he exclaimed,—

"Why, Julie, are you asleep? What were you dreaming of, and why such a sigh?"

"I was not sleeping; I was thinking, Allen," replied Julie, gravely, quite recovered from her fright.

"Thinking—and of whom?"

"Of myself, partly, and of *you*."

"Of *me*? and do thoughts of me cause sighs, Julie? Surely then, Miss Herbert cannot be pleased with the purchase; or father "——

"Oh no, Allen. I am sure Miss Herbert is very pleased; she does like the piano *so much*. She was so surprised, and says it is *such a beauty*."

"Oh, she does like it, then?" said Allen, with a glow of pleasure.

"Oh yes, I am quite sure; and do you know, Allen, I have really taken my first lesson; oh, it is so beautiful! I am so very glad!"

"Are you? So am I; but, by the bye, Julie, this is rather a different frame of mind to that I found you in. I was quite prepared to hear my taste in choosing the piano pronounced decidedly bad after that heavy sigh."

"Oh, were you? I did not know I sighed. But at any rate, it was not for that, I am sure," said Julie; "Miss Herbert said you showed very good taste."

"Much obliged to you and to her, Julie. Well— but what say father and Alf?"

"Oh, they have got over their laughing now, Allen. How very silly Alf is, though!"

Her brother made no answer, but quickened his footsteps a little. By this time they were nearing the house, and instead of walking towards the sitting-room, he went round the other side, still holding Julie's hand, and presently they stood together beside the study window. Allen placed his finger on his lips, and drew on one side a little, so that he could see within. Did he regret his purchase when he heard that low, sweet melody from its keys? Rather did he not rejoice that he had an opportunity of giving such pleasure, to Julie more especially—of course? No doubt it was a secondary matter that the little graceful hands within lingered so lovingly on the keys, now dancing, literally dancing along in wild gaiety, now hanging over the notes as though afraid to lose the melody. That had nothing at all to do with *his* rejoicing—oh no !

CHAPTER XII.

CHINTZ AND TACKS.

"The very instant that I saw you, did
My heart fly to your service; there reside
To make me slave to it; and for your sake
Am I this patient log man."

LIKE all other affairs in this strange world of ours, the novelty of the piano subsided, and the nine days' wonder having ceased, Mr. Burton's and Alf's tormenting banter was quickly over also. At last by common request the door of the sitting-room communicating with the study was thrown open every evening, and Marian's playing was a source of great pleasure to all through the winter. As to Alf, as if to make amends for his former laughter, the moment his brother conveyed a hint that it was too cold for Miss Herbert to play in a room without a fire, he obtained permission of his father, and with the assistance of one of the men, soon built up a comfortable hearth and chimney; and henceforth took upon himself the task of seeing that a bright fire glowed every evening upon the hearth. Allen, on returning from one of his excursions to the township, brought a large parcel back with him across his saddle, and threw it on the sitting-room table. Only the ladies of the house were present.

"What on earth have you there?" cried his mother in astonishment. "A draper's parcel?"

Allen smiled, and quietly untied the string; turned the brown paper slowly aside, and unrolled a quantity of striped chintz and binding to match.

"Chintz, I declare!" It was all his mother could exclaim in her surprise.

"Oh, how pretty!" exclaimed Marian and Julie together.

"What is it for?" cried Bessie climbing up by her brother's side, and smoothing down the shining folds with very admiring little hands.

"Why, Allen, is this for bed-curtains? Do you feel a draught to your head at night?" asked his mother, finding words.

"No, mother," replied Allen, laughing and colouring. "Well, I suppose I may as well tell you, for I am going to work immediately; this is intended instead of paper. I am going to clothe the study walls."

"Fiddlesticks! What a waste! How extravagant you are getting, Allen!"

"Oh no, Mrs. Burton—not extravagant; what a pretty idea!" said Marian. "How very pleasant it will be to study in our room, Julie!"

Allen turned from his mother with a quick glance of pleasure. What she had said was as nothing then; the last words had entirely effaced the effects of the first.

" Then will you give me your advice and assistance, Miss Herbert, in the performance? for I am
not sure of acquitting myself well in my new vocation."

" Most certainly—with great pleasure," and Marian
folded up the muslin she was working, and instantly
arose, while Allen produced from his pocket a paper
of tacks, and followed by Julie and Bessie, entered the
room.

" How very nice it will be!" said Marian, in a very
pleased tone of voice, after the first few tacks had
been put in, leaving the chintz depending from the
ceiling to the ground. " I am afraid the old sitting-
room will be sadly deserted."

" It will, at any rate, correspond a little better with
the piano," replied Allen. " I must acknowledge that
the unplastered walls looked rather unsuited to its
polished wood and rich blue silk." He glanced ap-
provingly at his work, which proceeded rapidly under
his hands and Marian's supervision.

" I bought enough, I think, Miss Herbert, for
cushions to the couch and sofa, if you and Julie will
make them; I know where there are plenty of
feathers."

" Mother is saving those for a bed, Allen."

Allen laughed. " Well, Julie, what then? Don't
you think she will give them to me?"

" I dare say," said Julie, doubtfully.

" We will make the cushions then," said Marian
smiling. " We shall have quite a pretty boudoir, and

the next thing we shall want will be a stand for flowers, to complete——"

"Yes; and, Miss Herbert, you know what you said the other day—a nice garden, a flower-garden, from here down to the creek."

Marian coloured and laughed. "You must not betray all my wishes and fancies," she said gently; "I only observed how pretty it would look, that was all."

All or not, Allen quickly got down from the step-ladder, and, walking to the window, pulled aside the curtain and looked out. How beautiful they looked in that clear, full moonlight, that grassy slope, the creek beyond, and the rough she-oak hill above all! He wondered he had never thought of a garden there before; but was there not a new house building? and all their thoughts of improvement were for that. Julie, as if she read his thoughts, had crept to his side, and now laying her hand on his arm, whispered,—

"The new house will be a long while building, Allen; why could we not have a garden *here?* If this is to be your house, won't you want it to be pretty?"

"I don't know, Julie. Why, do you think it possible of being made pretty?"

"Yes; and so does Miss Herbert. Don't you? I am sure I shall never like the stone house so well as this. Shall you?"—and the appeal was accompanied by an earnest glance into the face of her governess.

"Speak for yourself, Julie," said her brother, rather gravely; "Miss Herbert does not share in all your feelings."

"In this I do," replied Marian, rather embarrassed. "I almost wonder at your father and mother wishing for another house when they already have this nice one—one, too, capable of so much improvement."

"Do you think it is?" said Allen, eagerly. The old homestead was gaining new charms in his eyes, and he went back to his work with renewed pleasure, so that by tea-time the study walls were clothed.

Mr. Burton and Alf enjoyed, as usual, their masonic laughter that evening, as they discovered the newly-robed chamber. But they could not help acknowledging that, after all, Allen beat them "out and out" in taste and contrivance.

"I fancy I should have thought of a good many things, Allen, before I thought of a petticoat for the walls," said the farmer, stretching himself at full length on the sofa that evening, preparatory to being played to sleep by Miss Herbert.

"Well, Allen, that beats all!" cried Alf, in tantalizing admiration. "But I'd be bound, Miss Herbert, you put him up to the thing."

"Indeed I did not, Mr. Alf. I cannot claim the merit, I'm sure."

"Well then, you inspired him—that's the word, so it's all the same."

"I wish I could inspire you with a little common sense," said his brother.

"Wouldn't pay, Allen; I might prove too much for you," replied the provoking Alf, with a most impudent toss of his head towards Marian.

CHAPTER XIII.

BUILDING AND SPECULATING.

THE stone walls went up—not quite so rapidly as was intended, perhaps, but still steadily progressive. It was difficult in those days to meet with men of any building capacity, and labour was at a high premium. But notwithstanding all difficulties, the new house went on, and the winter months quickly stole away. In the spring they expected to enter.

One evening, a little before the tea hour, Allen and his brother Alf were slowly pacing the verandah which extended round the house. They were smoking and musing, and kept step by step together for a long time without speaking, a rather unusual thing for Alf; and it was he who at length broke the silence, making a full stop outside the study window, and gazing down the slope.

"This is certainly the most attractive part of the house, Allen," he exclaimed, laughing; "I vote to our limiting our walk to the boundary of its verandah. What was that you were speaking of the other day about a garden?" he continued, finding his brother did not reply.

"Why—that I should think it would be quite worth while to have a stone wall,—of course I mean loose stones, no mortar,—instead of a mere two-railed fence. I'm sure there are stones enough on the section, and they take no splitting."

"And look better," said Alf; "but there's a garden down at the other house; we shan't want this," he added, drily.

"A fruit-garden," replied Allen.

"Oh, I understand; you want a flower-garden here. But I say, Allen, what if you get ready your house and garden, and find no fair lady to put in it?"

Allen only quickened his footsteps by way of reply, but Alf could not be silent.

"Well, I don't see but that the wall can be done. You are so very quiet over your affairs: maybe the fair lady is already engaged, and in that case, if the garden is to have any flowers this spring, we must set to work at once. There's not much farm work doing just now, I'll speak to father, and get one of the drays."

"Oh, Miss Herbert!" cried Julie, running into the sitting-room, and throwing her arms round that young lady's waist, "I heard Allen and Alf talking just now by the study window, and they are really going to make a garden down the slope as you wanted. Alf is going to build the walls. I am so glad!"

"That will be an improvement, Julie," and Marian

coloured deeply as she spoke. " Well, by-and-by you and I will be able to offer our assistance. I have a large packet of seeds I brought from England, we can sow them, and then in spring, Julie, I can promise you lovely flowers indeed. I like this house; do not you ? " she continued, looking affectionately round the comfortable room as she spoke. " And with a garden, and that ugly stock-yard out of sight, what a pretty place it might be made!"

" Yes," said Julie, musingly; " I am almost sorry we have got the new house. It is so square and stiff after this, though of course it is better and finer."

" You are something like me, Julie; you would relinquish its finer appearance for the more graceful curves of this. Well, never mind, it will be some time before the Hall will be ready, and we can enjoy the garden meanwhile."

Anything that Alf engaged to perform was done in the face of all impediments, and he had not a little to oppose him this time in his father's expostulations.

" Really, Alf, you are as bad as Allen. Now what wild-goose chase are you after? What is the use of making a garden down here? No; let Allen and the girls set to work on the ground at the new place, if they want to garden. I can't spare time for foolery."

" But I thought you said Allen was to have the old place," replied Alf, with a laugh in his eye, though not on his lip.

" Well, so I did. Is he in so great a hurry that he must begin his improvements before we are out?"

"You know, father, a garden must have time to grow.   Besides," he continued, laughing, "Allen has taken such a liking to the old homestead, that I verily believe he intends to make a Bachelor's Hall of it, till —till something else happens."

" I' faith, does he? Well, he's such a strange, close fellow, I can make nothing out of him.   Is he not more open with you?   Do you think he is after Miss Herbert?"

" Not from anything he says.   If he is thinking of her, I fancy he takes it too coolly.   If it was me, at any rate, I should not act so."

" How would you act?" asked his father, with a quick twinkle of merriment in his eye, and knocking the ashes out of his pipe as he spoke.

"Make sure of my bird before I began to beautify its cage," replied Alf, turning away carelessly, and whistling a bar of that half-plaintive, half-defiant melody—

> " I care for nobody,
> Nobody cares for me."

But he took for granted that the work was to be done, and by evening had carted sufficient stone for the purpose, and built a long piece of the wall, from the creek, with the assistance of one of the men and his brother Frank, who chanced to be home for a holiday, and liked the "fun."   Alf was not one to slumber over his work, what he undertook to do he liked to do quickly, and on the whole, his father did not repent the tacit consent he had given, when he saw how little of his son's time it was likely to occupy. Besides, Allen's services were of too valuable a kind not to merit an occasional concession to his wishes. He retained, however, his own opinion respecting the folly of the business, and was inclined to take the same view of the subject as Alf, respecting the propriety of paying more attention to the winning of the bird than the gilding of its cage.

The question is, whether Allen would have thanked either for their opinion.

"Come and look at the wall, and see what you think of it," cried Alf, entering the sitting-room next day, and offering his arm with comic gravity to Marian.

"Not with that dirty jumper on, certainly," replied Marian, smiling and shrinking from the soiled sleeve and earth-covered hands.

"What, do you disdain the dirt accumulated in your service?" exclaimed Alf, turning away in apparent displeasure, but literally to hide the mischief of his intention.

"In *my* service? I don't know how you can prove that, Mr. Alf," replied Marian, crimsoning to the brow with vexation.

Allen raised his eyes from the account with which he was occupied, and looked earnestly, though covertly, at the flushed face.

"Surely you don't mind what that mad fellow says?" he quietly exclaimed, as his brother left the room and Marian rose to get her hat.

"Oh, no!" she answered, tying the rose-coloured strings very tightly; "I ought to know Alf pretty well now." But she did not say she minded a great deal more the question asked by Alf's brother, and felt far more inclined at that moment to shrink from the dark, spotless coat-sleeve that was offered to her than from the soiled jumper before presented. *Why,* she scarcely knew, excepting that there was something in the look, something in the manner, something in the tone in which this was said, undefinable enough, unpresuming enough, but cognizable to her delicate sense.

"See what it is to have a presentable coat-sleeve," said Alf, with a mock-rueful glance at his own, as Allen sauntered up with Marian to the spot where he had resumed his work. "Well, Miss Marian, have you forgiven me?"

"Forgiven you?"

"Oh, don't pretend you have not been very angry, because I know you have; but as I have been so unhappy as to give offence, have you forgiven me?"

"Oh yes; since you admit offence intentional," replied Marian; and Allen soon drew her away from his mischief-loving brother, to describe to her how he intended to divide and subdivide and serpentine the yet turfy ground, and to obtain her advice on the subject.

CHAPTER XIV.

A NOVEL FORD.

" WHO are those new neighbours I heard Alf telling your father about this morning after breakfast, Julie ? " asked Miss Herbert of her pupil, as once more they started off together, early one afternoon, for a rather long walk on a mission for Mr. Burton. They were not afraid of losing themselves this time. Their way lay entirely along fenced roads, and not across sections ; it was a road, too, with which they were familiar, and excepting here and there, where pools of mud and water covered the road, rendering it rather a difficult matter to steer clear of their stains, it was pleasant and dry.

" I do not know them," replied Julie, " but I think Allen does. Their name is Clare ; there is a large family of them up at the Burra, but there are only three of them here : the two eldest sons, and one of their sisters to keep house."

"But where is their house? since they are neighbours."

"Three sections from this. I do believe we shall
pass the very corner of their section, and shall perhaps get a glimpse of their house, for I think Alf
said they had put it up not far from the corner.
However, as Allen knows Edward Clare, we are very
sure to see some of them soon, for near neighbours
are so rare. Mother says it is a good thing to have
any."

"I wonder what Miss Clare is like," said Marian.
"How dull she must be when her brothers are away
at work!"

"I think she is pretty, from what Alf said. I heard
him talking about soft, brown eyes, and a small mouth,
and a colour like a rose-leaf."

"Indeed!" laughed Marian. "Alf is getting quite
romantic. Do you not wish very much to see this
pretty young lady who has so taken Alf's fancy?"

"I should like to see her, and shall soon ; but as to
her prettiness, we may not think her pretty. At any
rate, Allen has seen her a great many times, and I
have never heard him say she was pretty."

A very conclusive argument with Julie, not quite
so much with Marian. It was something, however,
which seemed to afford food for the quiet meditation
of each for a long distance on the road, for neither
spoke, though now and then Julie's hand was pressed
more closely on the arm she held.

It was a pleasant afternoon, winter though it was.

The sun shone out warmly and brightly ; so much so, indeed, that they were glad to remove their fur wrappers from their necks, and swing them on their arms. The grass, revived by the recent heavy rains, was of the freshest, gayest green, and here and there some of the earliest spring flowers were bending their blossoms to catch the breeze and bright sunshine. Glad were the two young ladies of their broad hats' shade, for that sunshine so eagerly absorbed by the flowers, looked down too hotly into their eyes and on their cheeks, dazzling and flushing with its cloudless beams.

They were walking along very silently and very leisurely, when by one of those obstructions, half mud, half water, their path was suddenly stopped. The bog extended from one side of the road to the other, and wandered off either way through young springing corn and lucern, so that there was little prospect of their finding a dry path on either side of the fence. They vainly walked backwards and forwards in search of one spot better than another.

"What can we do?" said Marian, laughing. "It would be a pity to go back when we are nearly at our journey's end."

"Oh, we can mount the fence, and creep along so;" and suiting the action to the word, Julie sprang upon the rail, and commenced a tottering walk.

"I can show you a more agreeable way than that, if you will allow me, young ladies," said a gentlemanly voice behind them.

Marian started and turned hastily round, and Julie sprang blushing from the fence, as the intruder, a young man dressed in a belted serge shirt and small oilskin cap, approached them from the other side of the road, leaping the fence by placing one hand on the top rail as he came. He raised his cap as he approached them, and looked inquisitively at Julie, and rather longer at her companion, and repeated his former offer.

Marian thanked him, rather wondering how he could make good his word. Her look seemed to say as much, for he smiled and turned again to the fence he had leaped; presently he came back with two or three long pieces of bark, which he busied himself in forming into a very passable bridge over the narrowest part of the slough. They crossed in perfect safety in a moment, and again united in thanks for the stranger's politeness.

He again bowed, and turned his gaze on Julie's fair face, as though there was something he recognized there.

"I think," he said after a moment of hesitation, "that it is Mr. Allen Burton's sister I have the pleasure of speaking to?"

Julie coloured and bowed.

"Will you tell him then, from me, Miss Julie, that when he has any leisure time to spare, an old friend, lately come into the neighbourhood, will be very glad to renew his acquaintance?"

Julie smiled her reply, and he continued gaily,—

"I need not speak for my sister, for I have no doubt she will soon find an opportunity for herself; nevertheless, Miss Burton, I am sure Mary will be delighted to see you, and your *friend* too," he added, with another earnest look at Marian, and a little emphasis on the word friend, as though a gentle reminder to Julie, that she had not introduced her. Julie did not heed it, however, and again raising his cap, he leaped the fence, and they pursued their way.

"Edward Clare! I knew it was, the moment I saw him," whispered Julie, as he left them.

"I thought so too. He was very polite. How do you think he knew you, Julie?"

"Only because I am considered so like Allen; and then meeting us here, you know, Miss Herbert. There are not so many young ladies in the bush, but that those there are may easily be found out."

"That's it, is it?" laughed Marian merrily. "So meeting two young ladies in these wilds, he thought he might easily find a Julie Burton in one of them."

Julie laughed and blushed. "Do you know, dear Miss Herbert, this road leads to our homestead, and he must have known that," she said, half doubtful whether her governess was laughing at or with her. "Do you like him?" she asked, after a moment's silence.

"I am hardly prepared to answer that question yet, and particularly of a friend of your brother. It would be scarcely fair to judge him after so short a time. He was very polite."

"Oh, you do not like him very much, I see!" said Julie, laughing slily, with a little of Alf's mischief in her soft eyes, "and I am very glad, because——"

" Because what, Julie? because you do ? "

" No, no. Because I should not like you to like him better than poor Allen."

Marian did not quite expect that reply, as the quick colour testified, but she only answered softly,—

" Do you then think it possible for me to like only one at a time, Julie? Are there not different kinds of excellence? And are you very sure, Julie," she continued, rallying, and smiling archly, " are you so very sure that your brother would like that epithet of ' poor Allen ' that you have given him, or that he would care so much as his sister, who liked or disliked him ? "

" I hope you ladies have not far to go," cried the same voice that before addressed them, now considerably in advance of them. They started, and looked about in vain, but could see nothing but trees before and on either side of them. It was from a cluster of wattles the sound seemed to come, and towards them accordingly they turned ; Julie with a very laughing face.

" Ah, you may laugh, Miss Julie! I can see you. —Never trouble yourself to look for me."

" Why do you hope we have not far to go, Mr. Clare? " asked Julie, silently prompted by Marian.

" Oh, you know my name, do you? and I only

know yours in return, and that you did not tell me: that's not fair, Miss Julie. Well, I hope you are not going far, because I see a storm brewing yonder, and if you are not very quick you will have it before you reach home."

"Oh, thank you!" cried Marian. "Come, Julie, we must waste no more time. Your father's message will not take long to deliver." And they set off at a rapid rate, which soon brought them in sight of the cottage they wanted.

"Who the dickens is she, I wonder!" was the muttered exclamation of Edward Clare, as pushing aside the branches of a tree he had climbed, in order to fix a white flag to be drawn up and down, as a signal for meal-hours, or *grub-time*, as he termed it, he showed his good-looking face and curly head, as rough as a carousal among the leaves and boughs could make it. "Well now, that's a little bit of Master Allen's slyness. To think of his having that young lady domesticated at home, as she evidently is by his sister's manner, and not so much as even mentioning her. Ah, ah! Allen, my boy, we'll be even yet. Well, that's a pretty little creature, too, that Julie. He has not praised her a whit too much. After all, it won't be so lonely here while the bush contains such *raræ aves* as these."

"Well, Julie, here we are at our novel ford again, at any rate," said Marian, once more tripping over the bridge of bark on their return. "But how the clouds are gathering now! See how black that large

one is over there!   Dear me, I am afraid, as **Mr.**
Clare said, we shall be caught in the storm."

"I felt a spot.   Oh, there is another, such a large
one—it fell on my nose.   Had we not better run?"
said Julie, laughing in spite of herself.

"I think we had, indeed.   I never like that low
moaning of the wind, and that whispering, uneasy
sound among the tops of the trees.   I always know
the shower is near," said Marian, almost breathless
with running.   "Well, never mind if we do get a
soaking; it will not be so bad as when we were lost,
will it?"

"Oh no; we know our way, even if it was dark.
But how fast the drops come!   I shall put on my
victorine, that will keep them from my neck."

"And so shall I, Julie.   Now for another run."

But run as they would, they could not outrun the
storm, which now came raging upon them, shaking
the trees, snapping the branches, hurling huge boughs
from the top of tall gums, and howling like a fierce
fiend.   They clung to each other, the drenching
shower pouring furiously over them.   Gasping for
breath, and almost beaten by its violence, they struggled
on.   But what could they do against such a storm?
Their strength was spent, they were both ready to
sink to the ground, when a clear, shrill whistle rang
through the trees, above the voice of the tempest, and
the next moment Edward Clare was by their side.   They
hailed him with most flattering delight.   Poor things,
they were only too glad of a brave heart to lead them.

"Now, Miss Julie, take my arm; come, hold on, and I'll keep you up. Please to make use of its fellow, Miss——. Really I beg pardon, but my little friend here has not introduced you."

"Miss Herbert."

"Thanks, Julie; better late than never. Well, on my knees (if it were not so muddy), Miss Herbert, I would entreat you to hang on a little harder. I should not like the job of having to account to certain friends of mine if you were missing."

There was not much time for ceremony in the midst of the storm, which every reader familiar with our Australian tempests will admit. Marian and Julie literally clung to their friend, whose stalwart figure was well able to support them. He put his arm round Julie to keep her up; of course he did not attempt the same liberty with Marian, but he helped her on none the worse for that. And through all the storm they went, till at length the homestead appeared in sight, and just sallying from the door came the two brothers.

"Who on earth have the girls picked up?" muttered Allen.

"Why, Ned! you don't mean to say that's you?" was the next moment's exclamation.

"I don't know who else it can be, then; though I don't feel very much *myself* either," was the rejoinder. "Well, don't you thank me for having taken care of the ladies? 'Tis well they were not washed away; and they might have been, for all *your* care."

"We have only this moment returned home our-selves, Miss Herbert," said Allen in an undertone to Marian, as he received her wet hat and cloak. She hastily threw them off, and ran from the room after Julie.

"Julie and I have nothing but adventures when we go out, Mrs. Burton," said Marian, laughing, as a little after, the kind, motherly woman came with warm spirits and water to her bedside, which she quietly insisted upon her taking to prevent the cold striking in.

"So it seems. I shall have to send Allen with you another time."

Marian lay long awake, speculating upon Allen's willingness to be her attendant. We will not record her conclusions.

CHAPTER XV.

A GENTLE NURSE.

THE storm passed away as even the wildest storm
will, and the morning sun shone upon the rapidly
flowing creek, more beautiful than ever in its full,
impetuous course. The birds chirped their pleasure
at the cessation of the hurricane, and the grass looked
yet greener. The warm sun-rays were rapidly drying
up the evidence of the storm of the previous night,
and there would not have been much to remind the
homestead folks of its fury and consequences, excepting
that miniature freshet and the closed window-blinds
in Marian's room.

It was Julie, however, and not Marian who had
suffered from exposure to the storm. But that she
might be near to wait upon her, they had carried her
in her little bed to the room of her governess ; and
since her removal thither, after a troubled, restless
night of wakefulness, she had fallen into a flushed and
heavy sleep.

It was Marian who gently tiptoed about the room, softly drawing the curtains to exclude the light from the sleeper, and stealing again and again to the bed-side, to consider the burning cheeks and parched lips and quickly-drawn breath that came from them, and then passed quietly out into the sitting-room to Mrs. Burton, as quietly saying,—

"Do you not think it would be as well for Frank to ride over to B——, and get Dr. Groom to call?"

It could not be concealed that Julie was in truth seriously ill, and her mother's worst fears were easily awakened. Frank was instantly sent off to the township, with instructions to wait there till the doctor's return, for any medicines he might order for the patient.

"It seems to me, Miss Herbert," said Alf laughing, "that you have quite a talent for adventures. I declare, as mother says, it's not right you should go out alone, you and Julie."

"Do you intend filling the office of attendant, Mr. Alf?"

"Me!" said Alf, with a comical shrug of his shoulders and a glance towards his brother. "No, that's reserved for a happier being than myself, I fancy—unless," he continued, teasingly, "Edward Clare constitute himself your attendant in future."

"I should think Mr. Clare will inquire whether such attendance is likely to be agreeable first," replied Marian.

Allen laid down the spur he was polishing as his

brother spoke, and with flashing eyes prepared to answer; but Marian's reply apparently satisfied him, for he again resumed his employment, with a slight smile playing at the corners of his mouth, which might, if seen, have told tales.

"By the bye, Allen," said Alf, as Marian left the room with the basin of arrowroot she had been preparing, "Ned Clare talks of coming down on Sunday, and bringing his sister here. What sort of a girl is Mary Clare?"

"You had better go and see for yourself."

"Well, I think I shall," said Alf carelessly, bending down to the boot he was lacing to conceal his smile. "It would not be quite the thing for you to monopolize all the ladies. If I were you, though, I would not let Ned have too much of *some one's* company; there's no knowing what might happen if you do."

"What do *you* mean?"

"Oh—nothing!—I think it's pretty fine now, and there's nothing particular to do, so I'll go and dig in your garden—make hay while the sun shines, you know," said Alf, significantly putting his head in again at the door he was closing, to give greater meaning to his words.

Who could so gently raise the weary, aching head, so softly smooth the pillow, so quietly move about the chamber of the invalid, as Marian? She had bought her experience at a dear school—the bedside of a beloved mother; and sometimes, as she flitted about the room of her little pupil, preparing cooling drinks and rendering more palatable the bitter potion, or moderating the light, that its glare might not affect the sufferer, her eyes would fill with tears at recollections that would come of the *one other* time when her whole soul went forth in her occupation, as if life or death depended on her tender nursing.

The gentle pressure of the burning hand, the glance of affection from the heavy eye of her young patient, was a sufficient reward for all these labours of love. But Marian had more than this in Mrs. Burton's gratitude and Allen's wordless thanks, not less eloquent for their *wordlessness*, whenever he saw her. As to Alf, he acknowledged her unremitting attention to his sister in his own way.

"I declare, Miss Herbert, it would be worth while to be ill, to have you to nurse one. I think I shall get up a fit of illness for the pleasure of it."

"You had better make sure of your nurse first," said Allen, rather abruptly, as Marian quitted the room, for he did not quite approve of his brother's free, impudent manner.

"Ah, that's what I wanted to say to you, Allen! That's what I think you are so guilty of not doing, the *making sure* business. It's not *my* way, anyhow, I should make sure of *my* nurse before I took ill, and what's more," he added, with the door open in his hand, "I should not rest till I had in verity made sure in *one other case*. But every one knows his own business best. Heigho!" and bang went the door behind him.

How Julie loved her governess! Her soft eyes would swim with happy tears, as waking again and again from her weary little day-sleeps, she discovered the same face by her side, either with book or work, quietly, untiringly watching her. Even the bitter draught with which she so often came to her side, was swallowed almost without a sigh or a sign of dislike. But weary, oh very weary, were those long days spent in bed! and Julie longed to be well again.

"Miss Herbert, I think I hear Allen in the garden. Are they getting on very fast with the wall?" she asked one morning, pushing back the soft light hair that fell in half-disordered bands on her pale cheeks.

"Yes, very fast; for it is quite finished, dear Julie," returned Marian, smiling; then rising from her seat, she slightly withdrew the curtain and looked out.

"You will see a great change when you are well," she continued. "Your brothers have worked so diligently that the whole plan of the garden is visible now, and I think your first walk in the open air must be to see it. We will take the seeds and bulbs with us."

"Oh, I wish I was well *now!* I am very tired of lying here; and I have looked at everything in the room till I know them by heart—every little nail, every little morsel of rough plaster, every knot in the counterpane. And I have thought of everything too. There is only *one* I am never tired of thinking about."

"And who is that, Julie?"

"*You*, dear Miss Herbert," exclaimed Julie, extending both her arms and clasping Marian's waist, for she had returned to her stand at the bedside.

Marian fondly returned her kisses, but still caressing her, she said rather sadly,—

"I was hoping, dearest Julie, that you were going to speak of *higher*, *better* thoughts."

"Ah! that is it, Miss Herbert!" said Julie, putting her thin hands as a shade for her fast filling eyes. "That is it; my heart cannot be in 'right tune.' I know it cannot, because those holy, happy thoughts do not come. But is it wrong then to love our friends very much?" Julie asked the question with an earnestness which served to convey an idea of the struggle it would cost her to diminish her affection.

"No, Julie, it is not wrong; it is right. Feelings of affection and gratitude and friendship are very precious, for they are gifts from God. But then, dear Julie, we are to love Him supremely, above all. We are not to suffer our love for His creatures to make our love for Himself less. Do you understand me, dear?"

"Yes, I do understand you; but how hard it seems! I know I ought not to feel so, and yet it appears so much more easy to love *best* those one is always with and seeing every day. I have a grand-mamma in England, but have never seen her, and am afraid I do not love her very much."

" And you feel as if grandmamma did not know you either. I understand the feeling precisely, dear Julie. But then, darling, this is not the case with God, be-cause His holy word tells us that He sees us—knows us—is acquainted with all our secret thoughts—knows every motive of our actions—understands our unbelief and fear, and *loves us still*. Ought we not then to love *Him?*"

Julie did not answer. With her long fingers veiling her face, she was thinking how wonderful must be that All-seeing eye, that could penetrate even into the hid-den thoughts of the heart, and a slight feeling of joy mingled with her reverence at the thought. " He can, perhaps, see then that *I* want to love Him, and when He sees the thought, the wish, perhaps He may show me how to do so."

" It is with our mental eye, the eye of our soul, dear Julie," continued Marian, "we can alone see Jesus while on earth. The veil is not withdrawn while we are in the body, and if we would hear Him speak to us, —yes, dear Julie, personally to us,—we have His sacred word we may hear His voice there. And how gentle are His words, ' I love them that love me ; those that seek me early shall find me.'"

" Does it say that ? " said Julie, with glistening eyes.

"Yes, dearest; is it not beautiful? Just what you want, Julie, is it not? To find this precious Saviour, this loving Lord; to know Him, to feel He is your Father, and loves you?"

"Oh, Miss Herbert! *yes—yes!*"

"And this seeking, Julie, is the inclination of the heart after Him. It is something deeper than words: something, perhaps, that our dearest earthly friends cannot see; but it is written on the heart, and He understands *heart-language*. Listen, dear Julie, and I will tell you a story, simple, affecting, and somewhat to the purpose. I want you to see that this kind Father is not *too far* distant to love, not too far distant to hear those who cry after Him."

Julie nestled down on her pillow, with her blue eyes fixed earnestly on her governess; and Marian, resting her elbow on the bed, and half shielding her face in her hands, in a low voice commenced:—

"Some time ago, dear Julie, in the wilds of Scotland, a minister of God, a truly good and devoted man, was accustomed to travel long distances, in order that those of his countrymen who inhabited mountainous districts might hear the glad tidings of the Gospel. Rough roads he had to traverse, rude receptions he often met, and his resting-places on his journey were only the small country inns—some doubtless with but poor accommodation. He was not, however, disheartened in his work. No; whenever he entered a little inn at night, he remembered his high vocation; he remembered in whose service he was engaged, and around the blazing ingle, he made it a rule to assemble all that were in the house to family prayer.

"A long day's journey found him one evening in the chimney-corner of a little roadside inn he had never before entered, and, as usual, before the supper appeared, he signified his wish to read and pray, begging that all who were in the house might be present. The landlord consented to the novel request, and the servants entered, and formed a group with the family.

"'Are all here?' asked the minister, hesitating to begin.

"'Yes,' said the landlord.

"'Are you quite sure *all* are here?' again asked the minister, doubtfully.

"'Yes; all excepting the little scullery-maid, and she is too dirty to come in.'

"'Call her in,' said the good man, 'call her in; dirty though she may be, she has a soul—a *precious soul*. If she has never been here before, more reason she should be here now.'

"The landlord hesitated, but at length the poor dirty little maid was brought wondering into the parlour; and the minister, perfectly satisfied, began to read. He felt strongly interested in that little dirty girl, whom no one appeared to care for or to notice; and after prayer, he called her to him, and made several inquiries. Poor girl! he found her sadly ignorant; she knew nothing about God, had no

K

idea she had a soul, and when asked if she ever prayed, replied that she did not know what it meant."

"Poor little girl!" said Julie, with tears in her eyes. "And did not he tell her?"

"Yes, dear Julie, he told her of the Saviour, and of His love. He told her what praying was; and then before he left in the morning, he promised her that on his return he would bring her a little present—a neckerchief—if she would promise to repeat a short prayer night and morning. The little prayer contained only four words, '*Lord, show me myself!* '"

"And did she promise?" asked Julie, eagerly.

"Yes, dear. She promised very gladly; and then the kind minister explained the meaning of the prayer, and how necessary it was that she should be able to see her own sinfulness, in order that she might discover her need of a Saviour.

"I hope he remembered that poor little girl, and the promise he made," sighed Julie, as Miss Herbert paused.

"He did, Julie; but it was many weeks before he returned to the little inn. However, when he did come, one of the first he inquired after was the little scullery-maid. 'Oh yes;' was the reply, 'she is here, sure enough, but little enough use she's been since you left. She's done nothing but cry night and day, and now she's so ill she cannot work at all.'

"'Let me see her! let me see her!' cried the

minister, and a flush of joy came to his heart. He guessed what was the matter with the little girl, and believed that God had answered her prayer. They showed him a hole under the stairs, where the poor girl lay on a bed of straw, very ill. He took her by the hand.

"'Well, Peggy,' he said kindly, 'I have brought you the neckerchief I promised you. Here it is!'

"'Oh no, sir!' cried the poor girl, her eyes streaming with tears. 'Take back the neckerchief. I cannot take it. A *dear* gift it has proved to me. God has answered my prayer. He has shown me *myself*, and I am miserable!

"Very glad indeed was the minister to hear this account, and so he told the sick girl. 'I will now teach you,' said he, 'another little prayer, which you must also promise to repeat as before. It contains only four words, like the other; but it will bring joy and peace with it. It is this, "*Lord, show me Thyself!*" It was, he kindly told her, a sight by faith of Jesus dying for her—bearing her sin in His own person on the cross at Calvary—pleading in heaven for her. That—that alone could restore peace to her agitated bosom. For this sight she was to pray, and that simple prayer contained all she could desire. That he prayed with her and for her there can be no doubt, and then he once more went on his way."

"O Miss Herbert! did he never see her any more?" Julie's tears almost prevented her asking.

"Years afterwards, dearest. She had become a

woman, had married and had four children. She took a long journey to Edinburgh merely to see him once more. He did not remember her, but she told him that she was the same little scullery-girl to whom he had once taught two short prayers. The last prayer had also been answered, and ever since that time she had been a sincere and happy Christian.

"So you see, dear Julie, it is not for our much speaking our Father hears. Oh no. It is the believing prayer, however simple, He loves to answer; and this last little prayer will just suit you, love, who feel as though you wanted to know Jesus, that you may love Him ; 'Lord, show me Thyself, that I may learn to love Thee !' " She gently wiped away the fast falling tears, and soothed the trembling Julie with caresses. Then shaking up the pillow and administering a cooling draught, she drew the curtains and left her to sleep, for which her excitement had disposed her. Her own prayers were fervently added to Julie's that night, not only for the gentle girl, but for herself.

CHAPTER XVI.

"I know by that golden wattle bough,
    That beautiful Spring is coming now;
    That the sun is dispelling old Winter's showers,
    And crowning the hill and creek with flowers.
    Oh dearer than ever will spring-tide be,
    For a Father's hand in His gifts I see."

NEARLY a fortnight's confinement in the house, and nearly the same time in her bed, were the consequence of Julie's exposure to the storm. It did not pass off so wearily as might have been expected. Her gentle nurse never left her self-imposed task, never appeared tired of soothing or administering. Could the walls of that little chamber have spoken, to how many sweet lessons would they have testified! How much of Jesus, His love, His tenderness, would they have discovered issuing from the lips of the gentle teacher! How fervent were her low-breathed prayers by the sick girl's pillow; how earnest and trusting was the voice in which the sacred page was read! In that sick chamber Julie learnt much; and, oh, higher, better than all other knowledge, she learnt to love her Saviour—she learnt to know Him as her Saviour. Between the pupil and her governess a new tie was stablished—they were children of one Father, bound for the same haven of peace, travelling the same road, understanding the same language. Julie could now bless the Hand that laid her low to raise her up to such happiness. And Marian's heart was overwhelmed with gratitude, that in bringing this one lamb into the Saviour's fold, she, humble as she felt herself to be, had been honoured as an instrument.

She had, indeed, been "sowing seeds," but little had she thought how soon they would spring up and bear fruit to everlasting life. She watched the young plant affectionately, prayerfully, it may be anxiously; that no frost might nip the blossom, that no storm might bend or break, oh, how earnestly she prayed!

Yet what had she done after all? the fallow ground had been prepared, she had only sown the seed. It was the continued influence of the Holy Spirit that could alone render the labour effective; and was not His gracious influence sufficiently evident in the new inclinations, the new desires, the new hopes of her pupil? Marian felt it was.

It was a pleasant change for Julie, from the bed-room to the little study, to sit in that comfortable easy chair—Allen's easy chair—by the glowing, well-built fire, the table drawn close within reach, her little Bible at her elbow, her volume of fugitive poems beneath it, the ripe oranges Allen had purposely ridden to the township to procure, temptingly diffusing their rich perfume; to exchange the closely curtained window of the bed-chamber for the gracefully lifted drapery of the window of their pretty blue room, through the parted folds of which she could discern green trees, and the dear rising hill, crowned with she-oaks, refreshing to look upon. How pleasant it was, too, to listen to the sweet-toned piano, to watch Marian's white fingers as they lingered lovingly over the keys; more than all, to hear her sing low, sweet, thrilling songs of Jesus and His love. How she loved her governess!

There were soft, warm, sunshiny days succeeding that storm. Indeed it appeared as though it was the parting outburst of the season, and though there was still occasionally a shower of rain, just to keep the earth refreshed and fertile, yet the violence of the winter had spent itself.

"Does not this remind you that spring is coming, Julie?" asked Allen one morning, entering the study, as his sister had seated herself in her accustomed lounge by its fire. He threw a small branch of golden wattle flowers on the table as he spoke.

"O Allen! yes. How beautiful. I am so glad. I did not think that there would be any wattle blossoms for a long while." The rich colour that glowed in her cheek sufficiently testified her pleasure. The sight of the golden blossoms did her good.

"When are you coming out, Julie, to see the garden?" Allen asked, placing himself behind his sister, and his hands resting affectionately on her shoulders.

"I don't know, Allen," said Julie, half mournfully "I want very much to come out, the sunshine is so beautiful. It is not wet, Allen, is it?"

"Wet, darling? no; the paths are as dry as a bone Try a walk to the window, pet, and look for yourself." He placed his arm around her, and gently led her across the room as he spoke. "There; is not that worth looking at, Julie? I'm sure it would do you good to be out. I'll ask mother and Miss Herbert, shall I? They will know best what is good for you."

"Oh yes, Allen! please do. I want so to see what you have been doing in the garden. Is the ground ready for the seeds yet?"

"Quite; and I want you and Miss Herbert to sow them. You see, Julie, I always think ladies manage those delicate sorts of matters best. They generally have more taste, especially among flowers."

"Ah! but gentlemen have taste, too," said Julie, with a slight archness in her tone and glance. "At least, Allen, Miss Herbert says *you* have."

"You will make me vain, Julie, if you tell me that," said Allen, smiling. "Miss Herbert wishes to please you, pet."

"But she would not tell an untruth, or say what she did not think, to please me, Allen," replied Julie, gravely.

"I did not mean that, darling, I'm sure she would not. Well, come and sit down again, dear, and I will go and consult your nurse as to the propriety of a quiet promenade. It is so very fine, I think I may promise you ' Yes,' for an answer."

And carefully wrapped in a warm shawl, with a close little silk hood tied under her chin, and her parasol to ward off the rather fervent sunshine, Julie was once more permitted to inhale the fresh air of heaven. With what new feelings she did so, welcoming each blade of grass, each tiny, insignificant flower, every leaf, every passing breeze, with the inward glad whisper, "My Father made them all. He who created all things is my God too! He loves even me." Could Alf have seen her that moment he would have better comprehended that term, "spiritual," Marian had once applied to his sister. Something of the heart's language was impressed upon her features.

Alf, however, was away at his usual avocation, and Julie was supported on either side by those she dearly loved, Allen and Marian. The paths had been left of a pleasant breadth; four might have walked comfortably abreast, for there was no deficiency of ground inclosed, and the purpose of all was pleasure, a very unusual one in Australia. Utility was here put entirely out of the question.

" I have been venturing a little beyond the pale of your advice, Miss Herbert," at length Allen exclaimed, as they turned into a path evidently winding round the whole of the inclosure. "Do you see what I have done?" and he pointed to either side of the path, along which were newly planted vines, rapidly putting forth buds and leaves.

"Grape-vines!" said Marian. "Well, but I thought you intended to have no fruit here."

"So I did; but you see, Miss Herbert, in planting these, I was thinking of something almost as agreeable in summer as fruit—I mean shade. I intend this to be one of the coolest, prettiest walks one could desire on a hot day. I shall have a trellis thrown overhead, the vines will very quickly cover it, and in the centre of the walk there is to be a summer house. Stoop down, if you please, ladies, and you will discover something else. Do you see those little unmeaning twigs, all putting out buds and leaves?"

"Yes. Why they are rose slips!"

"Every variety that I could lay hands upon," laughed Allen, highly gratified by the evident pleasure and approbation of his companions.

"How beautiful!" said Marian, with admiration. "How much I admire the idea! Can you not fancy, Julie, you see the roses in bloom, and the vine-leaves and tendrils interlacing above?"

Allen looked at her with unbounded admiration. His imagination carried him even a little farther than that, for hope was bright just then. It was something beyond roses and vine-leaves that was to reward his labour, or it was all futile.

They sauntered slowly through the walks. At intervals there were openings on either side, communicating with the other parts of the garden. Through one of these openings they came upon a little lawn in embryo. The grass had been left; it was of a particular soft, velvety kind, and had been newly mown into order. A ring had been marked in the centre by slender poles placed in the ground, round which, from pole to pole, wattle boughs, stripped of their leaves, had been securely fastened, forming a continuance of arches, and at the foot of every pole was a creeping rose-tree.

"You do not want my advice, Mr. Allen," said Marian, earnestly; "your design is beautiful. I can understand how perfectly lovely it will be."

"Oh, but there is much more to do. I fear I have exhausted my genius in the rose-walk and lawn. I hope you will not withhold your promised assist-ance.

"Certainly not if it is required; but it appears to me you can do so well without it."

Allen turned upon her a quick, penetrating, ear-nest look. It said more effectually than words, "That is impossible;" and there was so much more the eyes expressed, that Marian was glad to avert her gaze, and turn the conversation. Glad, too, she was to hear her name called from the house, that she might hide her embarrassment in a retreat.

"O Allen! I wish we were never going to leave this house," sighed Julie, as she slowly returned towards home with her brother.

He smiled. "Do you, Julie?" but he did not tell her he could not reciprocate her wish.

CHAPTER XVII.

WHAT THE RAIN BROUGHT.

> " And the rain, it raineth so fast and cold,
> We must cover the embers low ;
> And snugly housed from the wind and weather,
> Mope like birds that are changing feather."

SUNSHINE and fine weather did much for Julie, and she was no longer a prisoner in the house. As her accustomed strength returned, she was almost constantly in the garden, following out either Allen's or Marian's suggestions ; for he still persisted he could not do without their assistance. It was pleasant work those bright days, sowing seeds, and planting rose slips, young lilacs, and laburnum-trees. Allen was not at all times with them. He had his customary business to pursue, but he never returned from a journey without procuring some shrub or herb, some trifle for the garden, which he had either begged, borrowed, or stolen.

Just opposite the study window, in the centre of another plot of grass, he had formed a small circular bed, and in the centre of this he had placed a basket, on a pedestal of wattle boughs. Its shape was very ingenious, and green paint had greatly improved its appearance. This he had filled with mould, and decorated with two or three creeping plants, a geranium, and one or two dwarf rose-trees. It was attractive in its unfinished condition.

"We must have some more of your flower-baskets about the garden, Mr. Allen," said Marian with admiration, as she watched the completion of his design. "You will become quite notorious on account of this garden," she added laughing.

"I care little what others either say or think of it, if you like it, Miss Herbert," replied Allen, in a tone intended for her ear only.

She coloured highly. "What possible consequence can *my* opinion be on the subject?" she thought to herself. "I am not to be long here; or if I am, I shall be on the other side of the home section, in the new house. What benefit then will be the beauty of this garden? For in a short time it will be beautiful —it must be."

Marian stood with her hands resting on the top of the garden-rake. Imagination was busy at work. "It will indeed be lovely," she inaudibly murmured.

Allen rose from the basket around which he was twisting a truant spray, and looked earnestly at her. At that moment he would have thrown himself and garden and all he had at her feet. But whether or not Marian's quick instinct saw the danger, she destroyed the charm, and threw him back from his sentiment by suddenly exclaiming,—

"What do you intend doing with that large piece

of ground behind the house?   You have separated it from the rest by that long row of arches, which I see you intend to be covered with Cape ivy."

"I have not yet made up my mind," replied Allen, dashed down by the question from his sentimental position to common life again.   For in truth he had a kitchen-garden in view on that identical spot; and the completion of that was dependent upon an event, so uncertain that it would not do to speak of.

The new house was progressing rapidly.   The fine weather tended wonderfully to its completion.   All the exterior work was done, and the plastering of the interior was in some cases completed.   Mrs. Burton was satisfied to her heart's content.   She expressed her pleasure, and did not spare directions. and suggestions.   She was so often away at the new house with Bessie, Alf, and her husband, that Marian, Julie, and Allen were already almost left to the old homestead.   Allen was very contented it should be so.   If occasionally, on returning from a long ride, he found his mother absent, and on inquiring, heard she was not likely to return, he was in no way displeased. His dinner was too pleasantly prepared by other hands for him to miss her, his cup of coffee was none the worse for being administered by Marian.

The seeds, bulbs, flower-roots, and slips were just in their destined places, when down came the rain again—heavy rain, too—a sort of reminder that if the other storm was taken as a farewell to winter, it was a most decided mistake.   Work out of doors was out of the question.   Marian and her pupils returned more steadily to their studies, and the fire again burned all day in the music-room, for latterly Allen had changed its name, and by silent though general consent it had been adopted.

"Ah, come down—come down in bucketfuls! Who cares?" was Alf's exclamation on a very wet evening, as divested of damp boots and jumper, and in full enjoyment of warm, dry ones, he followed Allen's example, and sauntered into the music-room.

"Well, girls, this is what I call cozy," he exclaimed, throwing himself into a chair, a comfortable distance between the fire and lamp.   "I have had a vision of this music-room and its glowing fire and pretty faces," added he, with a glance at Allen, "all the time I have been in that wet stockyard.   The very prospect of it made me warm."

And so indeed it well might, for a very pleasant, warm picture of comfort was that little room ; the softened light of the lamp forming an agreeable contrast to the dazzling, brilliant, sparkling radiance of the fire.

Marian was seated between her two pupils, busily employed on a dress for Bessie, who was dividing her glances of approbation and pleasure between its soft blue folds and a large book of pictures which lay open before her.   Julie, in her accustomed seat, was leaning back among the cushions, with a small Pilgrim's Progress in her hand, in which she was deeply absorbed.   Certainly they were grouped very prettily together; the merry romp, with her flaxen curls, and the fair, soft-haired, delicate Julie, in strong contrast with their governess, with her rich, dark-brown ringlets and flushed cheeks. Allen silently thought so. Alf significantly expressed the thought, not only in looks but in words.

Characteristic, also, were the position and employment of the young men. Allen had seated himself opposite Marian at the table, with a small writing-desk before him. He usually had writing to do in an evening; but could the contents of that desk have been revealed, something besides calculations and business letters would have been discerned.

As to Alf, penknife in hand, he was very busily engaged carving the handle of a whip with all kinds of grotesque figures; his tongue meanwhile rattling on with its accustomed freedom, sometimes to the amusement, sometimes to the discomfiture of his companions. The fire blazed and glowed though the rain was descending still in torrents; it really made the atmosphere of the room very inviting.

"Hallo!" shouted Alf, suddenly, as a rather startling knock at the sitting-room door, followed by a rapid entrance of feet, broke in upon their momentary silence.

"I say, Allen, there are some friends of *yours*, I fancy," he continued, with a comic look at his brother, "three of them, Lady Mary and all!" He rose, threw open the door of their retreat, and discovered Edward Clare, his sister and brother, removing wet coats and habit before the large sitting-room fire. Allen left his seat, and went forward.

"We have taken you by storm, as the storm has taken us," said Edward Clare, shaking his friend's hand with double the warmth it deserved could he have known the feelings with which it was extended. "Frank and I have had a long ride, to bring this young lady home from Riverton, where she has been visiting; and this storm was so unmerciful as to half-drown both us and our horses. So, as the creek will be impassible, or at any rate, unpleasantly high to cross to-night, we have intruded on your father's kind hospitality. Do you and Mary need introducing?"

"I think not," replied Allen, making an attempt to smile, and approaching the young lady in question, who certainly had nothing either alarming or repulsive in appearance; for, as Julie had said, she had soft brown hair, banded neatly away from her brow, and eyes—not soft, that was a mistake—but quick and full of glee, and a cheek to which the storm had only given greater freshness, and whose colour might have shamed the rose. A tall, full figure, of very just proportions, did indeed give her something like a commanding aspect, and the ruby lips had not a little archness in their smile. Allen was, however, neither afraid nor bashful, and the other *nameless* feeling vanished before her first glance; and half laughing at her, half at himself, he bade her welcome to the house: then leading her forward into the music-room, at once presented her to Marian and his sister Julie.

"Allen, my boy," said Edward Clare, when he returned to him, in a low voice, "I had no idea you were so sly. To think of your having *music* and *beauty* here in the bush, and keeping it all for your own entertainment!"

"I never knew you were an admirer of music."

"No! Well then, you have discovered one of my dormant qualities. I am a passionate admirer of—of —of everything that is beautiful."

"I vote for our return to the music-room," said Alf; "father will enjoy his pipe and newspaper better if we go. Never mind what *we* shall enjoy," he whispered to Frank Clare, aside.

"I second the motion!" cried Edward, eagerly.

"Come, Allen, we have had the proof of eyesight that gentlemen are admitted: so please lead the way." And the whole party of them entered together.

Marian rose from her seat, and was formally introduced to Edward Clare and his brother; and then they all seated themselves about the room, Alf running the gauntlet of fun with Mary Clare, Allen talking gravely of horses and dogs with Frank, a young man of Alf's age, and Edward Clare devoting all his attention to Marian, who would rather have listened to his sister. Julie came in for a share of his attention. He had discovered that that was the most effectual way to secure the ear of her governess.

"You are like a veritable snowdrop, Miss Julie,"

he exclaimed, laughing. "All the prettier for your illness, if that is possible. Oh now don't blush so, or you will spoil my simile, and I shall have to think of another, or turn my snowdrop into a rose-bud."

"Julie does not care to be reminded of her looks," said Marian, taking compassion on her crimsoned cheeks.

He turned short round, and fixed a look of ill-concealed admiration on herself, but he said nothing, for the glance she gave was no encouragement to him to proceed.

"I suppose you will not venture out so far as your last walk for a long time, Miss Herbert?"

"Oh, I hope we shall; I should think this rain would close the winter. Have not you farmers had sufficient now?"

"Quite; we shall have a little too much if the weather does not become settled soon. Do you often walk such distances?"

"Not often; Julie is not very strong. But we can ride as soon as the weather is settled. We intend going to the little chapel at Evansdale as often as we can."

"What, to the Ranters?"

"No; the Wesleyans, Mr. Clare. They are a simple, earnest people, but I never heard of their ranting I am not a Wesleyan, but I like some of the people very much. At any rate I think it pleasant to worship God in a house set apart for His service, when I have the opportunity."

L 2

There was a little awkward pause for a few moments after this. It was broken by Allen suddenly exclaiming,—

"Miss Herbert, is it too much to ask for those sweet 'Bird waltzes,' of which we are all so fond? Miss Clare I am sure would like to hear them."

She rose instantly, and walked to the piano. Edward Clare started up, placed her chair in readiness, and opened the instrument; while Allen quietly took possession of her portfolio, and sought the desired waltzes, and then, to the evident disappointment of his friend, remained by her side to turn the pages of the book for her. Even Alf and his companion, Mary Clare, were silent as those sweet sounds floated through the room, rippling, quivering, dancing like things of life. Marian had often played, but never with more feeling. So Allen thought, as with one hand resting on the back of her chair, the other turning leaf after leaf, he stood watching the delicate hands in their passage over the keys, and determined to keep his friend Edward as much at bay as possible. A glance at him as he stood resting his head against the wall, with both arms folded, and his eyes fixed intently on the fair musician, not a little confirmed him in his purpose. How at that moment he wished that his own fate were decided, that he need fear no longer!

"How delightful it must be to have the power of bringing out such sweet sounds from those keys!" said Mary, with a sigh, after Marian had risen from her seat at the instrument, and returned to her former place at the table, Allen this time being by her side. "I wish I could play."

"*You*, Mary, with your great, fat, awkward hands! the churn-handle is better adapted to them," said her brother with a merry laugh.

"I am sure, Edward, you are very polite," said his sister, colouring highly, and looking down at the offending, but sadly libelled members. Rather large they certainly were, and—truth compels us to confess it—red; but they were not awkward-looking hands after all.

"If I were you, Miss Clare, I would pull his wool for that," said Alf.

"At any rate, he is glad enough to get the 'awkward, fat hands' employed in his service, and ready enough to eat the butter they make," replied Mary.

"To be sure I am; and when is there a time that I do not give you full credit for being one of the best and neatest housekeepers in the country?" replied her brother laughing. "I will say that," he continued. "Your dairy is worth looking into; but my dear sis, you must acknowledge your fingers were never made for piano-keys." And he gave a glance at the hands he was abusing, and then at the pretty fingers busily engaged on the soft blue merino, by way of adding force to his words.

"You must not think that your brother means anything else but compliment, Miss Clare," said Marian, indignant at the unwarrantable attack of Edward. "Many gentlemen think musical accomplishment waste of time, and that hands adapted for the piano are not fit for anything else."

Edward Clare shook his head.

"We know better than that, Miss Marian. Don't we, Allen?" said Alf, roguishly. "Do you remember last harvest—the can and the lunch bags?"

"Be quiet, Mr. Alf," said Marian, laughing and blushing; "you have no right to betray secrets."

"Or the winnowing machine?" persisted Alf, with a provoking glance from his brother to Marian.

"Alf, have you not sense to see you are making yourself very disagreeable?" said Allen.

"That's what it seems I always am," said Alf, with an affected sigh of resignation. "Was there ever such an abused being? Take pity on me, Miss Clare," he continued, turning with a most despairing countenance to the young lady he addressed, and flinging his arm rather impudently over the back of the chair against which she was leaning; "everything I say they tell me is wrong."

"And I shall join them; and add also, that everything you do is wrong," she exclaimed, laughing, and withdrawing her shoulder from his hand.

"No, don't do that, for it always has a contrary effect—it makes me *worser*. You have no idea how provoking I can be."

"I have: a very good idea," she replied, rising and attempting to cross the room.

"Oh, don't leave me," petitioned Alf, catching her hand and re-seating her. "I will be a good boy, indeed I will, if you will only stay."

CHAPTER XVIII.

WHO IS THE HAPPY MAN?

Not he who has all that this world can bestow,
  Its wealth and affection most lavishly giver,
But he who can look from a sojourn below,
  To a permanent treasure—to mansions in heaven.

"Who would not be a Christian? I have seen
Men shrinking from the term, as if it brought
A charge against them. Yet the honoured name
Is full of gentlest meaning."

"Good morning, Miss Herbert," exclaimed Edward Clare, moving towards the sitting-room door with a smile of pleasure as she entered. He was the sole occupant of the room, and had been silently and rather moodily watching the clouds, through which an occasional gleam of sunshine gave slight promise of improving weather.

"Good morning," replied Marian, cheerfully giving him her hand as she spoke. "The weather is not quite so bad as last night. I saw you were inspecting it."

"I was looking at the clouds, certainly, though not altogether studying the weather; about that there is not much question. The wind is in the right quarter; we shall have it fine again. I suppose,"

he added, laughing, "you would scarcely believe me
if I told you I was philosophising on *human life* when
you entered."

"Why should I not believe you?"

"Oh, I don't know. I thought perhaps you enter-
tained the same opinion of me as most other people
do, that I am a *harum scarum* sort of a fellow, into
whose head such a thing as philosophy could never
enter. Indeed," he continued, turning a very penetrating look into her face, "I still believe you think
so."

"Do you imagine then I can read character so
quickly?"

"Yes, I do—at least I think you form your judgment quickly, and have set down Edward Clare as
a very *shallow-pated* individual, with only a dash of
good nature as a redeeming quality."

"You affect to read my thoughts, do you?" said
Marian, laughing. "Will you, then, to counteract
those thoughts, oblige me with a little of your philosophy?"

"Has it ever struck you, Miss Herbert, that some
men are born under a particularly happy star, while
others have a clouded destiny from beginning to end
of the chapter?" Edward Clare spoke very gravely,
but not in reply to her question.

"Do you mean as to externals?"

Why, the internal is so dependent on the external, is it not? I should think there can be little
difference."

"Pardon me, *every difference* I imagine," replied Marian. "A clouded earthly career does not necessarily imply a lack of *mental* sunshine; and with regard to your first question, perhaps we differ respecting the 'clouded destiny' on one side, and the 'happy star' of the other; our estimate of each may widely differ. What is your definition of the latter?"

"I call that man born under a happy star, who is the favourite child of fortune, not only as to the possession of the baser metals silver and gold, but of the affections."

"I call that man a fortunate man, a happy man," said Marian, gravely, "who is a child of God—a favourite of heaven; who fixes not all his affections on earth, whose treasure is above, whose heart is there; external things can then indeed have little influence on him, he is beyond, superior to them all.

"Breakfast! breakfast!" shouted Alf, who had just entered the room; and not very well pleased, for his brother's sake, by the serious *tête-à-tête*, of which he was a witness, he broke upon them with the whole strength of his lungs,—

"Breakfast! breakfast!"

"For mercy's sake have pity upon one's head, Alf!" said Edward Clare, responding to his morning salutation, but most heartily wishing him at that moment sound asleep on his pillow, or at the other end of the section.

"Oh, it's nothing when one's used to it," replied

Alf, bustling about, upsetting the chairs and over-turning stools in his progress. "Come, Miss Herbert, let me escort you to your place; the coffee wants your attention. Here, Allen, come to your old post, can't you! I am obliged to take your office, you see. That comes of being late; however, now you are here, take your seat and do your duty."

Allen mentally, almost for the first time, was grateful to his random brother; he understood his intention. As to Edward Clare, it certainly was not a blessing he breathed on Alf's head for the officiousness that had left him only the opposite side of the table. He was obliged to content himself with his distant position, and answer, as well as he could, the questions with which Mr. Burton plied him during breakfast, respecting the produce of his farm and stock. It was a difficult task to be sure, and sometimes the answers he made were in danger of proving wide of the mark; for on one side he could hear a running fire of wit and fun between Alf and his sister, and on the other hand, nearly opposite to him, a low conversation was going on between Allen, Marian, and Frank. He would have given much to have heard what they were talking about.

After breakfast they had no plea to detain them; they therefore mounted their horses and returned home, Alf volunteering to accompany them.

Edward Clare had the satisfaction to hear his sister say, as she stooped from her saddle before they started, "I hope Miss Herbert and Julie will very often come and se_ me," and his satisfaction was by no means lessened at Marian's reply,—

"We will, as soon as the weather is fine."

"And let us see you often," said Mrs. Burton, kindly. "You young people must be rather dull by yourselves, but there need be nothing to prevent your coming here as often as you can, and your brothers too, Miss Clare."

"Thank you, Mrs. Burton, thank you," said Mary, with a beaming smile; "I shall certainly avail myself of your kind invitation."

"I am glad you include Frank and myself, Mrs. Burton. I shall certainly not forget it," said Edward, laughing.

"I hope you do not stand in need of invitation, Mr. Clare," replied Mrs. Burton, "you will be welcome whenever you come. Are you not Allen's friend?"

But Allen wished just then that his mother would not be quite so warm in her invitation to *his friend*. He stood by, and said nothing, affecting indeed to be too deeply engrossed in the arrangement of the bit of Mary's horse, to notice or even hear the conversation. It was a genuine sigh of relief he gave as the horses cantered away and disappeared among the trees. His spirits involuntarily rose fifty per cent. as Marian exclaimed,—

"Now, Julie; now for the garden. While this sunshine lasts let us see the good the rain has done."

Allen congratulated himself that he had thought of a garden, and gloried over Edward Clare, because it was *his* home of which Marian was the sunshine; it was by his possessions she was surrounded; and he had at least the benefit of daily intercourse with her, which Edward Clare was denied.

CHAPTER XIX.

MARIAN'S SHADOW.

"I would not wish
Any companion in the world but you."

Spring, with its buds and blossoms, was now fully in.
Occasional showers were now not deplored, but rather
welcomed. The little brown, unsightly seeds Marian,
Julie, and Allen had put into the ground, had now
sprung into beautiful being, and with all three the
garden was a favourite resort. Allen had formed a
very pretty bower of hop plants; he had chosen them
for their rapid growth, and closely around them he had
planted the choicest roses, and blue and white violets,
which, now in their full beauty, diffused delightful
fragrance through the air. Whenever the sun looked
warmly upon them, Marian and her pupils took books
and work thither. The girls were learning to love
flowers as well as their instructress.

Every fine evening brought other admirers to the
garden, admirers Allen could very willingly have
excluded, for he doubted, in one instance at least,
whether all the admiration was expended on the garden. Edward Clare was not one who waited for much
invitation. Motive with him was all; and a motive

he had in coming to the homestead which he chose to keep to himself; perhaps his own natural vanity prevented him from discovering that, to some parties, his visits were unwelcome.

"Well," exclaimed Alf to himself one evening, as he stood under the veranda, looking over the garden wall, where Marian and Julie were walking with Edward Clare by their side,—"well, if I were Allen, I be hanged if I would allow that! What a fool he is to let matters go on so. I doubt now whether he will not let the girl slip through his fingers!"

Allen heard his soliloquy, and was looking at the same scene in the garden, but he did not discover himself to his brother. "I am not quite such a fool as that," he thought; "at least I won't without a trial." Oh, it was rather a ticklish point, this ' to be or not to be ' part of the business; the courage might well require screwing up for the occasion.

"Promise me one thing, Julie, will you pet?" he whispered that evening to his sister, as he sat in the veranda, with one arm thrown round her slender waist, and her head resting on his shoulder. "Promise me one thing; whenever Edward Clare intrudes his presence on Miss Herbert, do you always keep close to her—don't leave her for a minute."

Julie's blue eyes opened very widely, and she lifted her head to look into her brother's face, in order to discover whether or no he jested. "Do you not like Edward Clare, Allen?" she asked in a tone of innocent wonder.

The colour flushed to Allen's brow at the question, but the shadow of the veranda prevented the moonlight from betraying it. He replied evasively to his sister,—

"I think he is rather tiresome in his attentions, Julie, that's all. Will you do as I ask you?"

"Oh yes, Allen. But do you think Miss Herbert will like it? I'm sure Mr. Clare will not, for he always looks as if he wished I would go away whenever he comes."

Allen bit his lips, and frowned, but he commanded his voice sufficiently to ask,—

"Do you think, then, Miss Herbert also wishes you away, Julie?" His breath came short and thick as he listened for her answer.

She hesitated a moment, and then replied, "No Allen; I do not think she does. She will always have me with her, and holds my hand, I remember now, very tightly whenever Edward Clare is with us."

Allen gave a sigh of mingled pleasure and relief. "Then, Julie, you will do as I ask?"

"Oh, yes."

And to her brother's secret satisfaction, though to Edward Clare's very evident annoyance, she most faithfully kept her promise. Thanks to her watchfulness, the latter gentleman never found Marian alone. "Her shadow," as he half playfully, half pettishly called Julie, was ever at her side. There was no such thing as a word in secret between them, and certainly

Marian gave no evidence of desiring it. She feigned no messages to get Julie from her side, but the more determined Edward Clare seemed against her shadow, the more determinately did she cling to it.

Julie's health had very much improved with the warm weather; they were once more enabled to resume their walks. And one very lovely Sabbath morning the horses stood ready saddled at the door, the hymn-books were once more safely tucked into the pockets of the saddles, and Marian, Julie, and the two brothers were again on their road to the little chapel among the hills. The wattle blossoms had all disappeared, but there were yet hundreds of unfaded flowers in the shade of the green boughs. Flocks of parrots of all colours, from the grass-green paroquet to the beautiful blue mountain, flew across and across their path. The little robin, with its breast of vivid vermilion, like a living gem, carelessly twittered among the wattle boughs; and sometimes a white cloud disturbed the blue of the heavens, attended by a discordant screeching, as a flight of white cockatoos passed over their heads.

Wide-brimmed hats and veils were found comfortable, for the spring was rapidly brightening into summer, and the sun looked very, very warmly from the heavens. Where the grass was unprotected by the shade of gum, or wattle, or cherry-tree, it had already begun to assume a yellow tinge, and its seeds were unpleasantly proclaiming their existence to the pedestrian. But on this Sabbath morning, a

M

pleasant breeze was tempering the sun's fervid rays; a breeze that lifted the veil, and fanned the cheek and lip and brow, and slightly dishevelled the ringlets beneath the hats, and was altogether a very welcome, refreshing visitant. So Marian thought; at any rate, it came so pure from heaven, albeit it caught some of earth's flowers in its way.

"I am very glad we are going once again to chapel, Miss Herbert, are not you?" said Julie, reining her horse to the side of her governess as she spoke, and placing her hand caressingly upon the mane. "It is only a little chapel, to be sure, but it seems so much nicer than spending Sunday as so many spend it in the bush—as once I liked to spend it," she added with a blush and sigh.

"Yes, dear Julie," said Marian, re-echoing her sigh; "that is just what I so much miss in the bush. The Sabbaths are still so strange, though we spend them a little more pleasantly than we used. But I must confess a strong attachment to the house of God, to a place set apart for His worship, where He has promised specially to meet His people. I can understand well the feeling of the poet, when he says,—

> 'I have been there and still would go,
> 'Tis like a little heaven below.''

"I think I can, too," said Julie in a low voice, musingly. "I felt so glad to think we were going to-day!"

"Yes, Julie; and we should remember whom we

are going to meet—not man, but our Saviour. He has promised to be there, and however poor the means, He can bless, and will."

Julie rode silently forward for a few minutes; she was evidently in deep thought, and for a little while no one spoke. At length she turned to Allen, and leaning slightly forward on her saddle, half coaxingly whispered,—

"Would it not be pleasant to have a pretty little chapel built on the home section, Allen?"

"Very pleasant," said Alf, satirically, for he had overheard the whisper. "I fancy I see it—Allen officiating as minister. By the bye, Allen, I verily believe you are cut out for the profession. Yes, decidedly, your cast of countenance is just the thing for a parson."

Marian glanced quickly at the embryo minister, a quick half-earnest glance; but, alas! the countenance wore anything but the meek, quiet expression of one of Heaven's messengers. With a quiet sigh she turned away again.

Allen was indeed prepared for a passionate reply; whether or not he caught the expression of Marian's eye is doubtful, but however he only answered,—

"I think you, Alf, are decidedly 'cut out' for a fool."

Alf laughed, and rode forward, amusing himself as he went by stripping all the boughs within his reach of their leaves. Allen turned toward his sister with a softened voice, asking,—

" What is that you thought would be so pleasant,
Julie?"

" A chapel on our home section.   Oh, it would be
nice, Allen! we should be able to go every Sunday,
and I dare say that after a little while all the people
within four or five miles would be glad to come.'

" If they all had hearts as warm as the little one
beating against your jacket, dear Julie, they would I
dare say; otherwise I fear they will prove very much
like some of the homestead inmates, rather lukewarm
on the subject."

" But you are not lukewarm, dear Allen?" Julie
asked earnestly.   Her brother, however, made no
reply to this, and she went on,—

" I dare say at first they would not all come, but
after a time they might, and I am sure some would.
Now, how seldom any of us can go to a place of
worship.   In bad weather not at all."

" Well, Julie, what would you have us to do?"
asked Allen, rather quizzingly, " ask mother to
throw open the sitting-room for the purpose?"

" That might do for a little time at any rate,"
replied Julie, gravely and thoughtfully, " but it would
not be half so nice as a little chapel; not half so nice,
Allen."

" But I do not believe that father would hear a
word of the scheme, Julie.   I hope you do not want
me to propose it to him, do you, pet?"

" Oh no!" said Julie, laughing, and then looking
suddenly grave again, " Oh no; not father, certainly,

but then you know, Allen," she continued, brightening up, and resuming her coaxing tone and manner, " you will soon be master of the homestead and the home section, and then of course you can do as you like, and build what you like."

Allen coloured and laughed, and playfully switched his sister's horse with his whip. It at once set off at a full canter, and his own fine steed gallantly kept company. They left their companions far behind.

" Will you do as I want you, dear Allen?" Julie resumed coaxingly, as they reined in their horses and stood waiting the approach of Marian and Alf, who were following more leisurely behind.

" When that time comes, Julie, and when the homestead has another inmate, ask me again," replied Allen, half playfully, half seriously.

Julie's blue eyes turned a very surprised look upon her brother; she did not thoroughly understand him; the " other inmate " perfectly mystified her. But she knew very well by the expression of his face, that she must not ask any further, and as she loved him too well either to trouble or displease him, the little homestead chapel was mentioned no more.

CHAPTER XX.

A PEEP AT "THE COURSE THAT NEVER RUNS SMOOTH."

> "Oh, how this spring of love resembleth
> The uncertain glory of an April day;
> Which now shows all the beauty of the sun,
> And by and bye a cloud takes all away!"

SERVICE had already commenced in the little chapel, when their horses stopped at its simple slip-panel, for it boasted no gate.   As they stood a moment or two while the brothers fastened the horses within the enclosure, Marian and Julie could distinctly hear the words of the sacred song.   The harmony was sweet, though the voices were rude, and to Marian especially the words were very dear.   Her heart leaped in unison with the measure and responded to the sentiment,—

> "I thirst, Thou wounded Lamb of God,
> To wash me in Thy cleansing blood;
> To dwell within Thy wounds: then pain
> Is sweet, and life or death is gain.
>
> Take my poor heart, and let it be
> For ever closed to all but Thee!
> Seal Thou my breast, and let me wear
> That pledge of love for ever there!
>
> How blest are they who still abide
> Close sheltered in Thy bleeding side!
> Who life and strength from thence derive,
> And by Thee move, and in Thee live,

> How can it be, Thou heavenly King,
> That Thou should'st us to glory bring?
> Make slaves the partners of Thy throne,
> Decked with a never-fading crown?
>
> Hence our hearts melt, our eyes o'erflow;
> Our words are lost, nor will we know,
> Nor will we think of aught beside,
> 'My Lord, my Love is crucified.'
>
> First-born of many brethren, Thou;
> To Thee, lo! all our souls we bow:
> To Thee our hearts and hands we give;
> Thine may we die, Thine may we live!"

They were comfortably seated within the little sanctuary before the hymn was concluded. Marian's eyes were resting upon the sweet words in her little hymn-book, and, as Allen turned towards her, he perceived tears on her dark lashes. He looked again and again, but unable to decipher the mystery, turned for information to the hymn-book in his hand,—

> "Take my poor heart, and let it be
> For ever closed to all but Thee!"

were the first words that met his eye. A shade of disappointment passed over his brow: he closed the book, and leant back in his seat. No, he did not, and could not approve of that sentiment, in his present state of feeling. "Why should the heart be closed to everything but God?" was the question his heart rebelliously proposed. He had yet to learn how possible it is to love earthly objects well, and yet for God to reign supremely in the soul. Perhaps, too, could he have learnt the source from whence Marian's tears flowed, a less gloomy shadow would have darkened his brow; and he would only have been too happy to have known that it was the thought of the ascendency of earthly affections above heavenly ones, that drew from Marian those silent tears.

Alfred's eye had been caught in another direction; he had exchanged a merry glance with a pair of laughing eyes a few seats off. Mary Clare and her younger brother, Frank, having taken advantage of the beauty of the Sabbath, and Marian's former recommendation, had entered the chapel a few minutes before them. He was pleased to see them, for there was a prospect of company home, and a merry canter with Mary Clare was just what he wanted. In his own mind, he at once appropriated her. Julie he gave over to the tender mercies of Frank, as he knew, young though she was, she was sufficiently attractive to him, her *snowdrop* style of beauty being his particular admiration, and he was perfectly convinced that Allen would be satisfied with his division of the booty.

Perhaps less of earthly feeling was mingled with Julie's thoughts than any of her companions. New to the heavenly road, all was bright and beautiful yet. It was a fair, a flowery pathway, with but few dark shadows or storm-clouds. Her young soul, melted by a Saviour's love, was yet unfrozen by the chill of worldly influence. She could feelingly respond to the words of the sacred page, " Her ways are ways of pleasantness, and all her paths are peace." Beautiful, childlike confidence, sweet early days of Christian life! Would that that delighful season, when the atmosphere in which the soul delights to dwell is an atmosphere of prayer, could always remain! And yet it is good for the Christian that he has to fight as well as to pray. Exercise is good for the soul as well as for the body, but the days of early love are never, never to be forgotten.

It was not one of the ordinary local ministers who this time ascended the pulpit, but a young and gentlemanly looking man, whose brow, from which a profusion of dark hair was carelessly thrown, bore the impress of thought, and whose eye glowed with intellect and feeling. He did not thunder out his message to his audience. He was evidently no Boanerges in the ministry, but he carried their hearts with him by his deep, rich voice, his persuasive tones, his affectionate exhortations. He placed before them a Saviour of boundless mercy, and exhibited Him in all His lovely attributes. He sought to throw around them the cords of love, not by awakening terror, but by enlisting their affections on his side. With those warm, pure, devotional feelings, think you he did not succeed? Even Alf was interested.

"Well, I call that something like a sermon, don't you, Miss Clare?" exclaimed Alf, after the usual salutations had passed, at the conclusion of the service, while they all stood grouped together before remounting their horses.

"It must be good, since you say so," replied Miss Clare, laughing, "though I perfectly agree with you.

I have been interested greatly, and I need not ask if Miss Herbert has." She added in an undertone, " Her beautiful eyes were glowing like stars—they would betray it—and my little friend Julie's look just like dewy violets."

" Well now, I declare Ned should hear that," cried Alf banteringly ; " I think he would see that his sister knew something besides the price of butter, or that at any rate *butter* and *sentiment* are not so uncongenial as he might suppose."

" Insolent ! " said Mary, playfully tapping him on the shoulder with her riding whip. " Let me see if you have improved in gallantry, and can hand me to my saddle in a passable manner."

They were the merriest couple ; though Frank was by no means lacking in fun and attention to Julie. The four were cantering along the homeward road before Allen had even assisted his companion to her seat. There was something certainly rather mysterious in the unadjusted state of Marian's saddle. How this belt had become loose, and that entirely unfastened, was exceedingly odd ; but Allen did not appear to be troubled about it, though a few moments placed the others beyond sight, and his companion began to be a little restless.

" What a distance they have gone ! " she said, rather uneasily, as Allen placed her at length in the saddle, handing her the whip, and gathering the reins in her hands.

" The trees are between us and them ; they will

easily be overtaken," he replied. But the quiet manner in which he allowed his horse to choose its own pace betrayed no intention of doing so. Marian's trod step for step with it.

A little way along the road, but at distant intervals, surrounded by gardens of fruit and vegetables, were the simple slab huts, familiar to every traveller among Australian scenery. These did not extend very far, and finally ceased altogether. Fenced roads continued some distance farther, and fine crops of wheat and newly-gathered hay attracted the attention. But presently even these marks of habitation ceased, and they were again in the bush among trees and hills, with nothing but nature—beautiful wild nature around them.

And where were Alf and his troop all this time? It was of no consequence, as Allen said, they would wait for them when they were tired of their wild gallop; and as to Julie, there was not the least cause for anxiety about her, she was so excellent a horse-woman, so familiar from her cradle with the saddle. And so they quietly pursued their way, talking about the service in the little chapel; of what might be done nearer to the homestead, and of all the fair scenes around them. But just in proportion as Marian became more perfectly at ease, Allen became more nervously restless. His face flushed, and grew pale by turns. He looked with anxiety into the distance, dreading lest he should catch even the shadow of a riding-skirt or veil. After all, how much pride is there in the heart of man in this dread of a refusal.

But he went on talking still of one thing or another, till at length the topic came nearer and nearer home. The new house, and then the old house and its improvements; Marian suggesting, and Allen eagerly grasping her ideas.

They were now far on their homeward course, and at any minute might come in sight of the rest of the party. Was this golden opportunity to be thrown away? It was not. It should not be. Allen, by this time, was desperate.

He turned suddenly towards Marian, with a countenance of intense anxiety, and laying his hand gently on the reins that were hanging carelessly from her horse's neck, exclaimed in a low, tremulous, husky tone,—

"It is not possible to go beyond a certain point of endurance. I must speak now, Miss Herbert. Dear Marian, it is in your power to make my life henceforth either very happy, or very, very miserable. Oh, let it not be the latter! Presumption though it may seem, I cannot help it."

Marian turned red, then pale, and finally slightly started from her saddle with surprise. The surprise, indeed, took away all power of utterance, but Allen had plenty of words now to plead his suit. She bent lower and lower over her saddle. There was a burning spot on either cheek, and more than one tear glistened on her dark riding-habit; her whip lay across her lap, and the hands were clasped closely over her heart. Little knew Allen the struggle she underwent with her earthly affections, before she had power to utter the words that seemed the death-blow to his hopes.

" I cannot—I cannot—you must not—I must not —we must not think of each other!"

"And why? What was there to hinder? Who?" were Allen's eager questions, but she only sorrowfully shook her head. The thought of Edward Clare flashed through his mind. His brow grew dark and troubled.

"Had another won her affections? Was she not free?"

There was none she preferred to him. She was free from all engagements excepting *one*.

And *that?* What other engagements could or ought to interfere with love?

She was turning over rapidly, though with eyes blinded with tears, the leaves of her pocket Bible. He watched her eagerly, and tried in vain to look into her face as she handed it to him. Another moment, and a look of blank disappointment passed over his countenance, as he read, underlined by her pencil, the decisive words,—

" *Those that marry, let them marry in the Lord.*"

At the same moment, the whole troop of missing ones rode into sight, and Edward Clare amongst them. What mattered his presence now? Allen felt indeed that he had to contend, not with him, but with a more powerful rival.

CHAPTER XXI.

THE TRIAL OF FAITH.

> " What may be my future lot,
> Well I know concerns me not ;
> This should set my heart at rest,
> What Thy will ordains is best."

In that homeward ride, neither Edward Clare, nor his sister, nor Frank, noticed any change in Allen or Marian, other than that Allen was in one of his reserved moods, and Marian particularly quiet. Alf and Julie were not so blinded. Under the shadow of her large hat, Julie cast many sad, perplexed glances, alternately at her brother and his late companion, wondering whether they were offended at being left behind, or whether they had quarrelled, or what indeed was the matter. As for Alf, one glance was enough, and " What the dickens is up ? " was his muttered exclamation to himself, as he took note of his brother's gloomy, clouded brow, and thought he saw a trace of tears in Marian's eyes. He began to conclude that after all he had better have left the saddle belt and buckles alone; or that at any rate he might have saved himself the trouble.

Had it not been for the Clares, the ride home would have proved but a gloomy one. It was, however, utterly impossible for Alf's buoyant, light-hearted nature to remain long with a shade upon it. He soon shook off the cloud, and was frolicking in sunshine again. The whole party rode home together, but they changed companions; Allen rode silently behind with Julie; Mary Clare, Alf, and Frank cantered on ahead; and Edward Clare for once found Marian divested of her " shadow." There was something in her face that prevented him taking advantage of the fortunate circumstance, however; something at any rate forbidding familiar approach. It was hard to Marian to bear his light, frivolous rattle, but she did bear it, and for the remainder of the day too, for she could not escape.

Allen was not so bound, or at least would not submit to such bondage. He absented himself immediately after dinner, and they saw him no more until very late in the evening, when he crossed the sitting-room, and went off to bed. He was to be up by daylight the next morning on his way to a distant station, and was not expected to return home for some days.

Marian passed a very sleepless night, a night of very mingled feelings. She could not disguise from herself that Allen possessed no second place in her heart; that she felt for him more than as a sister or a friend. But the one great barrier arose still strongly before her. They were thoughts, hopes, feelings, aspirations, desires, in which he could not share. He knew nothing of the inner life, the life of the soul, which was most precious to her: and "How can two walk together except they be agreed?" came again and again to her mind through the night.

Think you Marian trusted only to her own judgment in the matter? Oh, no; for her own natural inclination said enough for Allen. She knew that even for the simple actions of every-day life, it is well for the Christian to search for a warrant in the sacred page, to appeal to that throne whence no petitioner is sent empty away. "Be not unequally yoked together with unbelievers," were words that echoed commandingly in her ear, and she felt there could be no real happiness where the vital points were opposed. Yet it was a bitter, bitter struggle; and what was left for her? what hope? what consolation? She could pray for him. And when had she ceased to do so? though till that night his name never crossed her lips, even when alone and in prayer.

She had fallen into a tranquil sleep at last, and the dawn had stolen quietly in, and the earliest sunbeams were gliding obliquely into the room, when the prancing and neighing of a horse, and then a quick footstep outside the window, dispelled her slumber. She awoke with a start, and listened with a consciousness of pain to the sounds. She knew very well now she was aroused, who it was had risen so early. She lay breathlessly listening. There was a momentary pause at her window, and then the footsteps suddenly and heavily passed away; a few moments more and the quick gallop of horses' feet was heard, and Marian sprang from her bed to the window just in time to catch a glimpse of Allen's disappearing figure, and then her eyes rested on the little ledge outside the casement, where a small parcel lay directed to herself.

Ah! gently, gently, dear Marian! the sash of your little window is not of English manufacture, remember. It is fresh from the hands of one who has never handled work more delicate than a fence or a stile in the home country. Patience is a virtue, and it is sometimes meet that that virtue should be tried, even in the simple act of opening a stubborn window. Ah! patience has done its work, and that little parcel is safe in the eager hands at last.

Marian with glowing cheeks and trembling fingers tore away the paper, and discovered her own little Bible, the same she had handed to him during the ride of the preceding day, the leaf turned at the words which now seemed so terribly decisive. He had not re-turned it then. And now Marian eagerly turned over the pages—hoping to find she scarcely knew what. As she did so, a small folded paper fell from its leaves to the floor. She picked it up and read it through blinding tears; then throwing herself again on her pillow, she wept long, almost wildly; her whole frame trembled with emotion, and many, many bitter murmuring thoughts were mingled with her feelings. At some moments she almost resolved to let her affections take their own course; at some moments she almost reconciled herself to the reasoning of this too dear Allen. But at the very height of her passion, came the still small voice of the sacred word to her rescue: "Commit thy way unto the Lord, and He shall direct thy path." "I will guide thee with mine eye, and afterwards receive thee into glory." "The steps of a good man are ordered by the Lord." Marian recognized the voice, and was still.

"I cannot, will not, give you up, dear Marian," wrote Allen, " neither do I think a God all gentleness and love ever desired such a sacrifice. Did you not say (the ears of love are too quick to be mis-taken), did you not say you preferred none to myself? There is not another in the wide world, dearest Marian, that is worthy of comparison with you. If you cast me off, my ruin will lie at your door. I shall henceforth care for nothing; business or pleasure, *all* may go. Will you drive me from my home, Marian? The home I have been adorning with the hope that one day you will share it? Oh, can it be that religion teaches such harsh doctrines as this?

"I have marked passages in your own Bible, dear Marian, will they not plead for me? Surely they should do so. I shall return the day after to-morrow; if you can give me the shadow of hope (you know the old white gum-tree with the cherry-tree beside it, there is a small hole in its trunk) place there a letter for me, that I may know before I enter the house what I may expect."

CHAPTER XXII.

"A most auspicious star, whose influence
If now I court not, but omit, my fortunes
Will ever after droop."

THROUGHOUT that weary Monday Allen's words were incessantly in her ears : " I cannot give you up, dear Marian—will you drive me from my home ?—on you will lie my ruin." And many, many times she stole out of sight with her tears. She had an almost uninterrupted day, for Julie and Bessie had gone to visit the Clares. She was invited, but had excused herself; and the few little duties she had to perform, she went very listlessly about. It could not escape the quick motherly eye of Mrs. Burton that all was not well.

"Put down this duster, my dear," said Mrs. Burton, taking hold of Marian's hand kindly ; " you must rest yourself; you are not well, I am sure. Your hands are burning, and your head too." And she placed her own cool palm upon it so tenderly that the tears were nearly bursting forth again.

"I am not quite well, I believe," and Marian hid her tears and flushed cheek upon the kind bosom,

N 2

"This sudden heat, and you yet only new to the colony. Of course, dear, you would feel it. But did you feel well yesterday? you did not look quite the thing."

"Not quite well," faltered Marian.

Had Mrs. Burton looked at the face nestling against her at that moment, she might have been assisted to conclusions which as yet had never crossed her mind.

"Ah! what a pity I never noticed it; then Allen might have asked Dr. Brown to call. He will pass his door. What a pity! Alf is out too, and father is so busy."

"Oh I am not *ill*, dear Mrs. Burton," said Marian, hurriedly; "my head aches a little; but I will rest, and then I shall soon be better."

"Yes, do. Come lie down on the sofa in the music-room. I will draw the curtains and close the door, and if quietness will do you good you shall have it. Now if Allen were only here, I would set him to bathe your head with eau-de-Cologne, and he should have my old Indian fan to waft away the heat."

It was fortunate for Marian that as she spoke she was busily opening the window to its widest extent, and drawing the curtains closely over it; and then quitting the room, she presently came back with the eau-de-Cologne and a snowy handkerchief, and stood herself bathing the flushed brow; then stooping down, she gently kissed first the brow and then the lips, softly sealing the action by a gentle, " My daughter," and left the room.

" My daughter!" There was something beyond mere endearment in those words; there was an emphasis on them which shot a sudden thrill to Marian's heart. A mother's dearest wish was betrayed in that close kiss. Marian turned her head to the pillow and shed bitter tears.

What was she doing? Disappointing all this love and tenderness —turning ungratefully away from the pure affection lavished upon her! No, no! not ungratefully; for was it with no pang, no suffering to herself, she put this happiness from her? Was it no cross, that she laid all that appeared dear on earth at the footstool of her heavenly Father, exclaiming with faltering lips, " Thy will be done?" Rather was it not the heavy weight of her cross that sent the blood so wildly through her veins? Was it not this that made her temples throb so painfully? this that caused the deadly sinking of heart, which at times drove all colour from her face, as she lay stretched passively amongst the cushions heaped around her?

She lay there all day, quiet and undisturbed, excepting now and then by the kind entrance of Mrs. Burton, and the anxious glance of her eye. Now she had gathered a leaf of fine ripe strawberries, some of the first in the garden, of Allen's planting. Now she placed a slender glass upon the table near where Marian lay, with a stem from a beautiful and curious rose tree growing near the summer arbour. It was

but one stem, but there were on it two roses, one a
glowing pink, the other a pure white. That tree had
been formerly christened by Alf, in one of his provoking humours, " Allen and his Bride." The name
was familiar to the homestead ; Marian knew it very
well. Why that stem was gathered now by the
mother's hands she could not doubt ; or why, from
those roses to the couch where she lay, there were so
many wistful glances.

Marian slept much during the day, and may be
her sorrow made her heavy. Her intervals of wakefulness were generally peaceful. She had placed her
cause in other hands ; she felt sure she was right.
To what must inevitably be, her taking farewell of
the homestead, she closed her eyes. One hope per-
petually lingered to comfort her, that God would yet
touch the heart of him whom she had so well learned
to love, though that happiness seemed almost too
great for fulfilment.

And so passed away the long weary hours ; hours
of rest they were, too. The evening meal was over,
and the sun was already declining towards the West,
when Mrs. Burton came quietly into the room to
Marian, with her bonnet on, and a shawl hanging on
her arm. She came up softly to her, and seeing she
was not asleep, again tenderly kissed her.

" Do you feel better, my dear ?   Do you think you
would mind my leaving you for a little while ? Mr.
Burton wants me to go to Edward Clare's and fetch
back the children."

" Oh yes ! do Mrs. Burton, it will do you good; I can lie very well here. My head is a great deal better."

" You know the girls are all about milking now, but they will soon have finished, and I will tell Maggie to come and see if you want anything."

" Oh, thank you ! but I shall want nothing, indeed, and if I do, I can rise and get it."

" I shall send Maggie with the lamp, at any rate, dear, then you can light it if you wish," and with another kiss, Mrs. Burton went.

" You need not trouble about me, Maggie," said Marian, as the girl brought in the lamp and placed it on the table. " If I want you I will come and call."

" Will I not light the lamp presently, Miss ? "

" No thank you, Maggie; I can do that without troubling you. It does my head good to lie in the dark."

And so Marian was soon left alone in the house; quite alone, for the men were without at their various employments, just closing matters for the night, un-yoking the bullocks, after removing the last load of hay from the back section, or flirting with the girls who were milking a short distance from the stock-yard, sometimes with, and sometimes without their aid.

It was getting dark, but Marian was accustomed to the gloom. She forgot all about the lamp; she did not need it, but lay with her eyes wandering dreamily about the little room. They rested very lovingly upon the piano. It was open, showing its white ivory keys, but there was no music on the stand. It had not been played on that day, and they had forgotten to close it at night. A white shrivelled rose-bud lay on the keys; it was one Edward Clare had gathered her the evening before. It was withered and dead now; she had held it only for one instant in her hands, and a moment after it had been forgotten.

Near the window was a bouquet of flowers, still fresh and blooming, not a leaf injured. Marian had not seen them before, yet they had been gathered for her very early that morning. It was another assurance of Allen's devotion for her.

"Oh that that barrier, that only barrier were broken!" she sighed, and then closed her eyes. She lay so perfectly still, that at last she fell into a tranquil sleep, a sleep of mingled dreams. She was aroused by hearing a step in the room. She listened without moving, and her heart beat violently; but the dusk had increased so rapidly during her sleep, that she could at first discern nothing. At last her eyes caught a faint shadow of some one seated near the window. Whoever it was, the arms were leaning forward on the table, and the head bowed down upon them. Who was it? who could it be? Marian tried to speak, but failed; she half rose, and at the same time the figure arose, and drawing aside the curtain, the full light of the moon fell across the floor to her couch.

"Allen!" she exclaimed, in utter surprise and fear. He started, and came eagerly forward.

"You here, dear Marian!" he said, seizing her hand, and squeezing it far more than he was aware of. "They are all out. I thought you had gone to those Clares too. But you are ill—faint! Fool that I was, I have done this! Marian! dear Marian!"

She did not hear him; her head fell upon his arm. He lifted her up, and carried her to the window. She lay lifeless against him, almost like a child who had fallen asleep, had it not been for the deadly pallor visible even in the moonlight.

"I have killed her!" he again groaned, placing her on the couch; and steeping her handkerchief in the eau-de-Cologne, which he fortunately perceived, he bathed again and again her face, brow, and hands. He was presently rewarded for his anxiety by a faint sigh, and then life came slowly back to the pallid face. A moment or two more, and she was conscious who was beside her. She feebly raised herself, but he would not suffer her to move.

"Oh, when you are better! Not now, dear Marian. I thought I had killed you."

"I am better," she answered, trying to raise her hand to her temples. They were throbbing violently. She laid her head down on the pillow and wept. Allen was beside himself; he scarcely knew what he did. He drew her to him like a petted child, and tried to soothe and quiet her in vain.

"Marian, tell me one thing,—*do* you love me? Oh,

deny me not that!   I will wait—wait as long as you wish. You say you love no one else ; but do you not love me?   Say it, and I will not despair."

"Allen, you are unkind to urge me so," sighed Marian.

"Will you let me go forth without hope, Marian ? I had rather die at once."

"No, Allen ; if by saying that, I can save you to a *hope* of higher, better things, I will say it."   She hid her face on his shoulder, for he had drawn her to him again, and whispered almost inaudibly, "I do love you."

Allen's answer is not recorded, gentle reader ; we will look out at the open window, at the pure, clear moonlight, so tranquil in its loveliness ; or if it better please you, we can toy with the white ivory keys of the piano ; or better still, we will pass into the garden for a little while.   At any rate, it is no business of ours to listen to what is said.

Now we may enter again. Marian is half-sitting, half-leaning, against the sofa cushions, and Allen has drawn his chair close to the head of the couch ; one of Marian's hands is very fast in his, yet they are talking very gravely, for Marian adheres strongly to her first resolution. She has admitted the state of her heart, but that heart is not her own to give to him ; she owns allegiance to another, who long since had said, "Give me thine heart."   Her determination was fixed never to marry any other, but she was equally firm in her resolve not to bestow her hand on him till *she* should be thoroughly convinced he had experienced real change of heart. He was obliged to submit.

"At any rate, Marian," said he, bathing her hot forehead with the eau-de-Cologne, and pushing back the dark curls from her brow as he spoke, "at any rate, darling, you will let me enjoy the present. Do not be unkind, Marian; a little love, a little hope is sweet!"

She had not yet asked the occasion of his sudden return, and he laughed as he told her, that not being very well possessed of his senses when he left home, he had to return to find them. "I have a good excuse, however, for father. I heard news on the way of some cattle of ours which have been missing a long time, and it was worth while returning to make sure of the brands—at any rate father will think so; though, between us, I should never have dreamt of returning, had I not felt that I could not wait for the old gum-tree post-office, but would try and hear my sentence by word of mouth. And have I not succeeded?"

But just then came the sounds of voices and feet rapidly approaching. They were almost at the door. Allen started from his seat, and walked towards the window. Marian composed herself on the pillow, and awaited the intrusion with beating heart.

"What, still in the dark, love?" said Mrs. Burton coming quietly in. "I am afraid you must have been very dull, all alone."

"You did not expect *me* mother," said Allen, coming up to her.

"Allen! Why bless the boy—no! Why, is anything the matter?"

"Nothing, mother; only I have heard of those missing cattle."

His mother was looking searchingly into his changed countenance. There was too much happiness in it to deceive her, she turned and clasped him in her arms; and then throwing her arms round Marian, kissed her warmly, again fervently whispering, "My own daughter!"

"Who is that talking with father?" asked Allen, a moment or two after, when the agitation had a little subsided.

"Ah, I had forgotten! Some one you will be glad to see. He was coming here, when we overtook him, to see you."

"What name, dear Mrs. Burton?" asked Marian, pale with excitement.

Allen stood on one side, biting his lips, and trying to peep into the sitting-room.

"I did not catch the name. Here, stand by Allen, dear, and you can see."

"It is your cousin, Mr. Grenville, dear Marian,' whispered Allen, with a pleased countenance.

"My cousin William?" and pushing back her curls entirely forgetting their dishevelled state, she joyously sprang forward to greet him.

"Why, Marian! are you not surprized to see me up in the bush?" he exclaimed, laughing, and kissing her. "I am come to take you away. Isabel wants you."

CHAPTER XXIII.

THE OPPOSITION PARTY.

"No, I don't like you, naughty man! I won't like you!" said the romp and pet of the household, struggling to get away from William Grenville. He had caught the little bush nymph as she flew past him, and was holding her fast, to her infinite and laughable vexation.

"I don't like you, and I won't like you. Let me go, naughty man!" exclaimed the wild little Bessie, struggling like an eel to get out of his strong and somewhat rough embrace.

"'You don't and you won't like me!' eh, Miss Bessie?" laughed Grenville. "Well now, tell me why you won't like me?" he asked, after Bessie had ceased her struggles from sheer want of breath.

"Let me go, and I'll tell you," and seizing a favourable opportunity the little gipsy made a dive, and was beyond his reach at the other end of the room, laughing and dancing in triumph.

"Why won't you like me, Bessie?" said her tormentor, rising and approaching her corner, as though in the act of pursuit.

" I shan't tell you. I won't tell you. Go away, Mr. Grenville!" and Bessie danced up and down in excess of triumph.

" You will tell me, will you not, Miss Julie?" cried William Grenville, suddenly turning and throwing his arm round Julie, who was just coming in from the garden, with a bunch of flowers in each hand.

" Oh, my flowers! Oh, Mr. Grenville, please let me go, you are crushing my roses!"

It was too bad to tease poor Julie, bewildered with her flowers; but William was a thorough torment, and, as Edward Clare would have said, the snowdrop was transformed.

" Oh, please, Mr. Grenville, do let me go! Bessie, help me to get away."

But Bessie, secure herself, danced and laughed triumphantly in the corner. It was fine fun for her to see her sister in the toils she had so recently escaped, and she heeded not the plaintive cry, " Do help me, Bessie!"

" What do you want to know, Mr. Grenville? Please let me go, and I'll tell you," said Julie.

" I want to know why Bessie don't like me, and why she calls me a naughty man," said Grenville, laughing, but not releasing his prisoner one whit. " Oh no! I shan't let you go. Not I, indeed. That little eel slipped through my fingers; but I have got you safe enough."

" Bessie does not like you, because of something she heard you say last night."

" What was that ?"

" You are going to take Miss Herbert away, and for that I don't like you either.   Do let me go."

" You don't like me for that?   Then what do you like me for?   But do you know, Miss Julie, I have fallen in love with you, and have almost persuaded your mother to let you go also."

" Oh, I should like that very much!   Perhaps she will," said Julie, with animation.   " I will go and ask her,—no, I'll go to Miss Herbert first."

" No hurry, no hurry ; I want you to talk to me a little.   Now, Miss Julie, it is not fair to leave me to wander about by myself, and you seem the only young lady disengaged.   Won't you show me your garden ?"

" Will you let me put my roses into water first ?" asked Julie, colouring like a rose herself as she spoke, and with a parting struggle, Grenville allowed her to run off with her flowers.

She returned in a few minutes, having smoothed her hair, and tied the blue ribbons of her hat under her chin in a very becoming little bow.   She was already as tall as Marian, rather taller if anything, and her figure was slender and graceful.   Her beautiful complexion, ordinarily too pale, too unrelieved, had this morning a very decided rose upon it, which much increased her prettiness,—William Grenville thought so at least.   He knew very well that he himself had given the rose-bloom he so much admired.

"Now, Bessie, come along; your sister and I are going into the garden," said Grenville, springing up and offering his arm to Julie. " Come, you know very well where to find the ripest strawberries ; I know by those lips of yours."

The lips in question assumed a pout for a minute —only a minute. The romp had reached them before they had taken many steps, her curls all tossed about her face, and her hat tied all on one side. She turned back after she had got a little distance beyond them, and shook her head at the tormentor. Grenville understood there was to be a truce between them, and stopped also.

" Well, Bessie, what now ? "

" If I show you the strawberries will you promise to bring Miss Herbert back ? " she inquired, slightly stamping her little foot as she spoke.

" Oh yes," laughed Grenville ; " I apprehend she has found so many friends in the bush, I shall have a diffi- culty in keeping her now."

William Grenville, in fact, had come to take Marian finally away from the homestead. He had been very successful in his undertaking, had a pretty little house and beautiful garden in the suburbs of Adelaide, and all he wanted now was to show his newly-acquired possessions to Marian. Her cousin Isabella had something else to show her, a rosebud of a baby, the image, of course, of papa, and the best and sweetest little one ever seen, very much like Marian, too, as far as its little unformed features were capable of resemblance, its experience of life dating only a few weeks. The important business of fixing on a name was left till Marian should come and propose one. But Grenville was not quite prepared for the vehement opposition he met on all sides, and the tacit negative of Marian's quiet looks.

" Take her away altogether! " exclaimed Mr. Burton, looking up suddenly from his newspaper when he first heard it proposed, " be hanged to that! why, we can't spare her, sir! The mother and girls would be lost."

" And others besides the mother and the girls too," exclaimed Alf, who had been looking searchingly into his brother's face for some moments, and trying in vain to decipher its expression. " Say you won't leave us—do! " he continued, turning to Marian with a beseeching look, half-teasing too; for he saw as she leaned over the tea-table that her face was mantled by a deep blush.

Allen stood by and said nothing. He chose to say what he wanted when no other ears but hers could hear him. He chose his time when the moon threw a thousand shadows under the trees and round the house, when doors and windows were thrown widely open to catch the fresh breeze, and the whole household were scattered about enjoying the evening, and they would not be missed. Then, taking a mantle of his sister's from a peg in the sitting-room, he silently went up to Marian, as she sat for a moment alone under the veranda, and whispered as he threw it over her head,—

"I am going as far as the slip-panel; let us have one walk together."

She did not refuse. Dull indeed must be the heart that has no appreciation of our moonlight nights. How beautiful in the moonshine are those gaunt old gums, stretching their branches wildly across the path, and throwing far around them their dark, fantastic shadows! And then the graceful cherry-tree, the still more beautiful blackwood, and the drooping she-oak—most beautiful in that soft radiance. On the well-worn footpath that Allen had chosen (for they are not on the usual road to the slip-panel— there is too great a flood of light there) there is a complete tracery of leaves imprinted by the full, pure moonlight. There are a thousand rustling sounds here and there among the trees; the locust is singing its loudest notes of gladness, and from the distant creek the musical croak of the frog is heard. Then a more-pork sends forth its cuckoo-like note on the evening air, and the distant hooting of an owl makes Marian creep a little closer to her companion, so like a cry of human distress does it sound. And then, from bough to bough, the opossums are frolicking in the moonlight, sometimes almost leaping upon their shoulders or running across their feet. It is so warm she scarcely needs the mantle, and Allen has pushed it back already from the soft, dark ringlets. He loved to see all of that face the glimpse of moonlight would reveal.

"Will you go and leave us, Marian?" he at last

whispered.   It was the first word that had been spoken since they had quitted the house, and they were now far beyond hearing.

Marian did not answer for a few moments, she was playing with the button of her mantle—evidently there was something peculiar in its construction.   It was at last scarcely above her breath that she replied,—

"I must."

"Why need you? they are only cousins.   They have not a quarter of the right to you that I have.   You must not go; the homestead will be wretched without you."

"Will that be right, Allen?" Marian softly asked.

"Right or wrong, it *will be* so, dear Marian; how can it be otherwise?"

"Do you remember the terms of our agreement?" asked Marian, in a low voice.

"I have too good reason to remember!" said Allen, rather bitterly.   "Do not remind me of the cruel resolve.   If you go away, there will be less chance than ever of my becoming what you wish."

"No, Allen; perhaps not—without you forget me."

"Do you think I can do that?   No, Marian, that is impossible.   There is not a word you have spoken that I shall not remember."

"Remember all that is good, dear Allen, I only ask that.   Remember all I have said of the readiness, the willingness of Jesus to save; remember my little Bible, for I gave it to you.   You will read it, dear Allen?"

There were tears in the tone that uttered the entreaty. Allen clasped her to him, exclaiming in an unsteady voice,—

"Anything you wish, dearest."

"Oh! but not only for my sake; for your own, dear Allen.   Look for yourself, and find how sweet a thing it is to be a Christian."

"Anything, dear Marian;" and they walked on silently for a long while without speaking, till at last they stood side by side beneath the old white gum, on the other side of the slip-panel.   The soft breeze was increasing now, and slightly moaned among the branches, and one or two clouds flitted slowly across the fair face of the moon.

"And how long is this state of things to last, dear Marian?" at length Allen suddenly exclaimed, taking both her hands, and looking into the sweet face upturned to his.   "When are you coming back to the homestead?"

Her eyes fell under his beseeching glance.   "When you can rightly claim me, dear Allen,—when our agreement is fulfilled," she answered, in an almost inaudible voice.

CHAPTER XXIV.

JULIE ALONE WITH THE STARS.

"No unregarded star
    Contracts its light
Into so small a character,
    Removed far from our human sight,

But if we steadfast look,
    We shall discern
In it, as in some holy book,
    How man may heavenly knowledge learn."

EVENING once again, and an evening calm and beautiful as the last; but the homestead is not the same—some of its brightness is gone. There is one sweet face missing in the sitting-room, in the music-room, in the kitchen—everywhere. The whole household has a sense of shadow resting upon it; even the servants miss that gentle happy smile and cheerful word. Yes; certainly a change has come over the household.

Marian has really gone, and her absence, though so recent, has fallen heavily upon all she has left behind her. The "little light" has been shining clear and bright, though she knew it not; and it still shone in memory and influence, it still did its silent work.

Allen for worlds would not have encountered that

first dull day at home. He had suddenly discovered that his previous journey could no longer be delayed. His way lay partly along the road Grenville and his cousin had to traverse; at least, he made it do so. He rode several miles with them on their journey; and when he did part, it was because he could give no further reason for proceeding. A silent pressure of hands, and looks more eloquent than words, were all their farewell; after that, Allen's horse might well have comprehended, had he been capable of doing so, that sudden throwing off of rein, the sharp prick of the spur, which hastened him back for miles; for they had passed the right road a full hour before.

Allen was flying from his trouble, or seeking to do so; but was it in a right direction? Alas! no; for he sought it in excitement, whilst in the shadow of "the great Rock" it is alone to be found. At present there was only bitterness and rebellion in his heart. All soft, humble feeling was gone. He felt the discipline hard; the ride had no softening influence. Like Paul, he kicked against the pricks; but he only suffered more deeply for it. How certainly true are the sweet words of the sacred poet, who says,—

> "Law and terrors only harden,
> All the time they work alone;
> But a sense of blood-bought pardon,
> *That* dissolves a heart of stone."

At present Allen could only see the rod; ne discerned not Him who appointeth it, nor the reason for its appointment.

What a sight would that be to the Christian; if attainable in this world—a view of the road already traversed, visibly pourtrayed, with all those little way-marks of trial and trouble, and the cause for each clearly discernible! The cause? Love—love! pure and perfect love! and all leading to one glorious end— the upward progress of the pilgrim. But are there not now many Hill Mizars from which the Christian may contemplate his past footsteps? And can he not, as on a pencilled map, place his finger on *this* or *that* passage of history, and say, " Here God met me in the furnace, it is true ; but I can now see how lovingly that furnace was appointed, how carefully it was watched, that the fire should not be heated one whit beyond my strength."

Perhaps, of all in the homestead, Allen of course excepted, Julie felt most alone. Marian to her had long been as a dear elder sister, her daily companion in all her employments and pleasures ; now she had no one. Bessie was too much the romp, too wild to have the least sympathy for quiet pursuits. In her own little heart she had the greatest contempt for both work and books. It grieved her not at all to throw these on one side; she could now race Rover and Hector at her own sweet will. She could chase butterflies in their wildest flight, with her hair streaming to the wind, and her frock tucked up to her waist. Or she could go and dabble barefooted in the creek for hours together, fishing for crawfish, with morsels of meat tied to a string, and feel certain of but little rebuke. The question is, dearly as she loved her governess, whether there was not a little secret gladness in the corner of her heart, that for a time at least she was free again—free to be as wild as she chose.

But with Julie it was different. She was so quiet, so gentle, so thoughtful, of such delicate constitution. Before Marian came to the homestead, Allen was the only one who at all understood her. Many of her thoughts and feelings, be it remembered, were of his formation; but there had been a beautiful ingrafting, a careful pruning since, and the tender plant had learnt to expand in the beams of the Sun of Righteousness—had received into its bosom the soft dews from on high. To all who now surrounded her she was only more incomprehensible than ever. She wandered about the house, pale and spiritless, that first sad, unhappy day; her heart was longing after Marian; it was following the travellers on their way to Adelaide.

"I almost wish I had let that poor child go," ejaculated Mrs. Burton, as Julie wandered listlessly through the room from the garden that evening, and laying aside her hat, went into the lonely music-room.

"She do seem lost, ma'am!" replied Maggie, looking after her with tears in her kind, grey eyes. She herself keenly missed the sunny smile and encouraging word of the young governess.

"Yes, I am almost sorry; but I did it for the best.

I was afraid of that dusty Adelaide; and harvest will be coming on, and then it would have been impossible to fetch her had it been wanted ever so much. It can't be helped!" and Mrs. Burton sighed.

"Adelaide is a nasty, dusty place," sighed Maggie, thoughtfully; "I never heered any one in these parts as liked it, except Croaky Jimmy, and he boasts of being a Lunnoner—not much of a boast either if all the folks there are like him. When will Miss Herbert be home again, ma'am?"

"I don't know, Maggie, I hope before very long," replied Mrs. Burton, passing out of the room; and she sighed again, for Allen's last look, so despairing, at least so sorrowful, had puzzled her, and disturbed her sleep for many nights after. He had not even confided in his mother, he was too reserved for that, and kept his own counsel and his own sorrow.

Julie had the music-room and her griefs all alone that evening, she had not even her brother to sympathize with her. She felt, indeed, as if everything she loved was gone. Her first impulse on entering the room was to heap up the pillows of the couch and throw herself down upon them. The moon had found its way there before her; it was now sending a long, silvery beam across the room to the couch—just where it had fallen an evening or two before, only the curtains were now lifted higher and drawn farther back, and the sky was so clear that the bright, full face of the moon had not one shadow across it. It fell with full beauty into the room, just taking the little white hand that lay listlessly over the side of the couch, and bathing it in its soft light; then, gradually rising, threw into bold outline the delicate, reclining figure; and then higher—higher, till the soft bands of hair are glowing in its radiance, and it has fallen on the pale still brow, compressed lips, and closed eyelids, through which the first tears shed that day were slowly welling.

Julie opened her eyes then, and looked full into the clear, pure, cloudless sky, and its thousand little gleaming stars, so calm and bright. What was it there she saw that changed the current of those tears? that opened the hitherto compressed lips in half a smile—a trustful smile? A look of holy, childlike faith stole into those blue eyes. Julie rose, and went to the window; she quietly opened it, then leaning on the window-sill, looked long up to those beaming heavens.

> "Soft gleaming stars! soft gleaming stars!
> Emblems of God's unchanging love,
> Ye watch us from your throne above!"

she softly sang. Tears came with the words, for Marian had often sang them here. But there was confidence too, and the sweet refrain inspired it.

"God's unchanging love!" she murmured over and over again to herself, till sleep came and closed her eyes even to that happy thought; but peace was *left* behind.

CHAPTER XXV.

THE RIFLED PORTFOLIO.

"What are you doing, Julie? Anything of consequence?" asked Alf, coming suddenly into the music-room a day or two after the events of the preceding chapter. His sister was seated alone, as usual, and writing.

"No, nothing—of consequence, I mean," replied Julie, rising and hastily collecting her papers ; but the nervous haste in which she did so, and the blush that accompanied the look, betrayed her a little.

"I am glad to hear it," returned Alf, with a covert smile ; "I should be very sorry indeed to interrupt any correspondence carried on by the aid of Cupid, though truly I was not aware that you and Frank had got on so far."

"I don't know what you mean, Alf. Please let me pass. Do you want me ?" said Julie, visibly distressed.

"Yes, I do want you; but first I want to know what you are writing. Don't you know, my beloved Julie, that it is the privilege of brothers to watch over their sisters' welfare. Come, young lady, please hand forward your manuscripts."

"Don't, Alf! oh, please don't! I have not anything here you would care a pin for;" and she held her portfolio more closely than ever to her side.

But Alf was in a provoking humour, and besides, albeit of the masculine gender, he possessed not a little of the curiosity of Eve, in common with most of his brethren.

"How do you know what I care for, Miss Julie? I do care very much to see what love letters you are holding there so closely; so hand over!"

Julie only held the more closely.

"Oh, Alf!" she exclaimed, half-crying, "you know very well there is nothing of the sort. It is very unkind of you to tease me so."

"I know very well! no I don't; but I wish and intend to know. You had better yield gracefully, since you must. Dear me! you must have something extraordinary in this same portfolio, if you are so fearful of its being seen. Ah! here it is; now I'll only take a peep."

But Julie, unable longer to conceal her tears, had run out of the room, and Alf very coolly opened the writing-case.

Now for the honour of Alf be it stated that he had no intention at first of looking into the secrets, he was only indulging a little of his usual teasing, tantalizing spirit. But Julie's nervous trepidation and blushes spurred his curiosity. He could not resist the temptation when he absolutely held the clue in his hand.

He found no letters, but many little manuscripts—poetry in abundance, some signed, "Marian." He read those with interest; others, selections from well-known poets; and a very few bearing the initials "J. B." These were Julie's own.

"I did not think our Julie so clever," he said to himself; "I'm sure I could not write a line if I tried for a year." And he threw aside paper after paper, and read with mingled amusement and interest the manuscripts bearing that signature.

"Julie might have spared her blushes, at any rate," he exclaimed; "there is nothing objectionable yet." He took out another paper and spread it before him, stooping over the table to read. They were verses, with the simple signature, "Julie," appended to them, and of recent date.

> "I miss her in the early dawn
>   Of bright and rosy day;
> I kneel no longer by her side,
>   As once we knelt to pray.
> She is not in the garden walk
>   Where early rosebuds blow,
> I vainly mount the she-oak hill,
>   She is not there, I know.
>
> "I miss her when the evening sun,
>   Has poured his last faint light
> Over the far, far distant West,
>   He lately made so bright.

I miss her when the moonbeams fall,
　Amidst the study's gloom,
Like silver bars across the wall,
　And softly light the room.

"Yes, thou art gone, sweet friend, my own,
　We miss thee every day;
And I, yet more than all, alone,
　Can only weep and pray;—
Pray to be rendered meet for heaven,
　And agonize in prayer,
That if we meet no more below,
　Our meeting may be there."

Alf, with his hand shading his eyes, leaned thoughtfully for many minutes over the little plaintive piece of poetry. At length he rose, and walked to the window.

"How strange," he exclaimed to himself, "is this feeling! this faith in heaven, and in God, and in prayer! Something more it seems, than general belief in their existence, which I in common with most, I suppose, possess. At any rate my poor little Julie, your rifled portfolio has taught me a lesson. I must look more deeply into these mysteries; there must be something in them. Next time I go to the township I will get a Bible of my own. I have read little enough of it, I confess. Poor little thing! I am sorry indeed I have distressed her. I shall certainly respect her portfolio in future." He began to re-arrange the contents as carefully as he could. It was rather troublesome and unusual work for his hands, and Julie's neatly assorted papers were in great danger.

But he was in reality very sorry for having

troubled his sister, and after many efforts, he at last succeeded in his task.

He walked into the sitting-room with the portfolio carefully clapsed. His sister was still there, and alone ; her face hidden among the cushions of the large chair in which she had taken refuge when she ran from the music-room. He went gently up to her, and stooping down, he put his arms round her, and drew her to him.

" Will you forgive me, Julie ? I am sorry I teased you. Here is the portfolio."

She looked up, half-frightened, half-surprised, her face still wet with tears. It was so unusual a thing for Alf to act thus. She did not know whether or not he was jesting—whether or not he still intended to tease her. His grave face and really vexed look re-assured her.

" Oh yes, Alf ; say no more about it," she replied eagerly, softly putting both arms round his neck, and hiding her face on his shoulder. " I was foolish, silly, perhaps, in making such a fuss."

" No, Julie, you were neither silly nor foolish ; but I was thoughtless as I always am, and unkind too, I am afraid, and I doubt whether quite honourable. But, however, you may trust me ; I will never touch your portfolio again without your permission, though I hope some fine day or other you will grant that."

" But there was nothing to interest you, Alf!"

" Oh, I told you you did not know everything that I like or take an interest in, Julie. And now, if you will do one thing for me, the thing I came in purposely to ask you, I'll just tell you what will prevent your feeling sorry that I peeped into your writing-case. Something I saw there made me determine to get a Bible of my own and to read it for myself, that it may teach me something of that religion which you and Miss Herbert love so much."

He rose abruptly, for the quick tears were in Julie's eyes, and her hands clasped his tightly. With his usual determined carelessness he shook off his troubled feeling, and gave a forced laugh.

"Now, Julie, if you have forgiven me, we have been grave long enough, and I want you to put on your habit, and ride over with me to the post-office. There is something or other in the way of needles or tapes that mother wants, and you will understand better than I. I know more about packing-needles than about those fine things you run in and out of muslin. Who knows? there may be a letter from this dear Miss Herbert. Come, a good shaking up is just what you want."

CHAPTER XXVI.

MORE WORK FOR THE LITTLE LIGHT.

WILLIAM GRENVILLE had said truly that Marian
would like his new home. A very pretty home it was,
though aspiring to be nothing more than a cottage.
The garden was the glory of the place, and did great
credit to both his taste and diligence, though Marian
did not see it in its full beauty, when flowers of a
hundred different species filled the air far and wide
with their fragrance. But when once the threshold
was passed, all the spirit of beauty and order had
flown. It reminded one of the apples of Sodom,
beautiful in outward semblance, but within ashes,
nothing but ashes.

It was not that the house was ill-furnished, for
many a simple, neat article, had found its way from
the auction-room, and had taken the place of the
packing-case or trunk, since Marian's departure;
nor was it that there was a lack of cleanliness, for

the little maid, with the brisk movements and red elbows, who opened the door to them on their first arrival, did her best to scrub and clean all she could lay her hands on. But taste or order was nowhere to be found. There was no drapery, no carpet, no cushions; plain strips of muslin did service as window-blinds, and an ugly oil-cloth disfigured the table. Children's toys and articles of needle-work bestrewed the floor, and in one corner stood a rough wicker cradle, uncurtained, with a shawl for a coverlid, above which a sweet cherub face peeped out—the tiny rosebud Marian was expecting to see. This was the sight that saluted her vision on her first entrance to her cousin's new home, and it made her heart sad.

" Where is your mistress?" asked William Grenville, rather impatiently, as he walked into the parlour, and noticed its uncomfortable, disarranged condition.

" Law, sir! missus and Emeline are gone next door to Mrs. Tawson's. But, my word! she did not expect you home so soon."

" Go and tell her I am home then, and that her presence is wanted," replied her master, somewhat sharply. " I can't think what's come over Isabel," he continued to Marian : " she's always out gossiping, and I don't think much of those neighbours of ours, either."

" She is lonely—she must be while you are away," replied Marian, quietly ; " she has no one to talk to."

"One would think her children should be enough," returned William discontentedly, walking about the room, and removing the toys and work that strewed the floor, and trying in an awkward sort of way to put things to rights.

Marian said nothing in reply to that; she could not conscientiously. So she merely observed, as she approached a half-open door, evidently that of a bed-room, "I will go in here, and take off my things—shall I?"

"Yes, do, Marian; I declare it's too bad for you to come and see things in this state, after having been so long away. I can't think what Isabel means by leaving the house, when she must have known I should be home *soon*."

"She did not expect you home *so* soon, William, remember that," replied Marian quietly taking off her things. She would like very much to have bathed her face and hands after her long journey, but on looking into the jug she found there was no water, so she contented herself for the present with brushing out her curls, and shaking a little of the dust from her dress. She had not quite finished when the sound of voices and hurried footsteps were heard in the entry; and presently her cousin, flushed with excitement, rushed in, and threw her arms around her.

"Dear, dear Marian, how glad I am to see you! I was afraid you would not come."

"You were? What, when William came purposely to fetch me? It seems years since we met."

"And then to find me in such a condition! Yes, William has been scolding me shockingly about it. I don't know how it is, I can't keep places tidy; I was not brought up to it—I suppose that's it. Won't you wash? What, no water, as usual! Oh, that girl! Sophy, Sophy, where are you? Here—quick, fill this water-jug. Why don't you remember to do it?"

"Please, ma'am, I had to take baby," was Sophy's reply, for the girl with the red elbows rejoiced in that name. She made up for her forgetfulness, however, by speed, and Marian was soon enjoying the cool, refreshing water, as again and again she held her face in it, and poured it over her hands.

"I must leave you a minute, dear, just to see after Sophy and the tea; I dare say the fire's out, and no kettle on. I'm so very glad you're come at last;" and with another fond kiss she ran away again.

"Poor Isabel," thought Marian; "how can she bear to live like this! so unlike the Isabel of other days in that slovenly morning dress. No wonder William is so vexed and annoyed, and yet she is an affectionate creature."

Sophy and her mistress had bustled about to some good purpose, and things certainly wore a little better aspect when she quitted the bed-room

The parlour, which on their first entrance was close and heated, was now cool and pleasant. One of William's very first actions had been to throw up both windows, and as the green leaves of a luxuriant passion-flower, and a monthly rose full of delicate buds, crept round the window-frame, a very considerable improvement was made in the room, as the unsightly strip of muslin disappeared on the top of the window by the throwing open of the sash.   He had drawn the table, on which Sophy had just placed a neat tea-service, almost under the windows, and had filled a tumbler with water, and gathered two or three flowers for a centrepiece, just to please Marian.   He did not know how much he should contribute to her comfort and pleasure when he did that.

Sophy, more thoughtful than her mistress, had a bright fire in her wee kitchen, and plenty of boiling water, when Isabel went out to her.   She rightly divined that travellers from the bush must be both very tired and very hungry.

" Them'll want something else nor bread and butter or jam for tea, ma'am, won't them ? " she asked doubtfully.

" Oh yes, I suppose so; but what to get I don't know.   What have we in the house, Sophy ? "

" A little cold mutton, ma'am, that's all—just a bone, and two or three eggs."

" Eggs ! oh, I dare say Miss Marian's sick of eggs by this time ; and mutton, that won't do."

" There's the fish cart just below. The man's got some of those small fish master likes ; shall I get some of them ? "

" They'll do—quick Sophy, or the man will have gone. Here's the money ; I'll get out the pan while you're gone ; " and, stimulated by excitement and by the wish of appearing well in the eyes of her cousin, as well as by real motives of affection, Isabel did really exert herself more than she had done for months previously.

On Sophy's return from her fish mission, she brought back Emeline, with her face, hands, and pinafore grimed with dirt.

" For gracious sake, Sophy, don't let the child go into the parlour. Take her into the other room— Miss Marian's, and wash her, and brush her hair, and change her frock and pinafore. No ; you prepare the fish, and I'll attend to the child. Come Emeline ; " and she took the little thing in her arms, and carried her into the bed-room, where stood her little crib ; for she was to be under Marian's care.

" You don't know who has come," said the fond though indolent mother, brushing out the long golden ringlets, and tying a broad blue sash round the white diaper pinafore of her eldest born. " Do you remember Auntie Marian ? "

" Auntie Marian up in the bush," said the rosy lips knowingly.

" No. Auntie Marian has come to see little

Emeline, and make her a good girl. Papa is home too. Now you are pretty and clean, you may run in and see him," and away flew the little scampering feet.

"Go and get my barège dress, Sophy; I'll fry the fish meanwhile." And Sophy, who knew all about the wardrobe of her mistress as well as she did herself, soon returned with the required article. When Isabel appeared at the tea-table, certainly few would have recognised her as the same slovenly figure that had quitted the room half an hour before to prepare the tea.

"You are yourself again, dear Isabel," said William, caressingly, in a tone which made the bright blood come to the cheeks of the young wife. Alas! how seldom did she give him the opportunity for praise, not because she had ceased to care for his love—oh, no—but because she had grown careless and slovenly, dissatisfied with her home, adopted country, and everything around her.

Young wives, young wives! if you only knew how much love is cooled by this indifference to outward appearances!

The evening passed pleasantly enough, there were so many things to be said between the cousins, and the little baby to nurse and admire. His name appeared upon the tapis, and Isabel declared her choice was already made; Allen it should be, and nothing else. She had resolved it should be named after his uncle in prospective.

Marian found the less she said on the subject the better, for a word of hers brought William out full sail: he gave her no rest or respite.

"You might as well not keep your engagement so snug, Marian," he cried, provokingly. "Just as if we didn't know anything of the matter! Don't tell me; I knew directly I saw that young fellow, that you were nailed for the bush, and that we should not enjoy much of your company long. The only mystery to me is that they have allowed you to come off at all. I expected nothing less than a challenge from Mr. Allen, I can assure you. His eyes spoke if his tongue did not."

Marian did not choose to enlighten her cousin any further on the subject. She allowed him to say what he thought fit, and surmise as much as he liked, and she bore it all so patiently that at last he said,—

"Well, I declare, dear Marian, it is too bad to tease so, so I will stop. Only just tell me one thing— when is the wedding to come off? Whisper; you need not tell everybody, you know. But you remember my old failing—a fondness for iced cakes."

CHAPTER XXVII.

THE LIGHT DIFFUSING ITS BEAMS.

Two or three mornings after this, William Grenville
was standing out in the veranda waiting for the
omnibus. His wife was still in bed, so Marian had
made breakfast for him.

"Well, Marian," he exclaimed, "this seems like
old times again. I just want you to stir up this
little wife of mine a bit; she wants it, I can assure
you. Give her some of your own cheerful, happy
spirit."

"There is some excuse for Isabel, you must own,
William; she never liked the colony."

"Yes; but then, when we are doing well, and I
see no prospect of quitting it for years to come, what
is the use of making one's self miserable about it?
Why not take things as they come—dust and heat,
hot wind and scorching sun? Well, it's true we
have enough of them; but, dear me! what country
has a perfect climate, I should like to know? certainly not England. For my part, I think the wisest
thing one can do is to make one's self as comfortable

as one can, dwelling as little upon the disagreeable as possible."

" And this is what I am to impress upon Issy ? "

" Yes, exactly ; but in your own way, mind. Now good-bye, I must be off ; there's the 'bus, I don't want to lose that, or I shall quarrel with the heat and hot wind, too ; " and William darted through the little gate, just in time to take his place. Marian saw him safely seated, and then throwing something over her head, walked down the garden path to shut the gate which he had left open.

" There needs renovation, certainly," said Marian, musingly, returning to the house. " I am not afraid of Isabel ; I know very well she is as fond of a neat, pretty house as I am. She likes to see it well enough, but it is the energy she lacks. If I were of the medical profession, I should say there was a deficiency of iron in her composition, and no great mental power to make up for it ; and the thing is, to infuse that iron. Well, we shall see. I will at any rate put her in the way of it ; perhaps she may be excited to action before I leave her. Oh me! when will that be ? " and poor Marian went off into a fit of troubled musing which well-nigh banished the recollection of the present.

But it was the third day since her arrival in town, and she had scarcely commenced her work. This state of things must not continue.

She did not intend it should.

" If I had only a little of your energy, dear

Marian," sighed Isabel, languidly emerging from her bedroom, as her cousin entered the house.

"It would bring a little more colour to those pale cheeks, dear Issy, if you had," returned Marian, with a cheerful smile and kiss.

"Such weather! the heat is fearful—I hardly exist."

"You have lost the best part of the morning, dear Isabel. When William and I sat down to breakfast this morning, there was a delightful breeze, we had doors and windows open to enjoy it, which we did thoroughly. Does not this room feel cool and airy in comparison with that close little bed-room?"

"Yes; I confess it does. But it's hot enough anywhere."

Isabel, with her infant in her arms, sat down in the rocking-chair, which Marian had pleasantly placed by the open window, where she could catch all the freshest breezes, and whence the garden with its shrubs and few remaining flowers was in full view. The sun could not reach her, for the broad shade of the veranda interposed, and she could sit in comfort with her babe, and chat with her cousin.

All that could be done to make the little sitting-room pleasant had certainly been done that morning. Sophy's scrubbing-brush had been very busy, and the floor was perfectly clean. On the table, in the middle of the room, stood a glass filled with roses, in a bed of most natural-looking moss, Marian's handiwork, and long ago designed as a gift to her cousin. The chairs were tastefully disposed about the room, and a great change had taken place in little Allen's cradle. Marian had spirited it away into her own room the night before. She sat up late and rose early to complete it, and now how pretty it looked! She chanced to have material enough to suit her purpose in a large box which she had left with her cousin, not needing it in the bush. So the little cradle-bed was speedily lined, inside and out, and over head, with pink glazed calico. Two or three large anti-macassars, of which she had several, covered this very prettily, and another, lined also with pink, did duty as a quilt. Baby had never looked more lovely than when they placed him in his little bed, with the soft pink glowing on his innocent brow. Isabella's cheek was flushed with pleasure.

"Dear Marian, what taste you have! What a difference it makes! How you change everything you touch!"

"Do you not think, dear Issy, that this looks quite as pretty here as it would have done in England?" asked Marian, archly.

"Yes; to be sure it does," said Isabel. "Oh, but I know what you are thinking of. Still, my opinion remains unchanged. What is the use of taking trouble about anything here?"

"What is the use of taking our daily food?" asked Marian, gently.

"Oh, we must live."

"Certainly: that I suppose is a law of nature. But

do you know, dear Isabel, it seems to me quite as much a law of nature to live in comfort. *Live* we certainly might, in the same state as inferior animals. Live! no; I cannot call that living, it is merely vegetating, not worthy of the human species."

"Well, well, next to food, cleanliness, of course," said Isabel, rather testily; "that is another law of nature which few would be likely to transgress. Those are things which are *essentials* all the world over, but we are not discussing essentials, remember."

"Pardon me; I think we are—essentials to comfort and happiness, at any rate. Yes, happiness, dear Isabel; I repeat the term, notwithstanding those raised eyebrows. There is no knowing how much happiness is gained by attention to these external matters, or how much is lost by neglect of them. I am afraid you will think me very impertinent, dear Issy, but I cannot help mentioning it. Did you notice no change in William, no increase of happiness and pleasure in his manner, when you appeared in your pretty blue dress, and with your hair neatly arranged at the tea-table the evening I came?"

Isabella did not reply; she was recalling that evening. The look, the low tone of approbation, the smile her husband had then given, were not quite thrown away.

"I believe you are right, Marian, as you always are," she replied at length. "It would perhaps be better to make this place look more like home."

" You would like it better. You would be more happy and more contented, dearest, I am sure of it, and I know William would.'

" Do you think he would ? Do you think he would really be happier ? "

" I do indeed, dear Issy. Your unhappiness must affect him. Do you not think it would be far more pleasant for him to come into a prettily and tastefully arranged home after his day's fatigue, than to find a bare floor covered with litter ? You can spare a little money now, can you not ? "

" Oh, yes. Well, I dare say, if I once saw the house nice, I might grow more contented ; but I have not the spirits to put it in order."

" Will you give me *carte blanche?* Come, dear Isabel, I am not so extravagant that you need fear. I'll put on my bonnet, and take the next conveyance to Adelaide. I should so like to make a little difference in the house before William comes back this evening."

" Oh, if *you* undertake it, it is sure to be well done ; and for the expense, I have my own private purse to apply to, I shall not trespass upon William's. I give you unlimited power willingly, and free access to the purse. Here, take the keys at once."

" Very well," said Marian, laughing ; " I will not throw your money away, but use it pretty freely, I promise you, for I am bent upon making you happy and comfortable while I am with you."

It is a well-known fact that the most beautiful

articles lose half their affect if they lack tasteful arrangement; and this delicate art of arrangement, this gift of refinement, proceeds, we presume, from a keen sense and appreciation of the beautiful. We have lately been taught by the author of a curious work on "*Noses*," that this is the result of a certain formation of the nasal organ. Now, although we are not disposed to concede exclusive taste to the delicately outlined proboscis, we are yet ready to admit that it is generally found in connexion with a Grecian profile. Whether or not it is the result of that classic formation, or the formation is the result of the spirit within, is not ours to say.

At any rate Marian's profile was decidedly Grecian, and to her especially belonged the delicate power of diffusing the beautiful. Everything she touched, as her cousin said, experienced some of this magic transformation. She did not require a profusion of adornments—nothing costly, no extravagances; a few shillings went twice as far with her as with some people. But when she told Isabel she should use the contents of the purse with freedom, she was thoroughly acquainted with the Adelaide price of articles, and knew that some little outlay must be made at first to produce the transformation the cottage needed, to give it a title to the appellation of home, in her cousin's eyes at least.

It was with a heart not entirely free from palpitation that Marian entered the next omnibus passing the house on its way to the metropolis. She would have been very glad to have taken William into the secret, and have had the benefit of his company, if not advice, as she had a little dread of imposition ; and there was an indistinct fear of difficulty in the arrangement for the removal of the goods, but she checked it in its rise, for it was entirely contrary to her plan of surprisal for him to know anything about her purchases. She only hoped he would not make himself visible in the streets while she remained there; and cheering up her heart with the result that was to follow her morning's mission, she went bravely, earnestly, and well about the business.

She did not mind the heat nor the dust, though both were sufficiently unpleasant, and the reward for her toil was ample ; as having first seen her treasure carefully loaded in a cart she had hired for the purpose, she threw herself, both hot and weary, into the comfortable corner of a return conveyance.

Isabel had exerted herself considerably during Marian's absence. The house had undergone a thorough cleansing. Sophy's elbows were redder than ever with the excessive exertion. But she had found out that it pleased Miss Marian to see things nice, and she sang at her work as if it were only play, for she knew very well that her meed of praise would not be lacking. When Marian at length arrived, and placed herself in the rocking-chair to rest for a moment, all was perfectly clean, and on the table was a nice little lunch ready for her refreshment after her hot and fatiguing morning.

"Well, Marian, have you succeeded?" asked her cousin, after a moment or two allowed for refreshment.

"Oh yes, admirably. We shall make a little change in some things, I hope, before William comes home. Look, Sophy, and see whether the cart is coming. It must be nearly here by this time."

All Marian's fatigue vanished as, one after another, her recent purchases were carried down the garden walk, and placed at the door beneath the verandah. Her cousin's surprise at some odd-looking parcels, and evident pleasure at others, was to her an exquisite treat, and even Sophy's unsophisticated joy amused her. To pay the man and dismiss the cart was the work of a moment. She stood amidst her heap of spoil like the very goddess of bounty, flushed with triumph and happiness.

"Out of this heterogeneous mass, depend upon it, your home will arise, dear Issy," she laughingly exclaimed; "but you are forbidden to touch an article. I dismiss you and your cherubs to the bedroom; the parlour is mine for a *wee*."

"But, my dear Marian, you must be so tired."

"Not a bit now, Issy. Besides, I shall have plenty of assistance from Sophy, I dare say."

Sophy's eyes brightened very much at the implied compliment to her willingness and ability. She stood eagerly waiting for directions, while her mistress withdrew with the children to the back verandah, whither the rocking-chair and a little stool were despatched presently by Marian for their accommodation.

Isabel sat and rocked her baby. She was thinking —thinking deeply over the morning conversation she had had with Marian. Thought extended itself; it took wings and flew away far back, to the pleasant home of her girlhood; to the luxuries that then surrounded her; the taste she had then indulged—the fastidious taste that would have quarrelled with a bouquet if it was not arranged perfectly *comme il faut.* *Then* and *now*—what a difference! But was it not greatly her own fault? Was not Marian right, that it was her duty to make the home of her husband a happy one? and had she done this? Had she so adorned it, that through all those hours in the dreary office he could look towards it, as the one bright spot awaiting him to reward his toil?

Isabel drew her baby close to her, and a bright tear fell upon its little brow. She knew she had been guilty, deeply guilty in this particular. She knew that often and often on her husband's return, after a hot and weary day of close application, he was seldom greeted by a smile, seldom by a punctual and nicely prepared meal; untidy rooms, cross and repining words, were but too familiar to his ears. His only hope had been his cousin Marian.

Knock—knock—knock—what a time that hammering had continued. Little Emeline had sat for a long time nursing a new doll, a miniature of mamma, but the hammering at length attracted her attention.

She laid her doll carefully in her little stool, which she had turned up in humble imitation of a bed; then spreading her mamma's handkerchief over it, and taking a parting peep, and enjoining it to go to sleep, off she ran into the house to see what Auntie Marian was doing. Her mamma was too busily engaged with her thoughts to notice her.

She, however, did notice the clear, happy laugh that came ringing out to her from the parlour, and the sound of little feet gaily jumping up and down, and then the delighted exclamation,—

"Oh pretty! pretty!"

But for her promise to Marian she would have followed the little one to the scene of her delight. She was highly curious, for she had not been permitted to examine a thing. She had caught a glimpse, to be sure, of a pretty couch, of a little work-table, of a fender and fire-irons, and rolls of carpeting and matting. But there were draper's parcels and others which she could not peep into. It was rather provoking; she had, however, so much to occupy her thoughts that her curiosity was a secondary affair.

She was shaking a little of the dust from her mind. It had accumulated greatly since she had entered the colony. Necessarily it impeded her movements; the wings of her spirit were chained. She saw everything through a dust-cloud. All appeared to her gloomy. She had taken pleasure in nothing. Ought this state of things to continue? Young wife, for your husband's sake—*no!* Mother, for the sake of those little ones—thrice *no!* For the sake of your own health, mental and bodily—a thousand times *no!*

"Tum in, mamma; tum in, auntie says so!"

Isabel's fit of musing had been succeeded by a short nap, and the voice of her little one at first failed to arouse her. Little Emeline, however, was not to be baffled; she was too anxious that mamma should get a sight of the pretty things she had been permitted to look at. She ran forward and pulled her dress.

"Mamma! mamma! Auntie Marian says tum in."

Isabel woke with a start, and clasped her baby to her. She did not know she had fallen asleep, and it frightened her.

"Am I to come in? Is it true, Marian?" she called through the door.

"Oh yes; come in. We have finished at last;" and Marian appeared smiling at the door. "I am afraid I have kept you a long while. Are you not tired?"

"No; indeed, you seem to have been very quick. I believe I have been asleep though—" she stopped short, for she had reached the parlour door. Was it their little room? It had indeed undergone a transformation.

Over the floor lay a rich, soft carpet, whose pattern was composed of twining rose wreaths, on a drab ground. The hearth-rug was a complete bed of moss and flowers. The fender a Gothic bronze. From the round table in the centre of the room, the ugly oil-cloth had been removed, and a handsome cloth, to correspond with the carpet, hung nearly to the floor. Beneath the window stood the prettiest little work-table Isabel remembered to have seen, even in the home-land; and from those windows, curtains of the softest net Marian could procure were gracefully flowing. There was a pretty vase filled with flowers on the work-table, another on the table in the centre of the room; and fuschias and white roses commingled in the three crimson and gold vases on the mantelpiece. Opposite the window stood the couch, of which Isabel had already had a glimpse—a real, veritable couch, not the mere colonial sofa! Marian had been peculiarly fortunate in her visit to the auction-room that day. She might have gone many times afterwards without meeting with what she wanted. The couch was a very great improvement to the parlour. Isabel could find no words to express her pleasure. And to crown all, there was a treasure of an easy-chair. It looked particularly inviting, spreading out its soft arms.

"Just try it, dear Issy; this is my gift," said Marian, playfully seating her. "I thought it would be so nice for William when he comes home hot and tired. And now you have this pretty carpet, you will find those slippers you worked on the voyage very acceptable. Suppose you get them to-night, will you not?"

"Will I not? oh, Marian, I shall never repay you.

William talks about your being hereafter the ' Light of Some one's Home,' but I know very well you are proving the light of *ours*.   How shall I ever part with you?   I wish you would make me like you."

" You are both all I could wish," was the exclamation of a well-known voice, and the same moment Isabel and Marian were folded together in William's arms.

He had been standing an unobserved but charmed spectator of the truly magic transformation of his little sitting-room.   Scarcely able to believe the evidence of his senses, he had seen all, heard all, and his pleasure and happiness at that moment were too deep for words

CHAPTER XXVIII.

THE PLACE OF PRAYER, AND WHAT THE LISTENER
HEARD OF HIMSELF.

> "Some chord in unison with what we hear
> Is touch'd within us, and the heart replies."

THE old homestead looked the same, things went on
in much the same manner, and yet there was a blank
felt in its little society by every member of it. Marian
was missed everywhere, and missed as only one could
be who had gained great love. She had become so
entirely a portion of their every-day life, and they had
learnt to look upon that pleasing face with so much
affection, that to be without her, even for a short time,
seemed wretched—to lose her for ever had never
entered their dreams.

The greatest mystery and perplexity to most of
them was, that she could assign no definite period
for her return, that even the slightest allusion to it
occasioned evident distress both to herself and Allen.
Alf did not know which of them to be most angry
with—his brother or Marian; he could gain no clue
to the conduct of either. He could not discover
whether there was engagement or refusal in the

matter, though he was inclined to believe the latter, from his brother's silent gloom; and yet there were some reasons making him hopeful of the former.

"I wish they would settle it one way or the other," he muttered to himself. "They say 'love makes fools,' and I believe it now. But it's very hard that it should deprive us of Miss Herbert's cheerful company! One's evenings are not half so pleasant now. And as to the *piano*, it might as well be out of the house for the good it does; and I suppose Julie will forget all her playing if this state of things is to continue. Hang it all! say I."

Marian had been missed beyond the homestead. Edward and Mary Clare had called two or three evenings after her departure. They asked for her, and Julie told them that she was gone.

"Gone!" was their united exclamation.

"Not gone *for ever*, I hope, Miss Julie," said Edward Clare, with a countenance of deep anxiety.

"Oh no! not for ever," replied Julie.

"Why you quite frighten us, Julie. How soon do you expect her back?"

"I don't know, Miss Clare; I am afraid not for a long time," sighed Julie.

"You need not look so very grave, Edward, nor indeed, trouble yourself at all about the matter," said Mary, as they walked slowly home. "I told you before, that I thought things were all settled in that quarter, and I believe so yet. In these matters women can usually see farther than men."

"I am not so sure of your penetration in this case, however," replied Edward Clare, in a vexed tone. "What on earth should she go off for if it's all settled ; and why should Allen 'gang about like a ghaist' as he does, if he expected soon to make her his wife ? That's what I should like to know."

But Mary could as little solve the mystery as her brother, only she would not, out of that mystery, have him encourage false hopes for himself.

Allen was as little at home as possible. When he was obliged to be there, he was generally engaged with his accounts in the music-room. Julie was often there with him, seldom talking, but with work or book silently bearing him company. This silence and thoughtfulness was not good for her. She was growing thinner and paler every day. The brother and sister had *one* sympathy. Julie's anxiety was as great as her love for her brother.

"Where is Julie, mother ? " asked Allen, one Sabbath afternoon, walking quietly out of the music-room where he had been reading for more than an hour, and approaching the window of the sitting-room as he asked the question.

His mother was seated at the table, with the old family Bible spread before her ; for it was the Sabbath, and the Book of books, since Marian's arrival, always found its way out of the green-baize cover and little box on that day. So far had her little light diffused its influence, recalling many old memories of Sabbaths in the home-land—Sabbaths of *holy* memory—of God.

worship! and restoring something like a glimmering desire after that "holiness without which no man can see the Lord."

"Julie?" said the mother, looking up from the Bible. "She passed through the room nearly an hour ago, with her hat on, and some books under her arm. I dare say you will find her somewhere among the flowers."

Allen passed through the door, and slowly sauntered round the verandah, at the end of which was the entrance to the garden. He opened the little gate, and walked in.

How rapid had been its growth, and in what beautiful order everything looked. True, there were now but few flowers, though the sheltered position, the rich freshness of its soil, and the water of the little creek, which, from the many springs it contained, was never quite dry, prevented the arid appearance assumed by too many of our Australian pleasure-grounds in the summer season.

Allen turned into the favourite rose-walk—Marian's favourite walk. It was shady now; the sun only here and there penetrating and throwing a tracery of leaves at intervals on the path. There were plenty of monthly roses: they bloomed here in perfection, only just getting enough of the sunbeams, and sheltered from the hot winds, and carefully watered every evening by Julie, assisted sometimes by Allen, sometimes by Bessie, when the little wild one took it into her head to be useful.

He thought he should find Julie in the summer-house, for he knew she was fond of both rose-walk and arbour.   So he walked slowly along, musing gravely, sadly, for in truth though his thoughts were of Marian, there were many sad ones connected with them.   Her affection indeed he was sure of, but with what a condition was it clogged!   Change in outward deportment, in anything external, h. could easily have encountered; but change of heart, he felt, *that* must indeed be the work of a higher power.   He scarcely comprehended it.   It was so strange, and yet he felt it to be so real, so evident in Marian.

"Yes," he could not help sighing to himself, "it is true there is, there must be, something wanting in me.   Even the very feelings with which we regard the Bible are different.   She reads it as if it were the letter of a beloved friend, wherein wishes and desires and loving commands are expressed which it is her delight to obey.   *I* read it—but how dry it appears!   I cannot take it to myself.   There is nothing for me —nothing of love, nothing of joy, nothing of comfort; if indeed I take anything to myself, it is such passages as these :—

" 'The wicked shall be turned into hell, and all the nations that forget God.'

" 'For, behold, the day cometh, that shall burn as an oven; and all the proud, yea, and all that do wickedly, shall be as stubble: and the day that cometh shall burn them up.'

"'Every branch in me that beareth not fruit He taketh away.'

"'He that rejecteth me, and receiveth not my words, hath one that judgeth him: the word that I have spoken, the same shall judge him in the last day.'

"'But I know you, that ye have not the love of God in you.'

"Yes, indeed. I can find plenty of such passages —condemnatory!" He closed the little Bible and walked on again in silence.

He stood at the entrance to the little summer-house. How the passion-flower had grown, springing almost to the top with its dark canopy leaves. Julie had been there, but it was empty now; her pocket-handkerchief lay upon the seat. He sat down a minute and rested.

"I wonder what Marian is doing now?" he thought. "She is at chapel, I suppose—just what she likes. How lovely she looks with her dark eyes glistening with earnest interest as she gazes up at the minister. How humble, how lowly, as she bends forward during prayer. I wonder at those times whether she remembers me—whether my name mingles with her prayer!"

Poor Allen! how much of earthly love was mixed in those thoughts, and how new were all feelings of another nature—how little understood!

He presently rose, and taking the pocket-handkerchief with him, pursued his way slowly along the rose path. Julie had gone that way; two or three faded flowers that had fallen from her hands were his guide. Why was he seeking his sister in his present state of feeling? What was there in her presence that could relieve him? Ah! it was the one point of sympathy between them, if no other. They each loved one object, and daily, hourly, to that dear object their thoughts wandered. Allen could talk with his sister, though not with his mother, and by hints and half words, and by her own delicate perception, Julie had learnt more than half his sorrow and his love.

But where was Julie? Allen wandered on till he came to the little creek. It was not rushing wildly now, but murmuring tremulously along, with a low, complaining whisper. It suited Allen's mood. He threw himself down on the bank, with his elbow on the ground, and his head on his hand; then looking thoughtfully down on the slowly yet steadily trickling water,—

"Like life! like life!" he sighed; "flowing on, and on, and on, and emerging at last in the great ocean. But that ocean—what is it? What will it be for me? O Marian, Marian! you are right. How different we are—how different our destinations must be! Our lives' currents must indeed be turned into one before we can smoothly travel the path of life together, and together merge into the same great ocean, and thence to the land beyond. The land beyond! ah, what faith it takes to look beyond death's chilling flood with complacency!"

He rose abruptly, and leaping across the creek, began to ascend the hill, partly with the idea of finding his sister, partly from very restlessness. He could not remain long in one place.

He was more than half-way up the hill, and nearly approaching the little grove of wattles and she-oaks that mantled the top, when his footsteps were suddenly arrested by a low but well-known voice. He quietly seated himself on a rough mass of stone to listen. He could not see her, but within the shelter of those wattles Julie was concealed, and as he listened, he found that she, like her Saviour, had sought that elevated spot for prayer,—

> "Prayer is the Christian's vital breath,
> The Christian's native air."

So it seemed to Julie; for surely her whole soul was expressed in the simple language that reached her brother's ear. She thought that she was alone—alone with her God; but she little thought that the dear brother for whom she was so earnestly, so passionately praying, heard every word she said.

But hear he did. There was not a word, not a syllable lost to him. He stood rooted to the spot. The prayer itself, simple and earnest, the tearful and sometimes choked utterance of the speaker, and above all the subject of her prayer, touched him to the quick. He bent his head on a stone near, and tears rose to his eyes. Here was his little sister praying for him, when he could not pray for himself. How indeed could he, when there was not one good thought, one good action, in which he dare approach the throne? "Without God in the world—God not in all his thoughts." Ah, Marian's words were following him still, day and night, day and night, till it grew to be a terrible thought, this absence of God, yet he could not pray.

Allen had a deep lesson yet to learn—*that of utter destitution*, utter unworthiness, utter incapability of presenting anything of his own that could prove acceptable to a pure and holy God. After that, the *freeness*, the *fulness* of grace, of salvation *without price!* But there were clouds before the mercy-seat as yet.

He rose and sauntered back slowly and thoughtfully; his Bible sometimes open in his hands and sometimes tightly closed. When, an hour afterwards, Julie came home, she found him upon the couch in the music-room, fast asleep.

CHAPTER XXIX.

THE DESERTED HOMESTEAD.

"TIME and tide will wait for no man" is a very trite but true proverb, and so the people of the homestead found it; for heavily as the first few weeks of Marian's absence passed away, they still *did* pass, and with them brought the business of harvest.

There was not much leisure time for any one then. The boys, Frank and Charlie, were again recalled from school, the eldest to return no more. They and their father and Alf worked as hard all day in the hot sun as any of the farm men, but their appetites were none the worse for that, they were always ready when the great bell rang to call them to meals.

How much was Marian missed in those days when the lunch bags were opened! They were well supplied, to be sure, but not quite so delicately, not with so much variety. There were many quiet, whispering inquiries after the young lady who was here last harvest; for the same reapers, or some of the number, usually found their way to Burton's every season, and they had not forgotten the kind, gentle manner in which they were attended when they came hot and tired from their work that last year.

Then was heard again the dreamy, distant hum of the winnowing machine from the great barn; all day long it never ceased its drowsy rumble. The full sacks of corn were stowed away, and the pigs and fowls were allowed the freedom of the stubble. Alf worked as hard at the winnowing machine as ever, but he had hands less delicate than Marian's to attend him. He thought pretty often of that time though, and wondered a little how he could have been so thoughtless as to keep a young lady so long at work simply for his own selfish pleasure. He remembered Allen's angry exclamation, and how pale and pretty Marian looked as she lay on the heap of chaff at the barn door,—but she was far enough away now.

And then came a little interval of leisure to some of them. The work at the new house could be resumed, it was only the interior, and there was in reality little more to be done to that. The floors had been laid some time before, and the walls were all plastered; the painting, colouring, and glazing of the windows was all that remained. A short time would complete this, and with some little difficulty the men were at last procured, and set to work.

"Are we to have no flowers here?" Julie had asked.

"As many as you like, darling," replied Allen; "you have only to point out where you wish them."

And Julie eagerly pointed out the space in front of the house. The next time she walked that way she found her wishes accomplished, at least as far as they could be at that season of the year. The ground in the front of the house was tastefully laid out in beds and walks; and a close, neat railing, and two handsome gates, with one slip-panel for the present, occupied the place of the rude bush fence. It took off a neat slice of the home section; but Allen knew that was to be his property, and he cared not, so that he could gratify a wish of his beloved sister.

Poor Julie! she said little, but she shed many tears when alone, at the thought of leaving that little music-room, the dear garden, and the comfortable familiar old sitting-room. Not so with Bessie; she was glad enough to leave the "nasty old house," and she danced up and down in the empty rooms of the new one till she made their echoes ring again.

The new house at last was finished; there was nothing left to do but enter it, and this the squire said must be done before winter and the ploughing season came on. After all her strong ambition for the completion of the Hall, it was with something like a sigh his wife prepared to take a farewell of the old homestead, where so many years of her married life had been spent. She went slowly, almost reluctantly, about the work of removal, for though the Hall was only the distance of a section, indeed a part of it on that very section, a little care was required in packing those things too frail and brittle to be trusted to a wagon or dray without due precaution.

Poor old homestead! it was cutting work divesting it of its furniture. How chill, how desolate the wide hearth looked, now that the well-used easy-chairs and their companions were removed! What a void the long table has left; and how we miss those familiar, time-polished stools, which we cannot fancy any other places will suit so well.

But they all went—all by degrees, except the furniture of the music-room, and that by Allen's order was left untouched. It was his own property, it was independent of the new Hall, not an article was removed.

"Well, Allen," said his father, coming up to his side as he stood at the door of the now empty sitting-room, watching the slowly moving bullocks as they crawled off with their last load of goods in the direction of the Hall, "Well, Allen, I yield you full possession now. The old homestead is yours, my boy, together with the home and beech-meadow sections; and in my opinion the sooner you get your repairs done, your furniture in, and your little wife at the head of all, the better."

"It is not so easy, father, to do all this as you think," replied Allen, with so deep a sadness in his tone that it stopped any inclination to banter from Mr. Burton.

"Well, well; but I thought things had turned out

just as I wished. I fancied the lady was secured," he replied after a moment, rather gravely. "I don't wish to dive into any secrets, my boy, but I don't see the use of so much reserve, either. Of course, as a father, I must feel an interest in your welfare. Are not you and Marian Herbert engaged?"

"No, father, we are not; at least not as you mean."

"Not! well, I was never more deceived in my life What! you really don't care for each other?"

"I did not say that," replied Allen, turning away. "So far as love goes, all is right; but there is a barrier to matrimony notwithstanding—at present at least, and perhaps it may never be surmounted. However, father, that is a subject rather too deep for trifling."

"You shall hear no more from me, I promise you; but remember, Allen, a woman is full of caprice; they always shy a little at first. Tighten your reins, and you'll bring her up to the mark yet, mind you; so don't give up;" and the farmer slowly followed his dray.

"'Bring her up to the mark yet:'" Allen slowly repeated his father's words as he paced backwards and forwards in the long, empty room. "'Full of caprice:' oh, father little knows Marian! I honour her for the very sentiments most opposed to my own happiness. I would not have her different from what she is, even though I may have to suffer from her firmness to her principles; nor would I for a moment deceive her, or pretend to feelings to which I have no claim, in order that I might gain her hand." He turned abruptly into the music-room, and threw himself down on the couch. All around was perfectly silent. The servants were at the new house, the men belonging to the farm were scattered in their own huts, out of sight of the homestead. Allen was perfectly alone. Within and without there was no human sound; the wild cry of the night-hawk, the distant hooting of some prophetic owl, the whirr-whirr of a thousand locusts, and the croaking of the innumerable inmates of the creek were the only sounds that met his ear.

He had thrown the window of the room widely open. A sweet breeze stole in from the garden, and swept his heated brow, it waved his hair, and lingered so lovingly in his ear, that it was almost like a whisper, and that whisper, "Hope! hope! poor despondent one. Salvation is also for thee; thy name also is written upon the palms of His hands,—it shall never be erased.

> ' Those feeble desires, those wishes so weak,
> 'Tis Jesus inspires, and still bids you seek.'"

He rose hastily from the couch, and paced the room again. Whence came those words? what tempting spirit whispered them in his ear? No, the root, the foundation of any heavenward desires that he possessed was earthly, the inspirer was his love for Marian. There was no holy source. He wished to be a Christian, truly, but wherefore? was it from love to Christ? was it from delight in His ways? No! no! he dare not say that, he would not thus deceive himself. It could only be because she wished it, because she prayed for it. He shook off the feeling, the wish, as unworthy, dishonourable, hypocritical. He turned from the words the hope inspired, and even loathed himself for daring even for a moment to accept its consolation.

"No! I will at least be no hypocrite, dear Marian," he said to himself, as he continued his troubled walk up and down the room; "not even to gain you, the most precious gift of heaven, would I assume the mere name of Christian, while I am conscious of wanting that change of heart which you say takes place in every child of God. 'Ye must be born again,' is the language of Scripture: surely such a process can be no trivial one, and I have no proof that it has taken place in me. There are none of the signs of a renewed state, no love to God, no attachment to His word, no freedom in prayer."

Allen was learning that lesson—distrust of self, so painful to human nature, and yet so essential in paving the way for the entrance of a full and free salvation. Self must be rooted out before Christ and His Cross can be fully esteemed. But the struggle with this many-headed monster is often extreme. Hydra-like it springs to life again and again, and a large amount of grace is indeed needed to keep it subdued and humbled in the dust. There must be an empty heart and a full Saviour, the one ready to receive the other.   Thus God works upon the heart of the sinner. He Himself prepares the heart to receive Him, and then enters, to that heart's great joy.

Poor Allen, how lonely he felt !   She was gone, the whole house deserted, and the echo of those terrible words yet ringing in his ears, " Without hope, and without God in the world !"   If at first those words had cast a sudden chill when they were uttered, how much more so now, when he was beginning to discover their true import, the results connected with them.

He had written to Marian, and had received a long, kind, earnest letter in reply, dwelling much on the subject nearest her heart, and pointing out many passages of Scripture which she entreated him to study.   He never hinted at any of his feelings, never hinted at the singular manner in which her words pursued him ; no ! he guarded jealously against this. He shrank from saying a word even that should make her think of him other than he was.   And so poor Marian was praying and weeping in secret, wondering whether the answer to her prayer would ever be granted, wondering whether the harvest of her tears would ever come, and little knowing the deep under-current of feeling which had long since been stirred, and which one day should burst into existence, a clear, bright, sparkling stream.

" God will work, and who shall let it ? " was however a sweet promise that still afforded her consolation and hope.

Allen had once more flung himself on the couch, but it was growing late, the shadows were deepening every moment, and he at length again arose, this time closing and securing the window. He gave a parting glance to the piano, to the chair in which he had so often seen her at work, to the little row of books against the wall, to the flower vase, *her* flower vase, in which every day he still placed fresh blossoms, and then, locking the door, he passed once more through the empty sitting-room, awakening hollow echoes as he went, and thence out into the verandah. He turned the key abruptly in the lock, and silently took his lonely way to the new house, for a time his home too.

CHAPTER XXX.

THE SNOWDROP DROOPS ITS HEAD.

" I WONDER whether she will ever come back? I wonder whether we shall ever have our pleasant times again?" sighed Julie, as she sat at the open window of the best parlour in the new house, and looked sorrowfully out through the trees in the direction of the homestead.

"Well, if I were you, Julie, I wouldn't be long before I found that out," said Alf, who had entered quietly, and overheard her. "I should think you of all others might know."

"How can I? I only wish I did."

"Now Julie, that won't do ! You don't pretend that you have not seen this long while that there has been something up between Allen and Miss Herbert?"

"I didn't know for a long time," said Julie, looking down and colouring deeply ; "she did not tell me."

"No; but Allen did, I'll wager?"

"A little, a very little; hardly anything at all. I thought the rest."

"And you really don't know whether Miss Herbert will ever come back? I should say, Julie, you must be very frightened either of her or of Allen, if you have not asked that much."

"Ah! but I know. She will come back, if one thing"—— Julie hesitated, and stopped suddenly.

"If one thing?" repeated Alf; "if what, Julie? that is just what I want to know."

"I was not told *not* to tell," replied Julie, rather doubtfully; "but I know if you were to mention it again, Alf, it would trouble Allen very much, and Miss Herbert, too."

"Oh, you need not be afraid; I don't feel particularly inclined to meddle with the business again, and shall not speak a word. Nevertheless, as I cannot even guess the reason for the present state of affairs, I should like to have a clue to it."

Julie dropped her voice, and bent her head lower as she answered, "Dear Miss Marian is a Christian, and—and—poor Allen! she thinks he is not."

"That's it, is it? Well now, Julie, between you and me, that is not quite fair," said Alf, rather indignantly, "when, too, it's easy to see the poor fellow is over head and ears in the matter. If I were Allen I should give up the chase, hang me if I wouldn't."

"Not if you loved her, Alf."

"Oh, I don't know, a fellow can't make himself a Christian. To be sure he might put on a few sancti-

fied looks, go to chapel pretty often, and sit with his
Bible in his hand where he could be seen, get hold
of two or three cant expressions, too. Why on earth
don't he? the business would be settled."

"I don't think it would," said Julie, warmly; "besides, Allen would not do so."

"I don't suppose he would, but he might. I am
sure I don't know what more Miss Herbert wants
than she has in him. Why he's as grave and sober
as any judge on the bench, and, as I told her once,
has a regularly cut out parson-like face. He is a
teetotaller on principle; I quite shocked him the other
day, when we were in the township together, by asking him to take a nobbler."

"O Alf, did you? why you don't drink brandy, do
you?"

Alf laughed, "Never mind, Julie," he said, "depend
upon it there may be worse things done in the world
than nobblerizing."

Julie thought that was not possible. She looked
very sorry, too, and leant her head on her hands, as
in deep meditation. They were each silent for a few
minutes.

"Well," at length Alf exclaimed, with a sudden
start, "I don't see why we need trouble our heads
about their affairs, Julie; depend upon it, it will all
come right, no fear! We shall have a wedding by
and by, Julie, and then, instead of Miss Herbert, you
will have to say Sister Marian!" and he went away
laughing.

"'Sister Marian,' oh, how nice that would be! or Marian only. Would it be very difficult for her to say that?" She thought not. And Alf's last words plunged her into a pleasant reverie which lasted nearly an hour.

But there was a sad change coming over Julie. She was not like the girl of other days. Her cheeks were much paler and thinner; the blue veins were more distinct. She had become languid, and moved listlessly and wearily about, or lay for hours on the sofa in the best parlour, with no other companion than her Bible and two or three other books of Marian's or Allen's selecting. Her mother's watchful eye detected these symptoms with uneasiness, but when a little quiet cough began to add itself to the other symptoms, her uneasiness became positive alarm.

"I wish you would try to get Julie out, Allen," she exclaimed suddenly, one lovely evening. "It is quite painful to see her lying in that parlour all day, and taking no exercise. I don't know what will come of it."

Allen, who was seated with his account books open before him, looked up hastily, and then instantly closed and collected them together.

"I ought to have thought of it before, mother," he exclaimed, in a vexed tone. "Do you think Julie is ill, then?"

"I don't know what to think, I'm sure. She is not positively ill, but she can't be well, to be so weak and languid. She's no appetite either; I can't get her to eat; and she has a nasty cough at nights and mornings, which I can't say I like."

Allen gravely shook his head, " This ought not to be suffered to go on, mother," he exclaimed. " Shall I see Dr. Dean, and get him to call here ? "

" I shouldn't," exclaimed Alf; " I should take her to Adelaide at once, and get Dr. Bayer to look at her; at least, Miss Herbert said long ago that's what she should advise."

" Did Miss Herbert say that ? " said Allen.

" Yes—a year ago, but I never thought any more about it."

" But how to get her there ? "

" Easy enough, I should think, mother; is not Allen going to town to-morrow, and would it not be easy," he added half mischievously, " for him to call at Grenville's and ask Miss Herbert to take her ? "

" Yes, Allen; you might go there first without Julie. I think if Miss Herbert could be induced to go with her to the bay it would be the very thing. But, however, I'll ask father about it."

" I must know to-night," replied Allen, leaving the room with a thoughtful look.

To Marian ! was it possible they were sending him there ? Dare he trust himself ? Well, it would be something to look at her, and hear her speak once more. How he wished he could go to her, and say, " The barrier is surmounted, all is right, I too am a Christian." He could not say *that* yet, he felt he had no warrant to do so; and yet he was glad that he had a tangible reason for visiting her.

He went quietly out, saddled his sister's pony, and returned into the room where she lay.

"Come, Julie, darling! I want you to ride, and have brought Dapple round to the door."

Julie closed her book, and rose languidly.

"Are you going to ride, Allen?"

"I am going to walk by your side, Julie, the evening is too lovely to be passed in-doors. Here comes mother with your riding skirt and hat; you look as if you want a little of the fresh breezes, pet."

It was a beautiful evening, the air was delicious. A little flush stole into Julie's cheek as she once more found herself seated on her pretty Dapple, with her brother close at her side, talking and laughing somewhat as of old. She looked once or twice timidly into his face, as if she would like to decipher its expression, but she could not. He gave her a clue to this state of things before long.

"You have never been to the bay, Julie, have you?"

"No, Allen; I have never seen the sea."

"Should you like to go there for a while with Miss Herbert? Mother thinks it will do you good."

"Does she? with Miss Herbert? Oh yes, Allen!" and Julie's face grew wonderfully bright.

They were silent a few moments. Allen had evidently awakened pleasing thought by the mention of that name, and Julie knew the expression of his

face too well to wish to disturb his reverie; she wondered though very much what it all meant—wondered
at this sudden decision to send her to the bay—wondered whether Miss Herbert would like to leave her
friends to go with her—but she did not speak.

Allen walked on, with the bridle over his arm, and
the slender whip in his hand. He did not use it on
the pony, but switched the leaves from the wattles
in passing. He spoke at length, but without turning
round.

"I am going to Adelaide to-morrow, Julie; what
shall I bring you?"

"Anything you like, Allen;" and she added very
low and timidly, "I should like best if you could bring
Miss Herbert."

"Oh! but I can't do that," he replied, painfully,
the colour rising to his brow. "I can carry any message to her you like; and I hope next time I go to
Adelaide," he added in more lively tones, "to take you
to her."

"I will write a letter this evening, if you will take
it to her, Allen," said Julie, rather sorrowfully. She
waited a minute or two in silence, and when Allen
turned and looked at her inquiringly, he saw by the
expression of her face there was something she wished
very much to say to him, but failed in the necessary
courage.

"What is it, Julie? You want to speak, to ask
something; surely you are not afraid of me?"

"No, Allen," she replied, blushing very deeply, and

tears springing to her eyes, " I only wanted to ask you if you have not anything to tell Miss Herbert."

" What, Julie ? "

" That—that "—— Julie painfully hesitated, the colour came and went quickly, she turned her face quite away from her brother—" That you are a Christian now."

Allen started visibly ; he had not quite expected it. His old sad, desponding expression returned again, as in a low voice he answered—

" I cannot say that yet, Julie."

CHAPTER XXXI.

FRUIT, AND SOMETHING MORE AGREEABLE.

JUST five o'clock! one—two—three—four—five! The musical strokes of the little French clock, on the parlour sideboard (another gift of Marian's), told the tale. The clear tones roused her from a slight slumber, and scattered a not very pleasant dream. She quietly rose from her bed, and walked to the window, gently opening it, to allow some of the cool morning breeze to enter.

What a pleasing scene it was she looked upon! Cool, shady fruit trees. A few, very few, golden apricots peeped out from the green leaves; but there were rosy peaches in abundance, and large bunches of grapes, and nectarines, and plenty of figs, scarcely visible under their tropical-looking canopy. The veranda, stretching along the back of the house, was literally embowered in a grape-vine, all springing from one root. The rich purple clusters reached even to the chimney top, and hung temptingly down to

Marian's window. The air came in loaded with sweets.

There was more fruit in the garden than they could ever consume. Marian and her cousin had been busy with jam and jelly jars for a month past. A peep into the store closet was quite imposing, and would have perfectly enchanted an epicure. What was to be done with the surplus fruit? Marian found a ready answer to that. Why should they not sell it?

She took upon herself the whole charge, having only the assistance of the boy Grenville always retained about the place, for there was more work in the garden than he could possibly find time for. Since the commencement of the fruit season, it had been Marian's custom to rise before the sun, that being the most pleasant time to gather and pack the fruit. So she did not again return to her bed, though she cast one loving glance at the soft pillow, and gaped, gentle reader, rather unromantically—for our Marian is no creature of romance, be it well understood, but a being of flesh and blood—an embodiment of every-day life, with feelings and thoughts and actions in common with the rest of the extensive sisterhood.

She stood a moment by the little cot at her bedside, and watched the gentle sleep of the rosy Emeline. The long, light curls lay crushed under her head like soft silk, so fair and flossy were they, pushed far back from the open brow, and leaving the face entirely clear.

"God bless you, little sleeper, and make you His little lamb!" said Marian, softly throwing a light gossamer veil over the head of the cot, and tucking it in as a protection from the troublesome flies and mosquitoes, whose repeated assaults were sadly disturbing the little sleeper, and threatening to rouse her wholly.

She moved quietly about the room, and her toilette was soon completed. Then taking up her Bible, she sat down for a moment or two to cull a few words for morning thought.

She turned to one very favourite chapter in the Gospel of St. John—the fourteenth; there was such a rest for the weary, troubled spirit in the sweet consoling words; it reminded her so delightfully, that notwithstanding the troubles and trials and unrest to be experienced in the world, there was perfect rest and joy awaiting in those far-distant mansions, and that Jesus would assuredly come—come to receive His weary ones. But this morning it was the thirteenth and fourteenth verses that arrested her attention. She eagerly read them over and over again. How was it they had never appeared in the same light before?

"And whatsoever ye shall ask in my name, that will I do, that the Father may be glorified in the Son.

"If ye shall ask anything in my name, I will do it."

She sank on her knees, and buried her face in the

cushion of the chair. Tears came fast with the petitions that flowed from her lips—petitions that would have appeared unintelligible to mortal ears, but not so to her Father in heaven. Oh no! *He* can interpret the sigh, the tear. He understands the groan, that expression of "words that cannot be uttered." Her whole soul was in her prayer. She prayed that morning for Allen as she had never prayed before. It was a believing prayer. She asked as though she knew her petition would be granted; she sought as though she knew the answer would be found; she knocked as if already she could discern heaven's portals opened.

There were tears in her eyes when she arose, but heaven's own peace was in her heart.

After another look at her little sleeping companion, she softly opened the door of her room, and stole out into the garden. Hat on head and basket on arm, she could go lightly and cheerfully about her duties; for she had committed her great burden into the hands of One who knew best how to dispose of it.

It was a pleasant duty, at least so Marian thought, to go into the garden so early in the morning, while everything was yet still and tranquil, and only the tops of the fruit trees glowed in the golden light. So fresh and pure were those young breezes, that she often threw back her hat, or hung it on an apple-tree bough, that she might enjoy their breath to the full. No one was in the garden. The boy waited for six o'clock to strike before he made his appearance. So she sauntered slowly down the centre path, rendered dark and shady by the peach-trees on either side meeting over head, and little of the sun's beams could penetrate at any time. Marian could just see the golden sunlight on the upper leaves, as she looked up through the thickly clustered branches.

She turned out of this path into another, almost as shady ; and as it was at the other end of the garden, quite as secluded, or more so. The grape-vines grew here in abundance, and she at once commenced cutting off noble bunches, and loading her basket with green and purple clusters ; singing at her work a quiet, happy, trustful song :—

> " Come when thy heart is weary,
> Come when thy rest is brief,
> Come to the open portal,
> Knock, and obtain relief.
> Come with thy burdened spirit,
> Come with thy helpless plea,
> Turn in thy destitution,
> And find repose in *Me !*
>
> " Fear not to meet refusal,
> Fear no denial here ;
> Thy humble faith is precious,
> Precious each sigh and tear.
> Ask, and expect fruition ;
> Seek but in faith, and find ;
> Knock at the open portal,
> And leave thy fear behind.
>
> " Ask, and expect fruition,
> Seek but in faith, and find."

Marian softly repeated the last two lines again and again. They were in perfect unison with her feelings that morning, and suited the Scripture words she had so eagerly, so almost joyously opened on, half an hour before. They suited the whole tenor of her thoughts—of her prayer. How brightly do the wings of prayer spread themselves in the atmosphere of faith! It is against the cloud of unbelief they struggle—unbelief that impedes the progress, that stunts the growth of the soul. Marian was in faith's atmosphere now. She was longing to hear once more from Allen; perhaps there might be some *little* word, some little stray expression to confirm her faith. She felt almost sure of it, and was ready at that moment to believe anything, to hope anything.

Her basket was growing heavy, for with such thoughts as these, no wonder her work progressed rapidly. She spread a cloth on the ground, and carefully emptied her basket upon it. How rich, how tempting were those clusters, reclining amidst the green leaves! The delicate purple bloom was undisturbed, and how cool and refreshing they looked! Marian stood at a little distance to regard them to perfection.

"If our friends in England could only take a peep at these grapes as they lie here, how they would envy us!" she exclaimed, going back to her work, this time to rob the peach-trees of their soft, glowing fruit.

She should have seen herself as she stood there amidst that glorious display of fruit,—the pale pink morning-dress rising to her throat, its delicate frill of needlework, the dark ringlets falling round a face sweet and fresh with the morning breezes and her own happy thoughts. Yes; she should have seen herself, or rather, one of England's own artists should have seen her, and transmitted at once to his canvas the lovely picture.

But she thought only of the beautiful fruit; her own graceful figure was out of the question; she went on quietly in her work beneath the shade of the trees, heaping the rich, ripe peaches, and singing softly and almost unconsciously,—

> " Ask, and expect fruition ;
> Seek but in faith, and find."

Once or twice she thought it must be growing late, and half wondered why the boy had not made his appearance: once or twice, too, she had wandered to the end of the path, and looked down the peach-tree avenue. She saw the door was open, and caught a glimpse of Sophy's busy figure, but she did not care for help just then ; it was so pleasant to work alone, alone with her quiet hopeful thoughts, with those words ringing in her ears,

> " Ask, and expect fruition."

" I do, I do ; in humble faith I do," she murmured, as she stooped down to unburden her basket of its sweet load. Her lip quivered ; there were tears in her eyes as she added, " not my will, but Thine be done, O Father."

" Marian !"

She turned pale, and trembled all over as she sprang to her feet.

"You did not expect to see me! Only say, dearest, you are not sorry;" and Allen Burton took both her hands in his.

He had seen the picture; it was, however, not to canvas he had committed it, but to his own heart.

CHAPTER XXXII.

THE AVENUE OF ALMOND TREES, AND WHAT WAS SAID THERE.

> " Who ever asked for help in vain,
> Or weary sunk beneath his load,
> Or knocked, and could not entrance gain,
> Or hopeless died in seeking God ? "

ALLEN had arrived in Adelaide late the day before, having been unavoidably detained on the road. It was much too late to think of calling on Grenville. His only resource was supper and bed, and to those he immediately betook himself. Not so, however, the other inmates of the house. There was a ball held in a room but two removes from his, and as the steps were anything but fairy-like, and the music as little resembling the strains of Orpheus as possible, sleep fell not upon his eyelids till long past the hour of midnight; and even then it was not of a sufficiently enduring character to disincline him from springing from his bed, as the usual stroke of six was distinctly chimed from the clock opposite the door of his room.

He had resolved upon one thing the previous evening, that if his late arrival in town had prevented his intended visit, business should not cheat him of it in the morning. He felt, indeed, he should be none the worse for an early ride; and after indulging in a plentiful ablution, he left his heated chamber, and sauntered out into the cool, fresh air with very pleasurable feelings.

The streets of Adelaide were at present but little peopled by the busy multitude, and few of the shops were open, but Allen was not out for business. He soon left the city behind him, though he only walked his horse.

It was a lovely morning for riding, the sun's heat was so pleasantly tempered by the pure breeze. It came to Allen's brow, laden with perfume from many a fruit garden which he could see over the thick kangaroo hedges as he rode along, where blushing peaches, whose soft, downy crimson could not be concealed, vainly strove to hide themselves beneath their leafy canopy. But he was little sensible of their attraction, the eyes of his mind being busily engaged with a well-remembered image. How would she receive him? what would she think of him for coming? What had he to tell her? Nothing hopeful—his hopes and fears were not tangible enough to be spoken of.

His thoughts had turned into a rather melancholy channel by the time he reached Mr. Grenville's. He tied his horse carefully to one of the front railings, and walked in. Sophy was busy at the parlour window as he entered, and no one else was stirring about the house. She offered to awake Mr. Grenville.

"No; by no means, thank you," said Allen. "I can walk in the garden till the family's usual time of rising."

"Miss Herbert is in the garden, sir; shall I go and call her?" asked Sophy, innocently.

"Thank you, no; I am acquainted with Miss Herbert, and will go and find her."

He turned into a side avenue, and sauntered slowly along the covered path. The trees grew thick here, and he could neither see through very well, nor be seen, but he could hear; and he had not taken many steps before he was startled by a low, but sweet and well-known voice—

> "Ask, and expect fruition;
> Seek but in faith, and find,"

were the words which came through the leaves to his ear. He stood with folded arms and bowed head.

"Is she thinking of *me* now?" he mentally exclaimed; "and does she really *believe* she shall have what she asks for?"

> "Ask, and expect fruition;
> Seek but in faith, and find."

There was joyous, triumphant faith in the repetition of the words, in the sweet, clear voice. It seemed like an affirmative to Allen's question. The voice, to him, conveyed even more than the words. "Believe!" the sweet songstress seemed to say. "Oh, yes! I believe; for He who promised cannot lie. I believe that what I ask in humble faith shall be accomplished; and I have asked for you, Allen!"

"If I could only possess this beautiful faith!" he sighed, slowly sauntering on; "but how can *I* obtain it?"

"Ask, and expect fruition!" came softly and musically to his ear.

Ask for what? For faith? Why not? Yes, he would—he had never thought of that. Why, indeed, should he not? It was faith he wanted—faith to believe in Jesus—faith to render the atonement precious—

> "Faith to read his title clear
> To mansions in the skies."

A step forward, and he stood again rooted to the spot. Marian, in her pale pink morning-dress, kneeling amidst heaps of fruit, arranging and re-arranging, was the pleasing sight that met his vision. He stood, as we before intimated in the previous chapter, just long enough to transmit the scene to his heart, and then, moving forward, stood by her side.

"They are not up in the house; we need not go in," said Allen, after the first few minutes had passed.

"This fruit," said Marian, quietly.

"Here comes the boy. Leave it to him—you have already done too much. The fruit is all sorted; let the boy try his skill in packing for once."

Marian yielded, and suffered Allen to lead her to the path he first entered. Then drawing her hand through his arm, and taking close possession of it, they paced up and down, under the almond-trees, some moments in silence.

"Was I in your thoughts this morning, dear Marian?" at length Allen asked, in a low tone, looking down earnestly at the drooping head beside him.

She looked up instantly with a bright blush, and a half-reproachful smile, but he was perfectly grave.

"Tell me why you ask."

Allen replied by asking another question.

"To what did that *ask* refer, from which you seemed to expect fruition?"

The head drooped again, and the long lashes rested on her flushed cheeks, as she answered in a low voice,—

"I *was* thinking of you; I had been praying for you; and I was encouraging myself in faith in the Fulfiller of the promises when you heard me singing. Have you any happy change to tell me of, Allen?" she added, after a moment's pause, looking timidly up.

"Happy change? no," and Allen sorrowfully shook his head.

"Have you nothing hopeful to tell me?"

"You would not have me play the hypocrite, Marian? no, nothing as yet."

But there was comfort even in that "as yet;" it looked as though there was a reaching forward after a different state of things—something undefined— still in the distance—worth hoping for.

"Have you read all I asked you?" continued Marian, after a short silence—"all the passages I marked?"

"Yes, I have read them, but they do not come *home;* I don't feel them. I suppose it is because I lack the faith."

"Unbelief is the cause of all our woe," sighed Marian. "We can place a deeper trust in mere mortals than we can in God. How strange it seems!"

"Yes, it does seem strange, but it is so. I cannot give myself *faith,*—what can I do?"

"*Pray.* God hears and answers prayer. *Pray,* Allen, and then *watch.*"

Allen, according to his usual custom, quickened his pace, and said nothing. But he thought—thought how easy it seemed to Marian to pray—to believe; and even in this, what an unmeasurable distance there was between them!

"Pray!" he sadly repeated. "It is easier to do that than to *believe.* But what do you mean by *watch?*"

"Watching unto prayer," replied Marian, earnestly. "You know, dear Allen, if you had a favour to ask any of your friends, you would not, after asking, turn immediately away, forgetting all about your petition so earnestly asked for. No; the answer would be the chief anxiety—you would watch eagerly for a favourable reply."

"Certainly; but this is our earthly system of doing business."

"And of how much greater importance are the things we ask of God! And yet, how often we ask, and, rising from our knees, immediately forget all our petition. We have *asked* in all apparent sincerity, but, strange to say, we forget to look for the *answer* —for the *result* of our prayer."

" But answers are sometimes so long delayed. Do you not think it enough to occasion despondency or indifference to wait month after month and no reply? One gets cold and careless, as a matter of course—who would not ? "

" It is very trying, dear Allen, very trying to faith, but we cannot tell the wisdom of this," returned Marian, in low tones, for she could scarcely conceal the pleasant hope his words gave her. That there was evident concern awakening in his mind was very clear —concern which would prove the forerunner of better things.

" Is it not enough to make one doubt—to make one renounce all idea of Christianity ? "

"No, oh no, dear Allen. Remember, God sometimes gives us answers in a way and at a time we little expect. And we are not limited to *once* asking, you know. We are to come again and again, to prove our earnestness. There are to be repeated knocks. You remember the poor widow was avenged of her adversary by the unjust judge on account of her importunity ; and the Lord takes occasion from the parable to exclaim, ' And shall not God avenge His own elect, who cry day and night unto Him, though He bear long with them ? I tell you that He will avenge them speedily.' Oh no ; it will not do for us ' to be weary in well doing ; ' we must not grow languid in our supplications."

Marian would have continued, but hearing a foot-step in the avenue, she turned round, and discovered her cousin coming in pursuit of them. They stopped immediately. Allen advanced, and shook him warmly by the hand.

"I knew you were here some time ago," he exclaimed, with a sly laugh, "but I did not hasten up, being sure you would not be alone. Now, however, if the air has not made you hungry it has me, and Isabel will be calling out that her breakfast-cakes are either burnt or cold."

"I will run and see if my assistance will be acceptable," said Marian, turning away. She was glad enough just then to be quit of her cousin's nonsense.

Breakfast was not quite in the state of progress reported by William Grenville. He did not follow Marian, for he knew that fact well enough. His wife had wonderfully improved since Marian's return; he had not once been distressed by her untidy appearance, and she always now contrived to be present at the breakfast-table. But he knew that if there were any hot cakes to be concerned in the matter, they would have to pass through Marian's fingers, so he placed his arm through Allen's, and hurried him round the garden, detailing, with painful minuteness, the good points of each tree or plant, though he had an amused consciousness that he was contributing but little to the entertainment of his companion.

"I tell you what, Mr. Allen," he at length exclaimed in desperation, as they turned into the peach avenue,

T

in reply to a call from the house, " I don't believe we can spare our little Marian again ; she has proved ' the Light of our Home,' at least, and I am afraid if we let her go away too much, some one else will be discovering her excellence, and we shall be losers."

" It would require a very blind individual not to discern so much, sir," returned Allen, gravely ; " but you surely do not mean you would seek to prevent anything that might afford her happiness? "

" Oh, as to that, to tell you the truth, whenever our little Marian sees and feels she is right, she will act. I should not then have a voice in the matter, or very little."

Allen was not sorry to hear that--he believed it too ; he had a powerful consciousness that till she felt she was doing right in his case, she never would act, nor permit him to do so.   But of this Grenville knew nothing.   He thought in his own heart it was excessively strange, and decidedly not the thing, that Allen should have nothing to say to him on a subject to which he had afforded him so good an opening.   The fact raised a considerable doubt whether he had not mistaken the matter, and after all Allen was not engaged to Marian.   Be it how it might, he did not approve of this state of uncertainty.   For his cousin's sake he was determined to ascertain how the land lay, and turning round suddenly before they reached the house, after a rather awkward pause, he exclaimed—

" Mr. Allen, allow me to ask you one question.   I regard Marian rather as a sister than a cousin, which must be an excuse for my interference. You must know that I cannot be entirely unconscious of some things that have transpired; that, in fact, however blind I may have seemed, in reality I am not so. In one word then, are you not trifling with Marian?"

"Trifling, Mr. Grenville! I thought you had a better opinion of me. No; indeed I should have been too happy at the time I first saw you to have told you all, to have formally asked for your cousin's hand, but I have not received her permission for that. We are only conditionally engaged."

"Conditionally engaged! Why surely Marian is not capricious! I gave her credit for lacking that very usual feature of feminine character. Really I am surprised."

"She is not capricious, she is only steadfast to her principles. I honour her for it, though it is to my detriment."

"I think I can understand you," replied William. "I am very sorry, and I am afraid my little cousin is rather wrong-headed on some points. But don't despair, all will come right in the long run, you may be certain of that."

"I hope it may," thought Allen; but he did not look for the fulfilment of his wishes in the same way as his companion.

Marian did not raise her eyes for some minutes after her cousin and Allen entered. She busied herself in buttering hot cakes and dispensing the coffee —in anything rather than encounter a look from

William. Isabel took pity on her, and managed to attract attention to the little Allen, who for his part was busily munching at his fists as though he had decided cannibal intentions. The conversation soon became unembarrassed and general.

One subject was fully discussed—Julie's illness. Isabel gave a warm and unlimited invitation ; and after a little argument, it was agreed that Isabel and Marian should go at once to the bay, and engage lodgings, Allen arranging to bring his sister to town on the following Monday, and then, after resting a night, they could drive out early, and at once take possession of them.

Allen's farewell was not quite of so melancholy a character as it might have been had he not been assured of so speedy a return to town.

CHAPTER XXXIII.

JULIE'S FAITH.

"One more Sunday together, Julie. I suppose we shall not have another for some time," said Allen, quietly, as he sat by the open window, in the large easy chair, with his sister reclining in his arms.

"Do you not like me to go, Allen?" Julie asked.

"Oh yes, Julie. I want you very much to go; I hope to see you well again, and the fresh sea breezes will, I dare say, bring a little more colour to your cheeks. You will get strong after a few encounters with the waves; and then there is one thing I want you to do—not to tire yourself, though; you must promise that."

"What is it you want me to do?"

"Only to gather shells for *me*. If we could but get enough, I should like to line a summer-house. I am thinking of building another nearer to the she-oak hill, or perhaps half-way up."

"Oh, are you? I shall like that very much, and I am glad you have given me something to do: you shall see what a collection I will make."

"Are you well enough to take a ride in the garden on Dapple? The afternoon is not too hot. I will lead him under the trees, you shall not get much of the sun."

"Oh, I think I can walk, Allen," said Julie, rising, "I should like to walk. You know I have a long journey to-morrow; I must try to get used to it. Have you borrowed the gig?"

"Yes, pet, that is all right, and in the stable, but I hope by the time you are ready to come home again I shall have a pretty new conveyance of our own to drive. Father has commissioned me to order one."

"I am very glad. We can then take pleasant drives when we like;" and Julie walked slowly out of the room to get her hat.

They sauntered very quietly along. It was a lovely afternoon; the sun was not unpleasantly hot, and there was a cool, refreshing breeze. It rustled in the top branches of the gum trees, and whispered amidst the she-oaks, and shook the cherry-tree boughs beneath them. Julie said the birds were hushed and still, keeping their Sabbath, and, to her excited fancy, the grasshoppers subdued their chirping.

"Does it not make you think of that beautiful

exclamation of the angels to the poor frightened shepherds, Allen, 'Peace on earth. Good will to men?'" said Julie, in a musing tone of voice.

"What, Julie?"

"This quiet, calm afternoon—so quiet, one would think all nature was keeping Sabbath. It seems to me so like peace, so like the 'peace that passeth all understanding.' Is it not beautiful?"

"To those that can understand and appreciate it, yes, Julie. But do you know, my little sister, this peace, so beautiful in its nature, is not enjoyed by every one?"

"But all who truly desire, may have," Julie replied.

"How do you know that, Julie?"

"Oh, there is so much here to tell me," said Julie, clasping her little Bible to her. "Listen to me for one moment, Allen: 'Peace I leave with you, my peace I give unto you: not as the world giveth, give I unto you. Let not your heart be troubled, neither let it be afraid.

"'These things have I spoken unto you, that in me ye might have peace.'"

"But how does this prove that those who desire may have?"

"Such promises as these do, Allen: 'Whatsoever ye shall ask the Father in my name, He will give it you.

"'Hitherto have ye asked nothing in my name: ask, and ye shall receive, that your joy may be full.' Does not that seem enough, Allen?"

"It does seem so. Let me look at your Bible, Julie. I should like to study that chapter: it seems fresh. I do not remember to have read it before, though I suppose I have."

"It always seems fresh to me, and sometimes I could almost fancy Jesus Himself was saying the words to me. We need not be afraid of asking too much, or too often, while He says, 'Hitherto ye have asked nothing.' I am very glad of that, for it seems as if I were asking all the time."

Allen turned and looked at his sister, wondering whether her sweet, child-like faith would not soon be lost in fruition. Was not that peace, so certainly enjoyed, a foretaste of the peace above? Was not Julie gliding imperceptibly from his arms? Perhaps not. It may be she has a mission to perform—an earthly mission, such as those angels had, who were permitted to herald to a sinful world the first sweet tidings of " Peace and good will."

They had reached the homestead, Allen turned the key in the door, and they entered together. How strangely desolate the rooms appeared! Julie almost shuddered at their gloom.

"How I wish that these rooms were furnished again, Allen!" said Julie, with a sigh.

He echoed the sigh, and replied, "So do I, Julie."

She laid her head against his arm, and clasped his hand more tightly, as she timidly asked—

"Don't you think it will be soon?"

"I can't say, Julie. Why do you ask? You do

not think there is any approach to Christianity in me yet?" He turned an anxious glance on his sister as he spoke.

"I think you are coming to Christ, dear Allen," replied Julie, hiding her face and her tears on his shoulder. "I think it is His Holy Spirit that is drawing you."

"How can you tell that, Julie? Why do you think so?" Allen's coolness was only affected.

"From many things. First, because you like to talk about these subjects, and once you did not. You have a desire to be a Christian, but you hadn't always, Allen. You read your Bible, I do not mean *read* it only, but search it, and that is very different, Miss Herbert told me, to mere reading."

"Ah, Julie! it seems all simple enough to you. I wish I had your faith. But it requires more than words to make a Christian."

"Yes, Allen, I know. It is the precious blood of Christ. *We* have nothing to give *Him*. You remember what that beautiful hymn says,—

> "'Nothing in my hand I bring
> Simply to Thy cross I cling;
> Naked, come to Thee for dress,
> Helpless, look to Thee for grace;
> Black, I to the fountain fly;
> Wash me, Saviour, or I die.
>
> "'Not the labour of my hand
> Can fulfil Thy just demand;
> Could my zeal no respite know,
> Could my tears for ever flow,
> All for sin could not atone;
> Thou must save, and Thou alone.'"

"Yes, Julie, yes; I see it all. The plan of salvation is very beautiful. It only wants faith, and faith is the gift of God."

She knew not what to answer. She could only pray—she did that often and often. Even as she stood there, Allen saw her lips move, and her soft blue eyes turn heavenward.

"Allen," she said at last, following him into the deserted music-room, and seating herself beside him at the open window, "Allen, do you remember those sweet verses we used to sing with Miss Herbert? I mean, 'Nearer, my God, to Thee.'"

"Yes; I remember them, Julie."

"Will you sing them with me? I like them so much. The accompaniment is very easy. I can play it quite well, if you will please open the piano."

Allen removed the cover, and slowly unlocked the instrument, and placed the music-stool for his sister. He stood behind her, one hand resting lightly on her shoulder. Julie's voice seemed sweeter than ever, as she sang,—

> "Nearer, my God, to Thee,
>   Nearer to Thee;
> E'en though it be a cross
>   That raiseth me,
> Still all my song shall be,
> Nearer, my God, to Thee,
>   Nearer to Thee!
>
> "When in the wilderness
>   The sun goes down—
> Darkness comes over me,
>   My rest a stone;
> Still in my dreams I'd be
> Nearer, my God, to Thee,
>   Nearer to Thee!

" Then let the way appear
    Steps unto heaven ;
All that Thou sendest me
    In mercy given,
Angels to beckon me
Nearer, my God, to Thee,
    Nearer to Thee !

" Then with my waking thoughts
    Bright with Thy praise,
Out of my stony griefs
    Bethel I'll raise ;
So, by my woes, to be
Nearer, my God, to Thee,
    Nearer to Thee !

" Or, if on joyful wing,
    Cleaving the sky,
Sun, moon, and stars forgot,
    Upwards I fly,
Still all my song shall be,
Nearer, my God, to Thee,
    Nearer to Thee ! "

Allen drew his sister's head to his shoulder, and kissed again and again her white brow. Too little of earth there seemed in that sweet voice,—that spirit flying after God savoured too much of heaven.

"You would not like to leave us, dear Julie ?" asked Allen, sorrowfully.

"I should like to leave you only for one thing," replied Julie, gently, as she lay back exhausted in her brother's arms, "only for *one* thing, ' to be with Christ, which is far better.' "

"How can you tell that, Julie ?" asked Allen, in low, suppressed tones.

"Oh, I know !" replied Julie, and she closed her eyes, and lay quite still. Allen could almost read her thoughts, as a smile flitted across her lips, though she did not speak.

"Beautiful, beautiful faith!" he again thought, "brighter and stronger, as the pulse of life grows languid!" It was the expression of the same feeling, "I know that my Redeemer liveth, and that He shall stand at the latter day upon the earth: and though after my skin worms destroy this body, yet in my flesh shall I see God." The same expression, only from younger lips. Thus, in all ages, the children of God have experienced the same trials, adopted the same language, felt the same longing after their heavenly home. It is the family likeness visible in all the children, from ancient days even until now;—Was there any of this likeness in him?

CHAPTER XXXIV.

HOW THE WILLOW GREW BY THE CREEK.

IT was nearly six o'clock when the gig was brought round to the door, and all was pronounced ready for the journey. Some of the coldest hours of the morning were over, but Julie was none the less carefully wrapped up, though she declared she was not in the least cold.

"I think you had better, Julie. There are some unmistakable rain clouds round the head of that hill. It is better to be provided against them. Besides, that cloak will be of service to you on the sands. It is cold enough there sometimes. You will need wrapping up."

Julie permitted herself to be folded in the large cloak and lifted into the gig. Her boxes were safe in the seat behind, in company with a string of wood-pigeons, shot by Allen, as a present for Mrs. Grenville;

and these again in close companionship with a ham, a fine cheese, and fowls, from Mrs. Burton. Father, mother, Alf, and little Bessie, stood in a cluster at the door to witness their departure.

"Take care of yourself, darling, and mind and come back well!" were the mother's parting words.

"Don't forget the shells for me, Julie!" said Bessie, running a few steps after the gig, as it drove off.

Alf sprang up behind, with the intention of riding to the slip-panel.

"I say, Julie," he whispered, rather loudly, "if you discover any symptoms of a matrimonial tendency, just write and tell me."

"Nonsense, Alf; I don't know what you mean," said Julie, blushing, and vexed for Allen.

"Well, take care you don't get buried in the sand, and don't go far out into the sea. I should not like to see you come home minus a leg, and there are sharks, remember, in deep water," and laughing, he sprang from his seat, and tossed down the panels, one after the other.

The next moment they had left Alf and his slip-panels far behind.

How beautiful the old road looked with the sun shining upon it slantingly through the trees. Julie leaned back in the gig to enjoy it. Allen had carefully arranged the cushions so that she could do this with comfort. The wattles were not in bloom, but they were thick with foliage, and here and there little flowers peeped out from the dry, hard ground, as much as to say, " Hope on ! the arid desert has a termination ; the grass will again spring beneath your feet, a thousand blossoms will once more delight your eye. Hope on ! "   Julie imagined she could hear the song of these scattered little wildlings, and closed her eyes.   But there was a smile upon her lips.

Her brother looked at her once or twice.   He was doubtful whether she was sleeping, but the slight quiver of her eyelids and her mouth decided that. " Are you tired, Julie ? " he asked affectionately, after they had gone on some way in silence.

She opened her eyes, and returned his look of affection.   " No, Allen, not at all ; it is only very pleasant to travel as we are now.   I like to shut my eyes and think."

" What were you thinking of just now ? " said Allen, smiling gravely.   He knew very well his sister's thoughts were not of a merry order.

" I was looking a while ago at the tiny pink convolvulus, that grows by the sides of the road here and there," said Julie.   " It seems to look up so full of smiles, that I can almost fancy I hear it singing."

" And what does it sing, Julie ? " said Allen, smiling more merrily.

" Oh, a simple little song ; but I like it very much. ' Hope on, hope on,' that is the burthen."

Allen sighed.   " I expect, Julie, you feel a little like the author of these lines, for he talks of flowers having a voice.

> " ' By the breath of flowers,
> Thou callest us from city throngs and cares,
> Back to the woods, the birds, the mountain streams,
> That sing of Thee; back to the free childhood's heart,
> Fresh with the dews of tenderness! Thou biddest
> The lilies of the field with placid smile
> Reprove man's feverish strivings, and infuse
> Through his worn soul a more unworldly life
> With their soft, holy breath.' "

"Yes, I do feel something like that. But I was thinking just now of the 'hope that maketh not ashamed.' 'Which hope we have as an anchor of the soul, both sure and steadfast, and which entereth into that within the veil.'"

"That's the sort of hope, Julie," said Allen. "The sort of anchor my soul wants," he mentally exclaimed. He did not again interrupt Julie's musings, but drove on in silence. He had enough to think of; the billows and their surge beat wildly, and the anchor had not taken hold,—there was no steadfastness.

It was a beautiful country they were passing through. They had turned out of the road leading from the slip-panel, and were now between hills extending on either side along the track, and rising high, high above them. Here and there trees grew from the rocky sides, and tea-tree bushes, and clumps of the grass-tree, and the close little ground-berry bush. In other places, large pieces of rock had been quarried from its sides, the deep cavities in their variety of colour greatly enhancing the beauty of the scenery. They were shielded here completely from the sun; scarcely a ray found its way to them. But it was rather close and warm in the gully. Julie began to wish for a clearer prospect, so true it is, that even the most beautiful scenery wearies the senses if too universally repeated; we need variety to prevent ennui, and preserve our faculties in their freshness.

But between the hills they had to go.   It was the best path, and for a rough country road was by no means amiss in summer.   Winter travelling was not so easy.   A turn in the road brought with it a change. Allen had to alight at last and lead his horse.   They were coming out of the gully, and gradually ascending a hill which rose steeply before them, and Julie wanted to got out and walk too, but her brother would not allow her.

"It would hurt you to walk up the hill far more than it would hurt the horse to draw you, Julie," said Allen.

They continued ascending, and ascending; the gullies on either side becoming deeper and deeper.   It made Julie shudder to look down.

"It would be dreadful if the horse took fright at anything, and dashed with us down a precipice," said Julie.

"Rather so, I fancy," said Allen, smilingly, "but you are not afraid, Julie? you do not think Dandy an evil-disposed horse?"

"Oh, no."

Julie was not afraid to trust the horse, but she almost wished they were once more on the old road. It made her feel giddy looking down those thickly wooded gullies, clothed from the top to the very base

U

with dark green foliage.   But the scene awaiting her at the top was worth encountering a little difficulty, even a little fright, to obtain.   The sea, the broad, open sea, was visible, stretching widely across her vision.   The morning was so clear that the sun's rays danced and sparkled over the slightly agitated waters, and Julie could perfectly distinguish the white sails of a vessel bearing in for the port.

Between them and the sea there seemed to rise innumerable hills and gullies, wild and rude, but very beautiful, swelling and indented alternately, and forming a marked contrast to the clear blue of the heavens, and the sparkling, glossy surface of the sea.

"This is beautiful, is it not, dear Julie?" said her brother in a low tone, as he rested his horse a few minutes before descending the other side of the hill.

"*Very*," Julie frequently answered in hushed tones.   "It reminds me of those verses we sometimes sing,—

> "' Sweet fields beyond the swelling flood
> Stand dressed in living green!'

I can almost fancy I see the swelling flood and the gates of the Celestial City.   Allen, do you see them?" and she pointed to a spot from whence the whole strength of the sun's beams seemed to come.   An active fancy might easily have portrayed amidst the flood of light an archway and gates of pearl.   Allen looked till he almost shared her imaginations.

"You know," continued Julie, in a musing tone,

" the shepherds took Christian and Hopeful to the delectable mountains, and what a sight they gave them of the Celestial City ! Well, this hill reminds me very much of that. I often wish there were really shepherds, and really delectable mountains ; I would not be long away from them."

" Yes, my little sister, only you would look till you were so etherealized we should with difficulty hold you. We should, ere long, find that the angels had borne our darling away over Jordan."

" Well, Allen, and you would not be sorry for that, for of course it would be good for me, and I should be far happier."

" The little star has its duty to perform, as well as the brilliant sun. It will not merge into the blue ether till precisely the moment designed,"—Allen spoke gravely, and half to himself, as he again took his seat by his sister, and they drove on in silence.

Slowly, slowly down the hill, the gullies becoming less deep every moment. At the very foot of the hill Allen again brought the horse to a stand, for peeping through the trees, and just on the borders of a creek that spanned the road with its narrow stream, was a wayside public-house.

" Our first stage, Julie ! " said her brother, lifting her to the ground, and leading her through a little gate to a side door, whose porch was covered with a vine and jessamine. He had often been there before, and was well known, as well as perfectly familiar with the house.

There was a neat little parlour containing three windows, almost level with the ground, and they were open to their widest extent, admitting the breezes in all their purity and freshness. Allen wheeled a large arm-chair to one of them, and placing his sister in it, took off her hat and cloaks.

" Now, Julie, look out; there's a prospect for you !" he exclaimed, enthusiastically, as he turned the chair a little more to the window.

A prospect indeed! wild and romantic in the extreme, rocks and hills, and deep gorges, and the creek twinkling along like a silver thread among the whitest of stones, and hastening down the declivity in a tiny cascade. Massive gums, stretching their huge arms towards heaven, slender wattles with their broad green leaves, dark, gloomy honeysuckles, full of pine-like cones, and thick tufts of grass-tree, every-where.

Julie was silent with admiration and pleasure.

"Now, for one moment, come here, Julie;" and her brother led her to the opposite window. The scene was indeed magnificent here; a deep ravine, the hills on either side towering high, and one mass of dark underwood, stretching on and on as far as the eye could reach, and belted in, so it seemed in the distance, by the sea, clear, bright, glossy, dazzling. the brighter for the foil of that dark ravine.

"Oh, let me sit here, Allen !" was Julie's low exclamation of pleasure, but the flush on her cheek told that her enjoyment was very great.

Allen left her there.   Breakfast was only now in the course of preparation, so he had ample time to attend to his horse.

Julie could see him where she sat, as he led the animal down to the little creek, and stood with one hand resting caressingly on his neck, while he imbibed copious draughts of the clear fluid.   She thought it a pretty picture, well harmonizing with the lovely scenery.   Her handsome brother (for she did not admit even the possibility of any surpassing him in appearance) and his noble horse, whose fine sleek coat shone in the sunlight which fell upon it, and the bright waters rippling over the stones, now foaming and feathery, behind some mass of rock, now dark and deep as it was just where the horse was drinking, and now quivering and sparkling onwards in very gladness.   Oh! if she only had the power to take that sketch just as it was that moment!

There was a fine weeping-willow close by the creek, drooping its very leaves into the water.   Who could have planted it there?   Some one surely who had a love for the picturesque; but Allen knew the history of that tree better, and when he came in he told her the tale.

" On the first arrangement of the garden, through the centre of which ran the creek, a variety of vine cuttings and slips of trees of all descriptions were scattered about; a truant hen had ventured into the enclosure, and was busy tossing about the slips in all directions, when the youngest boy, an urchin of eight summers, perceived her, and intent on bestowing a severe castigation, chose the most whip-like slip he could see, and raced after the unfortunate tenant of the barn door.

"But, alas! he forgot the hen and the punishment designed for it, in astonishment and delight at the strange pliability of his whip.   He had been strictly charged on no account to touch any of the slips, and not daring to claim this without leave, he ran off to his father to obtain it.

"The publican took the slip in his hand.   It was evidently no fruit-tree, and considering it almost worthless, he carelessly returned it to the child with permission to do with it as he pleased.

"Full of his new acquisition, he for some time amused himself very well, but at last, getting weary, he begun to exercise its pliability on the legs of the stableboy, who, not particularly relishing the infliction, watched his opportunity, and snatching the switch threw it up high in the air to the other side of the creek.   It was winter, and the sides of the creek were embedded with deep mud, and into one of these mudheaps the willow slip sunk, and there it remained till the return of spring, when it began putting forth leaves so fast as to attract attention."

Such was the history of the willow-tree, and how it came by the creek.   Julie heard it while she was in the full enjoyment of hot cakes and coffee and delicious ham.   The fresh air had already given her an appetite.

Not a particle of fatigue was remaining when Allen once more brought the gig to the door. She was quite fresh and ready to renew her journey, though she had one glance of regret to give to the mountain gorge, the stony creek, and little wayside public-house, as they left it behind them.

CHAPTER XXXV.

HOW SOUNDS MAY DECEIVE.

Patience wanted a nightingale—Patience waited, and the egg sang.

How lovely was the sunset that evening, as roseate and golden clouds swept the whole western heavens. It was a sight of gorgeous beauty; but sadly prognostic of heat. The day had been sultry enough, but with the decline of the sun a slight breeze had sprung up. It was playing now and then rather fitfully with the leaves of the passion-flower, and one very full-blown rose had fallen to pieces, as it swept softly past, scattering the pale pink leaves over the window-sill, and even to the carpet within.

Doors and windows, all were left open to catch every whisper of the truant breeze. It entered at its own sweet will, wandering over the plentifully spread table with its neat china, through the flowers in the centre vase, and amidst tempting baskets of fruit—fruit that had been gathered in the early morning and still retained its delicious coolness. Something else it found to revel in—soft dark ringlets; it lingered lovingly there, waving them gently to and fro, over cheeks rather flushed, and eyes brighter than usual.

Allen and Julie were expected that evening. Marian was again to be united to her pupil. She had paced up and down the veranda for the last hour with little Allen in her arms, and had many times glanced through the trees in the direction the travellers were likely to come. She could see a long distance up the road, and even before any conveyance was visible would be able to hear the sound of wheels. But little Allen had fallen asleep, and she had placed him in his cradle; the sun had sunk gradually to the west, leaving the veranda in shadow, and yet they came not.

Little Emeline ran up and down the walk, from the veranda to the garden gate, each time peeping with her rosy cheeks pressed against the bars, and as often returning brimful of intelligence.

"They tumming, mamma! they tumming, Auntie Marian, they tumming!"

Auntie Marian was duped once or twice, but after that she learnt to disregard the little prattler. The shadow kept increasing, and yet they came not. William Grenville had been home nearly an hour. He had dined, and now came out upon the veranda.

"'Hope deferred maketh the heart sick,' eh, Marian?" he exclaimed, teasingly.

Marian smiled a little, and blushed a good deal, but did not reply. Her cousin took little Emeline on his shoulder and walked to the gate.

It was pleasantly cool now. The murky twilight was agreeable to Marian. There was a gentle little breeze playing among the branches and rustling among the leaves. She stood still in the centre of the path to listen.

Hark! was not that a distant murmur on the road? Yes; nearer and nearer, till it increased to certainty.

They were coming at last. Marian's heart fluttered almost painfully as William called out to her,—

"Here they are; they are coming now."

Her breath came short and thick, she held her hand against her heart to still its beating—and all this excitement for an empty butcher's cart.

William burst into a provoking laugh, which little Emeline echoed with her own silver treble, and Marian, too disappointed to watch any longer, slowly sauntered back to the house.

"How late they are!" said Isabel, coming from the kitchen, where she had been superintending some mystic operation. "Perhaps after all they will not come to-night."

"I should think not, as it is so late," said Marian, quietly seating herself in the large easy-chair, and leaning back as though she was perfectly satisfied with that arrangement.

"The lamp shall be lighted at any rate, and the curtains drawn," exclaimed Isabel; "and I should think, dear Mari, we need not wait much longer for tea."

"I should think not," was Marian's simple reply.

But as the lamp entered, the sound of wheels came again, nearer and nearer, till they stopped at the very gate, and William's hearty voice was heard in warm welcome. At the same moment came Emeline's little feet pattering down the garden walk, and this time truthfully exclaiming,—

"They tum, mamma, they tum."

Marian rose hastily, and went out into the garden to meet them, with her cousin Isabel. The moon had risen since her return to the house, and was now throwing shadows on the path, fantastic and strange. It served also to show the visitors, for the trees' shadows fell short of the gig, that was in the full, clear light. Marian saw with perfect distinctness the little figure wrapped in her mantle, still retaining her seat, while her brother busied himself in removing some articles from the back of the gig. She came eagerly forward, and the box Allen was dislodging nearly fell to the ground as he hastily turned to receive her greeting; and then lifting his sister out, gave her into Marian's care.

Into kind, thoughtful hands he had given her. Julie lovingly attended, and at last seated comfortably in the large chair at the tea-table, with her beloved friend, all but sister, beside her, seemed almost to forget her fatigue. Others did not forget it, though. Marian was much shocked at the evident ill health exhibited by the wasted figure, the pallid face, with a single crimson spot on either cheek, and the slight, but almost constant cough. She could with difficulty restrain her tears every time she looked that way. Allen watched her own countenance, and very grave indeed he looked when he interpreted its meaning.

Julie was with friends,—that was one comfort.

That little room would have revealed a pretty scene, could any one have pushed aside the curtain and peeped in. The soft light diffused itself through the lamp-shade over a circle of animated and happy faces. Julie, Marian, and Allen were by some means grouped together. William Grenville and his wife occupied the other side of the table. Little Emeline, weary of the indulgence of stopping up until the arrival of the lamp, had glided away unobserved, and was at last discovered lying upon the hearthrug, with her fair head resting contentedly upon the soft, woolly coat of her papa's large dog, Nero. That was a picture worth sketching, the child and the dog, but it wanted the colouring to make it perfect. The bright hue of the ringlets, like soft, flossy silk; the fair, dimpled face and arms; the rosy lips, parted in a half-smile,—it would have made a lovely picture.

In the happiness of the present, half the fear for the future was scattered. On such an evening, and with such bright, enlivening surroundings, hope lent its rainbow tint to everything. The sea air, the bathing, and daily walk upon the beach, were sure to prove efficacious. Julie was to recover strength and appetite and spirit in an incredibly short time. There was no medicine necessary in her case. Allen readily grasped the same sanguine views; he was prepared to return to his mother with all kinds of pleasant assurances, and left his sister next morning with a contented, happy mind, for he had left her with Marian.

CHAPTER XXXVI.

A GLIMPSE OF THE CROSS.

"ABSENCE makes the heart grow fonder," is a line from a well-remembered old song, whose words are familiar to most of those who have traversed the mighty expanse of ocean, leaving the shores of Old England behind them. Allen Burton experienced much of the truth of this, for certainly the dear absent ones occupied more of his thoughts than any of his daily avocations. They were so associated with everything at the homestead, it would have been almost strange had not their images frequently interposed.

At home, too, they were the daily theme of conversation. What they were doing; how Julie was getting on; if the sea-breezes were bringing health to her pale cheeks, and strength to her weak frame,— these were the subjects of daily thought and wonderment from Mrs. Burton; and as to Bessie, her little mind ran upon shells and sea-weed and starfish. She hoped Julie would get quite well and strong, that she might be able to get a *great* bag full. The question was, what the little bush lassie intended to do with her treasures when possessed of them.

Alf felt the loss of the missing ones almost as much as any of them, in one way at least.

"Hallo! all alone as usual, mother?" he exclaimed, in his customary noisy manner, one evening, as having finished work for the day, he came into the room where Mrs. Burton was seated at needlework.

"Yes, Alf, all alone, and have been all the afternoon. Bessie went with your father in the dray, to the she-oak section, directly after dinner, and I have not seen her since."

"You must be very dull, mother," replied Alf, rather gravely, taking possession of his father's chair. "I must confess this is a very unpleasant state of affairs. I hope it won't continue long."

"I hope not too," she replied, though in a rather unhopeful tone of voice. "I suppose we cannot expect all to go smooth with us in this world," she exclaimed, after a few minutes, with a deep sigh.

Alf had no answer for that; he continued silent and thoughtful longer than usual. He was not wont to be at loss for words on any subject within his comprehension.

"Is it not almost time you heard from the bay, mother?" he at length asked.

"Yes," said his mother; "Frank has gone to the post. I hope we shall have letters to-night."

"All right," cried Alf, jumping up; "then we won't cry out before we're hurt, mother. *I* won't for one, at least. Who knows? there may be good news in the letters brought."

With that hope Frank's return was eagerly looked for.

The post yielded nothing very satisfactory that night. Letters there were, but no tidings of Julie's improved health. These, however, were but early days. There had not been a fair trial yet. Mrs. Burton reasoned thus, and was less uneasy. Allen's satisfaction arose from the fact that his sister could not be in better hands than those of Marian.

The post brought a letter for him—not from Marian, but from Julie. It stood on the mantelshelf waiting for him. He caught sight of it as he entered the room that evening on his return from the run. Taking it up, and looking at the handwriting, he quietly put it in his pocket, and seated himself at the tea-table with the rest. His mother gave him what news there was.

There are some feelings too sacred to be trusted in the presence of others, even those nearest and dearest to us. Even Julie's letter was too precious for Allen to read while other eyes were upon him; so after tea he put on his hat and went out. He had loved his little sister, for she had looked up to him so long for love and guidance. But now, how things were changed! *He* was the learner, though scarcely in his inmost heart he admitted that. But he eagerly read her letters, for they always contained something suited to his state of mind. He liked to pore over them alone. And for this purpose he did not stop near the house. He walked straight on till he came to the door of the old homestead, when he turned the key, and went in.

Dreary, dreary old walls! The empty house threw a weight upon Allen's spirit as for some time he paced up and down what had once been the cheerful sitting-room. A few slant rays of the setting sun even now fell through the window looking towards the west, but they gave no brightness to the room. That parting sunshine only betrayed the desolation within. How hollow sounded his footsteps as he walked up and down! Allen could scarcely bear it; he walked into the music-room, and threw open the window. A shower of pink leaves fell to the floor from an adventurous climbing rose-tree outside. That rose-tree had thriven wonderfully; one would almost have imagined that a spirit of curiosity, such as that pertaining to our human nature, had become infused in the sap; that the aspiring stem was compelled upwards by a desire to peep within after the fair inmates, now no longer visible at the window or in the garden.

The breeze was welcome; it was soft and healing, and came in very sweet from the garden. There was desolation within, but not without. Even that music-room looked dreary. The empty hearth, the thick dust on every article of furniture, the untrimmed lamp, the silent piano, and the pretty vase, still crowded with the last-gathered flowers, now all dry and withered. Allen turned away impatiently from the dreary scene, and again looked out of the window. Not that anything in the garden attracted his notice; not the she-oak hill, with its whispering trees; not even the fair sunset sky, or pale moon, so slender and faint, making its first appearance. His bodily eyes gazed vacantly around him, but his mental vision was fully employed. It had no bright images to feast on; some of the dreariness of these empty rooms had crept into his soul.

And yet this place was really his own. Was it then always to remain desolate? No, no; it should not—it should not. From that day at least there should be a change; he would have workmen instantly. The old place she loved so much should not go to ruin, nor should it be empty long. He would furnish it, and live there himself till better days. Ah! that word brought a sigh with it. Better days! what right had he to think of better days? what right had he to dream dreams? Over the raging tempest of his mind had there yet floated the " Peace, be still "? Had the stubborn will yet yielded to the mandate, " Son, give me thine heart "?

That thought reminded him his letter was yet unread; he took it hastily from his pocket, that he might peruse it before the fast-fading light had vanished.

Julie's trembling hand! her own quivering hand! not a very long letter either—she had wearied while she wrote; it took scarcely five minutes to possess the whole. But there was one sentence over which Allen pored again and again; something therein needed more than a moment's reflection; something there touched him deeply.

"What, Allen, if I never should get better? I sometimes feel as if I shall not, sometimes as if I do not wish it; and yet, dear Allen, for one thing I do—for one thing I do wish to get well. O Allen, only for one thing—I couldn't die happy without it. I couldn't, I know I couldn't. I want so much to know you are a Christian. What keeps you back, dear Allen? Why will you not love this dear Saviour? O Allen, dear Allen, if it is the burden of your sins, take them, like Christian did, to the foot of the cross; there is an open sepulchre there, and they will roll, roll on, till they enter in the door of that sepulchre, and are quite, quite hidden. That's the place, dear Allen. I know it; you cannot lose your burden any-where else."

Had he been to that place? No; he felt he had not. With his burden heavily and sorely pressing him, he had wandered on all this time beneath the burning brow of Sinai. Fire and flames issued from every side; it was indeed a mountain that might "not be touched." The cross—how little had he thought of it! how little had he understood it!

There was yet sufficient light. He took a pocket-edition of the "Pilgrim's Progress" from the book-shelf, and sought the part his sister had indicated. He read with prayerful, tearful earnestness—read till he could no longer distinguish a letter—and then? Then, reader, he prayed.

He felt now he had indeed never come straight to Christ, like Christian bearing a heavy burden; he had gone the wrong way to be relieved of it; he had looked away from the cross. But now—ah, now, God helping him, he would do so no more.

Oh, could Marian or Julie have guessed what was transpiring in that old homestead, in that little forsaken music-room, what rejoicing hearts they would have carried! But "there is joy in heaven over one sinner that repenteth." Surely then in those bright realms, even at that moment, a glad heart-peal was ringing.

Ah, the cross had done its work—it was no longer a mystery. The scheme of salvation, beautiful as Allen had long considered it, was yet more lovely; it was something in which he was beginning to realize an interest. It was real; it was now all his hope: his heart melted as he dwelt upon the sweet theme.

> " ' My sins were the nail and the spear
> That wounded His side and His feet,' "

he repeated softly, the tears starting to his eyes. "Oh, never in this light have I viewed it," he exclaimed. "It was to cancel sin, even my sin, Jesus died; and if with the whole burden of my sins I come for His own name's sake, He cannot, He will not reject me! No; He died to save sinners."

Oh, how willing is the heart made, in the day Christ enters! how sweetly submissive to that entry! A sense of the love of Christ can dissolve even a heart of adamant.

Prayer went up from the foot of the cross that night. He who answereth prayer was beforehand with His blessing, and with the prayer there was a sweet commingling of praise.

What a new world of happiness had opened up to Allen! He was no longer the same; a few moments' glimpse of the cross, a look by faith to Him who hangs thereon, had changed the whole current of his existence. Strange that he had never looked before; strange till now he had been unable to realize how the death of Christ brought life to every seeking sinner; how the sting of death had been destroyed and eternal happiness secured; and that in all this he, too, had an interest.

> " God moves in a mysterious way,
> His wonders to perform."

But so certainly as He had said it shall the promise be fulfilled—the seeker shall find. Humble faith, weak faith, trembling faith we may have, but the promise is the same; the simple look upturned to the brazen serpent, results in a perfect cure.

But, like Mary of old, Allen kept all these things in his own heart; he kept the precious assurance safe in his own breast. Not that he feared the shame of the cross, not that he dreaded its reproach; oh, no; he was jealous of its honour, he wished to prove he was indeed influenced by the love of the cross, and not by earthly gain. He wished to prove, not only to others, but to himself, that he was under no momentary delusion, influenced by no evanescent feeling; that it was not the mere hope of worldly happiness, dearly as he yet cherished that hope, that had wrought the wondrous change, but that higher, heavenly motives, sweetly constrained him.

Marian heard nothing, therefore, of the glad tidings —heard nothing of that answer to her prayer for which she so earnestly longed; she still wept and prayed, believing through all.

And Julie,—was there no word to her?

Yes; a hint, nothing more. It made her hopeful.

"Pray on, my little sister," wrote Allen; "who knows what God may yet do for me? Nothing is too hard for Him, Julie. You may live, dearest, to see wondrous changes. God will not take you from us yet."

Poor Mrs. Burton was again lost in wonder. What had happened to remove that gloomy look from her son's face? Nothing that she could discover, nothing apparently in external things, no brightening of his prospects, as far as she could discern. She watched in astonishment the calm, quiet expression of his face as he went about his usual avocations; the air of dejection was gone,—but how?

There was more astonishment yet in store for her, when a few mornings afterwards he quietly signified his intention of procuring workmen, and at once proceeding with his old plan of improving the homestead.

"Have you heard anything? is anything settled, Allen?" she asked, with pleasure very visible in her face.

"Nothing fresh, mother," he replied, with a little smile, "but I may."

"Bless you, even for that, my boy!" said the fond mother; but after all it was a very strange mystery to her, past her comprehension.

CHAPTER XXXVII.

"NO MORE SEA."

"And I saw a new heaven and a new earth: for the first heaven and the first earth were passed away; and there was no more sea."

JUST in sight of the beach and the broad open waters of the bay stood a little cottage-built house, covered with white stucco. Its situation was its chief charm, for the few flowers in its sterile slip of garden looked withered and blighted, as though the salt air did not agree with them; and the two or three trees were of the saddest and most gloomy class, throwing a melancholy shade over the front windows.

These front windows, however, commanded a beautiful view of the sea, whether in its placid or wildest moods; whether curling in playful snow wreaths, or swelling high, high in surging billows. A picture of life—ripple and billow, storm and calm, like the heart's restless motion—was that broad, open sea.

At one of these front windows many times during the day Marian and Julie appeared, sometimes standing, the younger leaning on the circling arm of her companion; more frequently seated, one in a large cushioned rocking-chair of American construction, the other on a low footstool close by, both with eyes of intense interest resting upon the ever-changing scene before them.

They had been thus employed in silence for a long while, one rather overcast afternoon about three weeks after their arrival. The waves had been rising higher and higher for the last hour, and were beating towards the shore with a wild, restless motion, sending forth a low, hoarse murmur. They could distinctly hear it where they sat. Hither and thither the rude surges swayed; the almost lead-coloured billows, crowned with a crest of foam, came riding over the sand, nearer and nearer with every heave of the mighty waters. The wind was rising; it moaned round the house, and through the solitary honeysuckle by the window. There were dark clouds over the face of the heavens— dark, looming clouds, ominous of a storm; and towards the horizon was a long line of bright orange tint, lurid and angry-looking, as it mingled with the black. The rough billows, the howling winds, the angry heavens, all foretold a tempest of no little fury.

Julie was the first to weary of the prospect. She sank back into her rocking-chair and turned her face away, closing her eyes.

"Are you tired, dearest?" asked her ever-watchful companion, turning an affectionate and anxious gaze upon the little thin figure in the great chair, thinking as she did so, that those strong sea breezes had brought no colour to the pale cheeks, no strength to the weak frame, much as they had anticipated of their health-restoring qualities.

"I am tired of looking out," said Julie, opening her eyes and fixing them lovingly on her governess. "I like to shut my eyes, because then I fancy I see the dear old homestead, and its trees, and hill, and flowers. I wonder how the garden is getting on?"

"Nicely, under your brother's care, I dare say, Julie. Do you not like the sea? There is something very magnificent in this approaching storm. I rather like to see those wild billows curling so gracefully, and the white foam at the top, such a contrast to the hue of the waves."

"Do you? I like it best when it is calm, I cannot bear to look upon it when it is rough," said Julie, still with averted face. "I like it when the little waves come gently, gently one after another, as if they were at play; when the sun shines on the tiny ripples, and turns them into gold, and the white crest is full of the colours of the rainbow; but these terrible billows make me sick. They frighten me; I feel all the time as though I wanted to escape from them. I like that Sabbath lay of the Hon. Mrs. Norton so much, 'No more sea.' I can understand it better than ever now."

"The words are very sweet," replied Marian, and she softly sang them,—

> " Like the wild restless motion
> Of the deep heaving waves,
> Is the heart's restless beating,
> From our birth to our grave.

Tossed by strong stormy passion,
  In the swift winds we flee,
Till life's bark reach the haven,
  Where is ' no more sea.'

" O calm distant haven
  Where the clear starlight gleams
On the wild restless waters,
  On the heart's restless dreams:
How oft, gazing upwards,
  My soul yearns to be
In that far world of angels,
  Where is 'no more sea.'

" There the storm threats no longer,
  There the passions lie still,
There the meek wings are folded,
  Waiting God's holy will.
There from grief and temptation,
  The soul shall be free,
In that calm world of angels,
  Where is ' no more sea.' "

Julie's face was turned towards the window again while Marian sang, but her head rested on her thin hand, and her eyes were closed to the billows. Two or three tears were falling silently, and rested on her black silk apron, like drops of dew. Marian presently put her arms softly round her, and drew her head to its wonted resting-place on her bosom.

"Of what are you thinking, dearest?" she quietly asked after a few moments.

The blue eyes looked up calmly into Marian's, as in a low voice she answered—

" ' That far world of angels,
  Where is 'no more sea.'

Oh, how my soul yearns to be there!"

"It is sweet 'to wait God's holy will,' dear Julie,"

said Marian. "These billows and surges of time, beat about us as they may, only bring us ultimately nearer port. No soul in Christ Jesus is ever made shipwreck finally. The little vessel may be tossed about, and rudely divested of its sails, but the pilot is on board, and shipwreck is impossible!

> "' Thou art my pilot wise,
>   My compass is Thy word,
> My soul each storm defies,
>   While I have such a Lord ;
> My anchor-hold shall firm abide,
> And I each boisterous storm outride.'

"Are you afraid now, Julie,—afraid of shipwreck to your little vessel ? "

"No," said Julie, in low earnest tones ; "no, I am not afraid."

And she lay quite still in Marian's arms, too exhausted to say more ; but the calm eye, the play of the mouth, spoke more eloquently than words.

The sea breezes had indeed wrought nothing in her favour, she was wearying for her home. Sometimes Marian thought home was the best place for her. She feared that terribly quiet, hot, tormenting cough. She feared that white brow, the blue veins of which were more than ever visible. She feared the etherialized attenuated figure. Night and day she was an anxious watcher, till the colour in her own cheek waned, and her heart grew very sad.

It was beginning to be evident indeed to her, that the air so life-imbuing to some invalids, was too strong for Julie. She longed for Allen, or Mrs. Burton, or

even Alf to come to them. She wanted the counsel of
other eyes besides her own. William Grenville came
every week, Isabel now and then, for after the first
week she could not be spared from home; but Marian
could not very well depend upon the judgment of
either.

They were obliged to give up bathing altogether;
for after the first immersion in the sea such fits of
sickness succeeded, followed by prolonged shivering,
that it would have been highly imprudent to repeat it.
The walks on the sands became less and less frequent.
Julie could endure but little fatigue, and the heavy
sands of the beach, particularly the approaches to it,
were very wearisome, especially to an invalid.

Marian was sadly disturbed by this state of things;
she at last determined to write and tell Mrs. Burton
her thoughts. They as yet had neglected to consult
a medical man. How much she regretted that. It
certainly ought to have been the first object; but it
might yet be done, and to request permission to do so
was one motive of her letter.

Julie was not unhappy, she suffered comparatively
little pain. Her cough occasioned her most trouble.
It was at times very distressing. Her chief pleasure
was reclining in the rocking-chair with Marian at her
side, either singing or reading or talking to her. There
was one theme of which she was never weary. The
words of the poet who says,—

> " Jesus, I love Thy charming name
> 'Tis music to my ear,"

were very expressive of her feelings. Even at midnight, when the one from suffering, the other from anxiety, was deprived of sleep, that theme soothed and tranquillized. Like Paul and Silas, the two friends often had "songs in the night," and the angel came down to them also, unloosing the chains of their unbelief, and illuminating the darkness of the night with his presence.

The homestead was another favourite theme with both. They often chose the hours of twilight for that. Julie, resting in Marian's arms, could have talked for ever on the dear familiar scenes, of her mother, of Alf, of Bessie, but chiefly of Allen. She always found an attentive auditor in her companion. Marian loved to hear all she could of him, everything of a hopeful character,—and there was very much to encourage her hope in what Julie had to tell her; though little was evident, it was very precious to her. She had prayed; she was on the "watch tower" praying still. "They who wait upon the Lord shall never be ashamed." How this promise had already been fulfilled they had yet to learn.

And Marian little knew how earnestly Julie was hoping and wishing for her brother's happiness; how she was watching for the signs and evidences which she knew were all-important to his heavenly felicity, and even to his earthly bliss,—to that final consummation which she now more than ever longed after. Little knew Marian, as she watched her leaning back

in her rocking-chair, and fancied her sleeping, what
waking visions were before her eyes; the dear old
homestead re-furnished, with Marian and Allen for
its inmates; Marian as Allen's bride, the mistress
of his home. Julie was wondering, and sighing
as she wondered, whether her little thread of life
would linger out so long as to witness all this in
reality.

CHAPTER XXXVIII.

HOMEWARD BOUND.

"I AM not sorry, dear Marian, that mother has decided on having doctor's advice for me, for I think then you will all know what I have been sure of so long, and you will get used to the thought, and will not mind it so much."

Julie had her arms round Marian's waist, but her face was turned upwards, and a calm, sweet smile rested upon her lips as she said this. They were seated together in the large rocking-chair in the old position. The morning sun was playing pleasantly over the rippling waves, and little feathery flakes of foam were receding from the shore, snowy and rainbow-tinted; groups of ladies and children were busy on the sands gathering shells, or inhaling the soft sea-breeze. It was yet early, but our two young friends had not ventured out. They were going to town, and knew not whether they should again return to the bay. That rested on a word from the medical man.

Julie hoped not. She was sighing for her native hills, the dear familiar old hills, far surpassing to her in loveliness the exquisite picture of wave and sunshine before her. All but that beach was so wearying, so uninteresting, at the bay; no trees, no flowers, no green slopes, no high hills, no deep gullies. It seemed to want all those traits so dear to Julie. She had not a sigh to give as they took their departure in one of the earliest conveyances to Adelaide, excepting one of weariness and weakness.

Mrs. Burton had written back to Marian in great anxiety. She entreated her not to delay a moment in procuring the necessary advice, and concluded,—

"Allen will be in town by Thursday evening, the day after you get my letter. Without the doctor's orders are contrary, I wish him to bring my child back to me. I cannot longer endure the agony of separation under the circumstances,—and will not you, my dear girl, come too? You, who have been such a blessing to the homestead, who have been such a blessing to my poor Julie, to us all—you cannot refuse us; your cousin has her husband to take care of her. But there are those here whose hearts are very sad at your absence. My daughter, come back to us."

Mrs. Burton's letter was bedewed with Marian's tears; it was prayed over. After that she saw her path of duty clearly.

"If Julie goes," she at length said to herself, "I will certainly go too."

When at last they stopped at the little gate of her cousin's cottage, Isabel came forward eagerly to meet them. She had been long looking out for them, for the doctor had appointed to meet them that morning, and she was afraid he would arrive first. William had promised to see him before he went to the office.

"You have not come away from the bay too soon, dear Mari," whispered Isabel, as she looked sorrowfully at the pale face and attenuated figure reclining on the couch, for they had laid her down the moment they entered. A slight faintness had succeeded her fatigue, and taking off her bonnet and mantle as best they could, they were bathing her brow and hands with eau-de-Cologne.

"I wish she were at home among her own hills," sighed Marian.

Julie heard the whisper and the sigh, quiet though it was. She opened her eyes and looked anxiously up into the sorrowful face.

"Not without you," she faintly murmured.

"Not without me, dearest," was Marian's tearful reply, as she bent down and tenderly kissed her pale brow.

But the doctor's opinion was yet to be obtained. Marian's heart beat quickly as, a short time after their arrival, she caught a sight of him advancing up the garden path. She stood by trembling exceedingly, as he kindly and quietly examined his patient by q_estioning and stethoscope, for he had been fore-warned of some of the symptoms of Julie's illness, and had come prepared to test them.

Marian turned absolutely pale as she followed him out under the verandah to hear his opinion, after the examination was over.

" There can be but one opinion, I am sorry to say, my dear young lady," he replied gravely ; " your little friend's lungs are extensively diseased. I should advise her return to her friends as soon as possible."

" You apprehend no immediate danger ? " asked Marian, the tears coming to her eyes.

" No, no ; with proper care, judicious treatment, a nourishing diet, and her native air, she may be spared for months. Of ultimate recovery I can hold out no hopes. Take her home at once. I will not answer for her being equal to the journey a fortnight hence. Besides," he added, pointing to Marian's own pale face, " the anxiety is too much for you, it will do you harm ; and the young lady will be better with her mother. Good morning, ladies ; " and the doctor abruptly withdrew.

Marian had a difficult task to compose her counte-nance on her return to Julie. It was almost impossi-ble to force back the tears as the question was eagerly asked by the gentle invalid.

" Was I not right ? "

She evaded the answer, replying,—

" You are to go home, dearest, as soon as we can start."

"And that will be to-morrow. I am glad of that,"
replied Julie, "very glad! I want to see them all
again.   I would rather die at home."

"We want you to get well, Julie," replied Marian,
no longer attempting concealment of the tears that
would come.

"It must be as God pleases," said Julie, gently,
but she clasped Marian's hands tightly in her own
thin ones, and covered them with caresses.

"What He wills is indeed best," sighed Marian to
herself. "Even life and death must be trusted in
His hands, and it is certain all will be right He orders;
but it is better that we know how matters really stand.
Dear Julie! I always feared it would end thus. Oh
well! she will be a fair flower to gather into the
heavenly garden. It will be our loss, indeed, but her
gain."

"You surely are not intending to leave us, dear
Mari?" exclaimed Isabel, in consternation, as she
watched Marian slowly taking one thing after another
from the chest of drawers in her room, and packing
them up in her portmanteau.

"Yes, Issy.   Are you not tired of me?   I must go
with poor Julie, and Mrs. Burton wishes it so much."

"Now, Mari," returned Isabel, laughing, "acknowledge at once that Mr. Allen is the attraction, and
that *he* is wishing for you. I am sure it is selfish
enough of him."

Marian blushed deeply; she had nothing to reply
to the unjust suspicion, and so said nothing. She

could not help thinking, however, that if there were any room for a charge of selfishness, it must certainly devolve on the lady who made it. She went on quietly with her employment, filling her own and Julie's trunks, and preparing for the anticipated journey as though nothing had been said.

"Oh!" sighed Isabel, after an interval of silence, "I suppose William will be saying again, that the light of his home is gone."

"I don't think he will," replied Marian, quietly, "for you will be its light."

"I know this," returned her cousin, "I shall never be so good as you, never half so good;" and she seated herself on the side of the bed, and burst into tears.

Marian rose from the box at which she was kneeling, and came and threw her arms round her cousin.

"My dear Issy," she exclaimed, "you are too unconscious of your own merits, too little aware of your own ability, and far too extravagant in your ideas of mine. You little know the pleasure you are giving William by the exertions you are now making for his happiness and comfort, and all this will be more evident than ever when I am away."

"Ah, Marian! but I don't indeed know what I shall do without you."

"Better than with me now, dear Issy," said Marian, laughing.

"And I am sure, very sure, those Burtons will never let you come back again. I shall never expect you any more."

That was another subject on which Marian preferred silence, so she went back to her boxes and business again.

She was determined to do all the packing at once. The evening would be free if all were prepared Julie was sleeping quietly on the couch, so after she had finished her task, she sauntered out into the garden alone. Into the garden, and through the avenue of almond-trees, up and down, up and down. It was her favourite walk, from its loneliness and entire seclusion, and she had many things to think of.

She was really going back to the homestead, to everything most dear to her. How she had longed to do this, deeming it almost a hopeless case, and yet after all she *was* going! But the conditions, they were yet unfulfilled; would they ever be fulfilled? and if not, was not her happiness endangered, might there not be a fear of her own decision relaxing its firmness, when in constant association with Allen's importunity? She hoped not; she prayed that this might not be the case. She felt that at least she was in the path of duty, and feeling assured of this, she left it to God to strengthen and protect her.

She little knew that, better to her than all her fears, better than all her hopes and desires, God had designed great good for her. Little knew she, praying still, that her prayers had been registered on high, and that the answer was also recorded there.

Encouragement for *you* here, praying ones: praying

parents or praying children, praying sisters, or praying brothers,—whatever you are, pray on, pray on. It may be while the prayer yet lingers on your lips the answer will be given ; it may be while you are perhaps tearfully exclaiming, " God shutteth out my prayers," that the little cloud has arisen in the sky, destined by and by, to " break with blessings on your head." We must not always expect an immediate answer to our prayers. Our Father sometimes exercises the graces of His children by delay ; but He will answer in His own time, and in His own way. His promises are sure.

The sun had set, and it was nearly dark when Marian at length sauntered back to the house. Her cousin William met her at the door, and seizing both her hands,—

" So, Marian, I find there is a little mutiny on board. I hear you are going to leave us."

" Yes, William, for a little time. I am sure you must think it is right I should."

" Well, I don't know ; I suppose it is right, but I do not know what we poor mortals shall do without you. But it seems they are just in the same kind of quandary up there ; you can't be spared, child, on either side, that's the mischief ; and perhaps, after all, *one* up there has waited long enough."

But Marian had no reply for that, except the quick blood that sprang to her cheeks. She tried to get her hands free, and run in.

" Stay a moment. I was sent to call you. You

don't know who is in the parlour," cried William, mischievously keeping her back.

" Let me go and see," replied Marian, as gently as the motive of the case would admit, but she presently freed her hands and ran past him.

Not Allen, though, but his father, arose to meet her. A warm greeting he gave her ; her hands tingled with the tightness of his clasp.

" I am come for you both," he exclaimed, earnestly, " You will not let poor Julie go alone ? You are coming with us ? "

" Yes ; Mrs. Burton wished it," Marian answered.

" And I wish it, we all wish it, my dear girl ! " said the farmer warmly, leaning his hand affectionately on her shoulder. " The homestead has been but a poor place without you."

CHAPTER XXXIX.

TRANSFORMATIONS.

"Love is a lantern of the magic kind, dealing in wonderful changes
and transformations."

THE grass was getting green again, and the roses
were some of them in full beauty. Everything
looked fresh and fair, for a thunderstorm had been
in the neighbourhood of the homestead, clearing the
heated atmosphere, and causing the herbage to spring
with renewed loveliness.

The showers had been continuous and heavy, last-
ing through the night and part of the following
morning. Down they came, swelling the nearly exhausted creeks and watering the newly-ploughed
furrows. The hard, dry ground eagerly drank up the
delicious moisture. The trees in the garden and the
flowers and shrubs grew fresh and beautiful as the
large rain-drops fell upon them. And at length, as
the last peal of thunder died away in the distance,
and the last faint flash shot across the bosom of a
disappearing cloud, the little birds in the wattles
burst into an ecstasy of joyous chirping, rendering
the air vocal with their grateful notes.

There was a refreshing coolness in the air—a balmy freshness not only agreeable to the birds in the branches, but to the heart of man. Allen was enjoying it to the utmost as he stood at the open window of the music-room, and looked out through the trees and shrubs to the creek, at the extremity of the garden, once more rushing wildly along, dashing and foaming as it rounded the hill.

His business had commenced a fortnight ago. There was a considerable change in the homestead already. The very window against which he stood now opened from the floor, in the French style, and was ornamented with ground and stained glass. There was now another window similar to it, for Marian's little chamber had been thrown into that room, making one large one, and this had not only been floored, but ceiled and plastered. The old blue hangings were down, and an elegant paper supplied its place. The chief change was at this end of the house, as though entirely to complete this room had been the main intention. It was now finished, even to the furniture. A soft carpet to correspond with the tone of the room, silver-grey leaves with veinings of crimson, spread over the whole apartment. The chimney was removed to the place once occupied by Marian's little bed. The piano retained its old place, so did the work-table, full as it was of Marian's work, and the newly-varnished book-shelves chiefly ornamented with her books.

Allen had felt many qualms of conscience about

these books; they were not his, ought he to retain them? was it not rather his business to place them under his mother's care? He puzzled and troubled himself for nearly an hour, in the end resolving to leave them where they were. It might be that the owner might come to claim them one day; it might be yet that the work-table, in the very spot it now stood, might again come into use. That thought resolved the question. They remained where they were. The same old easy-chair was there, which Marian had long since made respectable by the dark blue cover she had neatly fitted to it. New chairs there were, bright polished and horsehair seated; but Allen liked the old chairs best, with their blue cushions—they must remain; so he placed them there among the others. The draperies of the windows were beyond his genius; he had to get his mother's advice and assistance, which she readily gave. He more willingly did this, because she never teased him with questions, though there was often a searching look in her eyes, which seemed to say, " Is all right yet?"

There were many other new attractions in the room, among them a stand of basket-work for flowers, well replenished with the loveliest blossoms, for he had not forgotten Marian's former suggestion There were two or three well-executed drawings, neatly framed, hanging against the wall, some of the fruits of Allen's pencil, and sketches of all the loveliest points of scenery some distance round the homestead. But there were two heads in crayons, surpassing all the rest, placed side-by-side above the piano. A glance was sufficient to prove their beauty and truthfulness. Julie's had been taken long since; she sat for her sketch "under the greenwood tree;" but Marian knew not even of his talents; he had never ventured to ask her permission, memory had therefore to make up for the lack of oportunity; those rarely occurring opportunities, when unseen, he could add to the secret sketch, which was again and again thrust under the business papers in his desk. It was completed at last, in spite of difficulty, and very exact was the whole; from this little sketch the larger drawing had been made. These faces once seen above the piano, and the room would have looked incomplete without them.

In the other rooms a transformation was taking place, but this was complete. Plastering, whitewashing, and flooring, were going on in all directions; in the sitting-room, and in every other but this. The keys were in Allen's possession, so the music-room and garden were sacred from the steps of the workmen.

Still greater was the internal transformation, the transformation of his own heart. It was swept, garnished, newly furnished. At last, like the poor maniac among the tombs, he was "sitting at the feet of Jesus, clothed, and in his right mind." The first joyous outburst of wonder and amazement had indeed passed away, but what a deep peace had succeeded,—peace, that like a sweet flower, blossoms best at the foot of the cross.

Amidst all these transformations came tidings of Julie's health. The father's anxiety overweighed all business impediments. Mr. Burton chose himself, as we have seen, to fetch home his child. They were expected that very evening, and Allen, after dismissing his workmen for the week—it was Saturday evening—was taking a parting survey of his pet room, and enjoying the calm beauty of the sunset, and the intense quietude around him.

He did not know that his mother had written, urging Marian to return with Julie. He expected his sister, for he was certain his father would not dream of allowing her to remain from home longer. Would Marian allow the sick girl to leave her behind? How he hoped not! What would Julie do without her? What would he?

He stood leaning against the window-frame, pulling to pieces a fine rose he had just gathered from the tree at the door. Had there not been a change since Marian had left them? After all, were not those parting conditions fulfilled? He thought, with a feeling of softened pleasure, "Yes." Might he not now call himself a follower, a humble follower of Christ; not a follower for worldly gain, but from real love to the Saviour? Were they now unsuitable to each other? No; they were not. It was for Marian now to fulfil her pledge. Julie should yet see her wish accomplished.

A thrill of pleasure ran through Allen's heart at the thought. He was glad he had not removed the work-table; it was in its right place. He inwardly hoped it might never again be used till its fair mistress sat beside it where it then was, as his own little wife.

The moon had risen, and the soft beams were now falling full into the room, but the theme was an engrossing one. Many fair pictures of future days were arising before him; scenes in which he and Marian were sharers; scenes of domestic happiness he scarcely dared hope for.

And all this earthly happiness heightened by Christian communion. Ah, Allen knew now why there could have been no real happiness in a union, when on such an important subject there was no agreement. The sacred injunction, "Those that marry, let them marry in the Lord," no longer appeared harsh; it was only a beautiful part of a beautiful whole. He could see it all now.

Had he forgotten his sister in his pleasant dreams? No; or if for a moment, it was but for *that* moment. The sudden recollection of *why* she was returning home restored the grave look of care to his brow. "My poor Julie!" he exclaimed to himself, "we must take care of her. I cannot yield to the feeling of losing her; I cannot resign her so easily. She *must* get well; that is," he added more gravely, "If it is God's will."

But his happy thoughts had flown. He closed the

window, and locking the door after him, turned towards home.

The evening was beautiful, for the moon was particularly bright. He walked slowly home, for he thought it wanted an hour to the time the travellers were expected. His thoughts now were sad enough; Julie occupied them all. His dear little sister, the companion of so many of his wandering hours, the sister who loved him so well, who studied his wishes so constantly,—was it possible that she should one day be beyond his reach, beyond his love, beyond his care? Was it possible that little foot was already outstretched to step into Jordan? Amidst these troubled thoughts came others, of angel-attendants on the banks of the river, and of the Celestial City beyond all. But even in prospective, that river looked cold and dark, and the brightness beyond somewhat paled in the distance.

"As thy day, so shall thy strength be," was the inward whisper that soothed and tranquillized him. He went on in the strength of that promise, committing, as he went on, all to his Father's hands. The issues of life and death, he knew, were in His keeping.

He did not even look towards the parlour window as he approached the house, so entirely absorbed was he with his thoughts; he did not see the corner of the blind uplifted, and Bessie's happy little face peeping out to spy if he was anywhere near, nor did he hear her exclamation as the light fell upon him.

"Here's Allen, mother."

He walked quietly into the house, as quietly hung up his hat, and opening the parlour door, stood in its entry. He changed colour then, as well he might. The whole party was there—his father, Julie, and Marian.

CHAPTER XL.

ALF, AND HIS BUDGET OF NEWS.

> " Speak on, speak on ; I'll listen to tho tale
> Till morning dawns again."

MARIAN was too fatigued with her journey to make much comment, or bestow much examination on the new house, or Hall, as it was designated. The nights of watching which had been so long allotted to her, rendered perfect repose a luxury. Mrs. Burton took Julie under her own care, and Marian's head was scarcely placed upon her pillow before her eyes closed, and she fell into a deep sleep.

But a feeling of strangeness came with the morning's light. She opened her eyes to behold nothing familiar—not even the furniture of her room. That was replaced by a more costly arrangement. Her plain little white bed had gone, and curtains were now looped around her. There were many new things in the room, for Mrs. Burton had exerted herself to the utmost to render her comfortable; yet, after all, there was not the home-like appearance of her former little chamber.

When Marian sprang from her bed, and up-

lifted the window-blind, cautiously looking out, how
beautiful everything appeared! grass and trees in
abundance, but nothing in comparison with the view
from her homestead sleeping-room—no garden, no
laughing creek, no she-oak hill, with its boundary of
blue sky. No; all was strange here, and unhome-
like.

With a sigh for the old homestead, Marian returned
to her bed—not to sleep; she lay in waking dreams.
Scarcely more than a month ago, she had wondered
whether it was possible for anything to bring her
back to that spot again; and now, here she was, but
little had she deemed the occasion that would bring
her. She hardly dare glance even at that; it was not
to be dwelt on. It is so hard to relinquish those we
love to the cold hand of death—so hard to watch the
dear ones fade before our eyes, and feel that all our
tender care, all our devotion, our love, can do nothing
to stay the destroyer's hand. And yet, how many in
this wide world of ours have this sorrowful task assigned them! Happy they who can feel firm footing
on the Rock of ages, and who know that death to the
beloved one will prove but as the opening of the portals
to eternal life.

But Marian found that tears laid too closely connected with thoughts of Julie, so she put the thought
away, and took up another scarcely less tearful subject—that of Julie's brother, Allen. Sorrowful enough
it proved to be, when with it came the memory of her
own partial engagement, and the little probability

there was of its ever proving more. Where was her faith? Had the cloud come between her and the promise? or was the arm of God "shortened that it could not save"? She hid her face on her pillow as that thought came to her mind, ashamed and distressed. Where, indeed, was her faith? "Lord, I believe; help Thou mine unbelief," she humbly and earnestly groaned. But the clouds were very dark and lowering that morning.

It was something, however, to meet all the same faces at breakfast. Even Julie was not absent—they could not persuade her to be. She had most wonderfully recovered her fatigue, and her spirits were in excellent flow. Alf declared, as he looked at her flushed cheeks and brilliant eyes, that, "in his opinion, the old Adelaide doctor was a most decided humbug, and that his sister was better than ever."

"I always said I believed you were all frightening yourselves about nothing," he exclaimed, after breakfast, as he stood under the verandah at the back of the house, near where Marian was seated. For what purpose she had chosen that position was best known to herself; but certainly a little glimpse, a tiny little glimpse of the homestead was perceptible through the trees from that spot.

"What makes you think so now?" asked Marian.

"Her looks; faith! I should think that ought to satisfy any one. I always go by looks."

"Not always the best or truest guide, Alf," replied Marian, gravely. "I wish *I* could feel as hopeful.

Unhappily, those very appearances which seem to indicate health to you, are the fatal symptoms of consumption.   The flush you speak of quite frightened me this morning."

" Why should it ? "

" It is a strong symptom of fever, hectic fever, and speaks too truly of the progress of the disease."

" Does Julie know all this ? " asked Alf, gravely, for her cheerfulness, he thought, was at variance with such a knowledge.

" She does," answered Marian.   " She knew it before I could believe it, but she is not less happy.   You know, Alf, she has a heavenly home awaiting her, and looks forward gladly to that."

" Strange ! strange ! " muttered Alf; " it beats me altogether ; I can't make it out at all.   Why, Miss Herbert, these sort of things were never heard of at the homestead till you came."

" Does that make them less true ? " asked Marian, quietly.

" No, no—of course not ; only I am thinking, since there is truth in religion, what a lucky thing it is you came here."

" God makes use of very feeble instruments," returned Marian, humbly.   " But you remember, Mr. Alf, that religion is a personal matter."

" I know what you mean.   Well, maybe, my turn will come some day.   I am afraid there is no hope of its having come yet."

" What if death comes first, Alf ? "

Alf uttered a long, low whistle, and walked to the other end of the verandah. He had nothing to say in answer to that. He came back in a few minutes with an altered countenance.

"Have you heard what has been going on up here since you left us?" he asked, with a wicked, mischievous smile in his blue eyes.

Marian coloured slightly, and smiled. "Nothing more than your removal from the old house."

"Nothing more? Oh, you have not heard half the news. Ned Clare's made his exit, and left the farm to Frank and a younger brother; have you heard that?"

"No," replied Marian. "I hope his sister has not gone too."

"I hope so, too, but I fancy not; at least I saw her yesterday. Somehow, I don't think Allen and Ned had been very good mates lately," he added, with a saucy look into Marian's face; but though her colour rose, she only answered,—

"That is a pity."

"Perhaps so, and perhaps not. Anyhow, he's gone," replied Alf. "Well, but that's not the best though. There are fine doings down at the homestead; if it were not Sunday, you would hear the hammering, for the wind lies this way."

"The hammering?" asked Marian, greatly confused.

"Yes. What, is that news, too? I shouldn't have thought it. There are a few changes taking place down there, I promise you. I suppose," he added with a sly laugh at Marian's crimson cheek, "that Allen is going to play mine host of bachelor's hall; but for my part, let him beautify as he will, the place will be nothing without a fair lady. What say you, Miss Herbert ? "

Marian was too embarrassed to answer anything, so her reply was another question,—

" Has anything else happened ? "

" Oh, yes. I have not told you all; one thing re-mains, that, in my opinion, caps the rest, and that has to do with Mr. Allen himself. Talk of changes, I never saw such a change in any fellow in my life before."

" Surely not for the worse," Marian managed to say.

" Not according to your judgment, at any rate; and, for the matter of that, I suppose not according to mine. The change has wrought him no harm ; he was always tolerably grave and sober. Don't you remember my telling you one day that his face had decidedly the parson's cut ? "

Marian's first answer was a look of great eagerness ; her second,—" What has this to do with the change, Mr. Alf ? "

" This much, that if before he only looked the par son, I believe he is one in reality now, or something very near it. Black Jack says he gave him a sermon half a yard long the other night, because he slipped out an oath or two while feeding the horses; and Tom, the mason, told me they have more work in prospect when they have finished the house. It seems that wish of yours, or Julie's, is to be accomplished after all, and a veritable chapel is going up."

There was a moment's deep silence.

"Are you sorry for that?" Marian asked, in very low tones, as soon as she could command her voice at all, and still, as she spoke, looking down to hide the tears with which her eyes were fast filling.

"No, I don't care; it can't matter to me,—about the chapel, I mean."

"And your brother, Mr. Alf?"

"Oh, I suppose he's right too. At any rate there is nothing of the hypocrite about him. What he says he means, as I told Black Jack. I was pretty nearly overset myself with him. I happened to overhear him in the night, praying. I think he thought I was asleep, but I wasn't; and that prayer was a little more than my ears bargained for, for he didn't forget to pray for me."

Alf turned away with some show of feeling, and sauntered from the house.

"Not to have even told her that!" was his mental ejaculation as he walked away. "Well, I don't know but I like him all the better for it. It looks as if it were the genuine article, and not assumed for any particular worldly purpose; however, I knew all along Allen was no counterfeit. I am not sorry though that I have put that spoke in the wheel, for if he didn't tell her, she ought to know. There's the genuine article on her side too, and no mistake. I couldn't stand by though, and see her tears dropping quietly down when I gave her a hint of what had happened."

As Alf turned away, Marian ran to her room, and locking fast the door behind her, threw herself upon her knees in a perfect passion of tears. She could not utter a word for a long time, and when at last she began, words seemed too feeble to express the joyous thanksgiving she uttered, while she recognized, with humble gratitude, the answer to her many prayers.

Yet, why had Allen told nothing to her? why had he not even hinted at a change capable of making her so happy? was it possible his own affections had changed? That was but a momentary thought; it faded away before the recollection of what her reception had been the evening before, of his quiet, gentle manner, even that very morning. No; it was not possible, he had not changed in that particular. He had his own motives, no doubt good ones, for his silence. By and by, maybe, those motives would be revealed.

That hope roused her. She got up and bathed her face, re-arranged her hair, and soon removed all traces of her former discomposure. When quite recovered, she went to look after Julie. She found her alone in the parlour, reclining upon the sofa, her Bible in her hands; there were traces of tears in her eyes and many had fallen upon the pages of her book.

"Julie, dearest!"

She looked up at that, and a bright smile spread over her face. She stretched both arms towards her governess.

"What is the matter, love? Have you been alone long? How thoughtless of me to leave you!"

"Oh no; I have not been lonely; Allen has been with me, and he is only just gone.   I am so happy, dear Miss Marian, so happy, I can hardly believe it."

" What, dearest ? "

" That Allen is a Christian."

CHAPTER XLI.

THE OLD WHITE GUM.

THE Sabbath passed away, and left no opportunity for even the slightest private conversation between Marian and Allen. The news of the return brought visitors to the Hall, in the persons of Mary Clare and her two younger brothers; and two or three settlers from distant stations dropping in during the day caused the house to be one scene of confusion and bustle, very uncongenial to the spirits of either Marian or the invalid. Throughout the day Marian had to subdue her feelings, and to take her share in the entertainment of the guests; at the same time she was longing, oh longing, for a little quiet retirement. There were words, words that had been breathed that day into her ear which were glowing in her inmost soul; through the merry laugh, the cheerful jest, through Alf's banter, and the cheerful conversation of Mrs. Burton, those few words came again and again, and all day she looked forward to the quiet hour in her own room where she could pour out her thankful aspirations.

But the longest day will come to a close. Evening's shade at last relieved her. The horses were brought round to the door, and with one exception the guests departed.

Marian lingered a moment or two on the doorstep, to watch the last of the visitors depart. It was a most lovely night, the moon was at its full. She just caught a glimpse of its silver head as it rose, fair Queen of Beauty, behind a cluster of young gums. The sky was not entirely cloudless; there were a few slight snowy flakes on the deep blue, and one or two fair stars had stolen out like jewels, vexing not the eye with their tranquil light. She turned instinctively towards her favourite spot. Those moonbeams, she knew well where they were falling now. She caught a glimpse, only a glimpse, through a long vista of trees, of the distant homestead; her heart leaned towards it as towards a dear friend. She clasped the hands tightly that would fain have reached forward to it; they were presently clasped by another.

"All this day, and not a word together!" exclaimed Allen, in a low, complaining voice. "See, I have stolen one of mother's shawls; wrap yourself up, and let us take a quiet stroll together."

"But your mother, Allen, will she not think it strange?"

"Do not fear mother, dear Mari, she will be only too glad;" and he carefully wrapped her in the large, warm shawl, and again taking possession of her hand, passed beyond the bounds of the garden into the road.

"I little thought to have you back here so soon, dear Mari; I little hoped it," he at length said, breaking the long silence that ensued after passing into the road.

"I little dreamt it, little dreamt of poor Julie's illness being the cause of my return."

Her voice was very low and tremulous, and there was no answer for a very long while to this.   They walked on, and on, no sound but their own footsteps, or the rustling opossums overhead, or the night-bird with its cuckoo-like note, disturbing the silence.   Perhaps the beating of their own hearts was the most audible sound to themselves.   So strangely excited is the human heart by an approach to confession, of whatever nature that confession may be, and however insignificant it may appear when among the things that have been.

"Do you remember the night we parted, dear Mari? our last evening stroll?" Allen again exclaimed, after a long silence.   "Do you remember the spot we had reached when I suddenly stood still, and asked you when you would come back to the homestead?"

"I have not forgotten, Allen."

"Nor your answer, Mari?"

"Neither—have you?"

"Do you think I could have done that?   No, indeed, not I!   Despair enough it cost me at that time, though, even then, I believe there was a strange little wavering hope in my heart, not that *you* would change, but that *I* might. Look, Mari; here we are again, only we have reached it by another way. Here is the old white gum beneath which you stood as you uttered words which then seemed the death-blow of my hopes. Now," and he stood still and clasped both her hands in his, "now, dear Marian, now, humbly before my God, before you, I may breathe the hope that this engagement is fulfilled. Dearest Mari, 'tis surely not presumption to believe that even on me God has been pleased to shed abroad His love!"

Ah! language was too poor for such a moment. Tears were more eloquent, and mute caresses, upon which the calm, sweet moonlight might freely look down. What have we to do with such holy, joyous moments as these? Tears?—ah! but how often are tears but akin to the joy-bells that murmur sweet music in the depths of the heart. Joy-bells, indeed! was it nothing to Marian that he with whom all her heart's earthly affections were entwined, had also learnt the heavenly language, had become free of the Heavenly City, and that now she might safely commit herself to his love, his companionship?—a companionship not for this world alone, but for the world to come. And did not Allen, in those few precious moments, again and again welcome that passage to his heart, "Only in the Lord?" for he understood its sweetness now.

Yes—together under that old white gum, together

in that still, quiet moonlight they stood. With his
hat dashed to the ground, and his fair hair uplifted
by the slight breeze, with eyes upraised to heaven,
still sustaining with firm arm his trembling companion, he prayed—prayed for them both unitedly,
for sustaining grace, for humility and trustfulness,
that they might first spend a life of usefulness
together on earth, and then together enter their
heavenly home.

Think you not a union commenced with prayer was
likely to prosper?　Think you not there were smiling
angels to witness that betrothal?　Let not the sceptic
laugh.　"The blessing of the Lord, it maketh rich,
and He addeth no sorrow with it."

Julie was alone in the parlour, when at last they
returned to it.　Her father and Alf were still absent
with their guest, and her mother had left the room a
moment before, to prepare the drink she usually required during the night to relieve her cough.　She
sat leaning back among the cushions of her large
chair, her thin crimson cheek supported upon a little
shadowy hand, and her large eyes intently fixed on
the glowing embers.　It was of the absent ones she
was thinking, and sometimes a smile stole over her
face, though a very April smile, for the tears lay near,
ready to burst out on the least occasion.

She was musing on the old theme, her old desires.
Allen's happiness was uppermost.　Would Marian
have him now?　Oh yes! she thought so, for he was
a Christian, so *that* was a settled point.　But then

how long would they be arranging matters? should she live to see it all? the homestead finished, and the bride brought back to its walls?

She bowed her head on her arm as she asked the question, and hid her face from the light. But even then she shed no actual tears; there was only dimness in her eyes, for she was schooling herself in this particular to say, " Thy will be done."

But she was presently lifted from this position, and taken into her brother's arms. He had entered so quietly, with Marian, that she had not heard them. She looked eagerly into his face, and from that to the sweet blushing countenance in the vicinity.

" I am going to run away with your governess, Julie —will you give her to me? " asked Allen with a smile.

She stretched out her arms to Marian with a look of intense joy. She had no words, but the clasp of those arms was enough.

" Will you take Marian for a sister then, dear Julie?"

" Oh yes! if she will only be my sister."

" She says she will, Julie. You must love her dearly, for she has made your brother very happy."

A fresh caress and kiss was the reply, and then Julie lay back among the cushions, faint and exhausted with excitement, her soft eyes resting on them, and still retaining a hand of each.

" Will it be long first, Allen? " she at length whispered after a silence of some moments.

"I hope not, Julie—not as far as *I* am concerned. But why do you ask?"

"If I have to leave you, you know. I should not mind so much after that," whispered Julie, hiding her face on her brother's shoulder.

CHAPTER XLII.

" Coming events cast their shadows before."

" There's something up among your folks, Alf! I'm sure of it!" said Mary Clare, coming forward to the fence where her brother Frank stood in deep conversation with the young farmer, one very chilly, cloudy morning, two or three weeks after Julie's return home.

" Your reasons for so thinking, Miss Clare?" inquired Alf.

" Reasons? oh, I've plenty of reasons, and that's more than you can say of every woman, you know. Only look at the old place, the homestead, don't you call it? I declare I couldn't have thought it capable of such improvements. I don't know, if the choice were given to me, which I'd take, the new house or the old, whether I should not decide for the last."

" For the matter of that, so should I, so far as prettiness goes, but the other is more substantial, Miss Clare."

" More substantial! Oh, but that's not what a

woman looks for; at least, not all she looks for. We want our eyes pleased, sir! Brick and stone walls are good enough in their way; but there is nothing to feast the eye in mere bricks and mortar. Now that homestead has something quaint and ancient-looking about it; I like its deep-set doors and windows, and its garden is lovely."

"If you saw the improvements within, Miss Clare, you'd be still more in love with it. The workmen will finish this week."

"They will! and what then, Mr. Alf? I'm dying to know! Do you think it is such a secret? I can assure you, sir, it is not. I have my spies, like a true woman as I am;" and Mary Clare laughed heartily.

"Come then, out with your secret!" said Alf, holding her fast by both hands, "maybe you know as much or more than I do myself. What have you found out?"

"What have I found out? More things than *one*, sir!" laughed Mary, trying to release her hands. "In the first place, did not three loaded drays of carefully packed furniture arrive at the homestead last night? and were they not duly unpacked under your mother's own eye this very morning?"

"Well, for my brother's bachelor's home," replied Alf, slily.

"Very well, sir,—very well! The next thing, you will try to persuade me that the exquisite little work-table, which was so carefully carried in, is part of a bachelor's arrangements. I happen to know better.

I know that the homestead will soon receive a bride —a pretty little bride too—but I want to know how soon."

"Oh, you will receive due notice no doubt;" Alf laughed and sprang on his horse. "I say though, Miss Clare, when shall you and I try matrimony?" he exclaimed, as he rode off, not before he had re-ceived in his face a whole handful of roses from the young lady, who had been unconsciously pulling them from a bush by the fence as she talked.

It was really thus. Things were in this state of progress. But little remained to finish the house, and Marian's position as bride-elect was a very con-spicuous one. It was soon whispered round the neighbourhood, and reached even the distant town-ship. Many a visit Mrs. Burton received, which would have been unpaid but for the promptings of curiosity. A peep at the intended bride was a point which, once gained, was sufficient to render the happy individual a lion for a season. Marian was the talk of all the social gatherings for miles round; when the wedding would come off; what would be the costume of the bride; if the ceremony would be performed by banns or special licence; in town or country, at church or at the squire's house. All these were the topics of the day, and were freely discussed long before the bride herself had formed an idea upon the subject, or even consented to name the day.

Perhaps amidst the general talk and bustle, no one

was more calm than Marian. She left everything to Mrs. Burton, who was quite in her element unpacking and arranging; and seated at her needlework, away from all the confusion, she sought companionship with her young invalid, who grew neither better nor stronger, and yet seemed no worse.

Many times during the day Allen would come and sit down two or three minutes with them. They always welcomed his coming, and he gave them the whole of his company every evening.

On one occasion he came into the room with a face beaming with happiness. Julie was lying at one end of the sofa, with Marian at her feet; room was soon made for him, and he placed himself between them.

"Everything finished at last!" he exclaimed. " I left mother and Maggie putting up the window curtains; that's the finishing-stroke, I presume."

" Everything finished! Oh, I am so glad," said Julie, softly. "Now you will do what you promised, dear Marian ? "

" What I promised, dear ? "

" That's what *I* have to ask her," said Allen, quietly possessing himself of one of her hands. " I am going to Adelaide to-morrow. I want to fetch Mr. and Mrs. Grenville back with me, but you will have to give me licence to do so first. Will you do this, dear Mari ?"

" Oh, not yet," replied Mari, bending a very blushing face over her work. " I don't think Isabel can come."

"Will you permit me to try?"

But he got no answer to that, the fingers went nervously on with their sewing. Julie quietly slid from the sofa, and crept from the room.

"Do you think the agreement is not properly fulfilled?" asked Allen, after a few moments' quiet observation of her drooping curls.

"Why do you ask?" she inquired with a reproachful look.

"Because I think you are doubtful about me. I often am myself. You think my religious feelings have not had full time for development—you fear a relapse, a declension."

"Stay, Allen; you have no right to interpret my thoughts so. When and how have I shown such sentiments? This is unkind."

"No, dearest Marian, not unkind. I know you act from the best of motives; I know you have a right to be suspicious of feelings that have had only two or three months' existence."

He leant his head on his hand as he spoke, and heaved a deep sigh.

"I have no right to be suspicious, neither am I, Allen," she replied.

"Yet if you are not, why not let me do as I entreat? If you do not doubt me—if you have no fear of my steadfastness—why not consent to be mine before winter sets in?"

"I forgot," said Marian, smiling, "that you farmers have regard to the seasons in everything. Is it so very important that the event take place before winter ? "

"Yes," replied Allen, with a smile, and returning to her side, "*very* important—the state of the roads, remember. We shall not get your cousins up here if we wait much longer."

"An excellent excuse for your haste ! "

" Excellent, and I have another quite as good : I want you and me to enjoy our evenings together in our own house this winter. Now, will you let me tell your cousin she must return with me this day week ? "

" Nonsense ! too soon—too soon, Allen."

" This day fortnight—there, that is a fair compromise—no, not a word more." And Allen sprang up and left the room as his mother and Julie entered.

" This day fortnight, mother," he exclaimed gaily, as he passed her on his way to the door.

CHAPTER XLIII.

SUNSHINE AND WHITE ROSES.

" Then, before all they stood—the holy vow
And ring of gold, no fond illusions now,
Bind her as his."

WILL it be a day of sunshine or cloud?   How difficult
to tell in that early dawn, so grey and sombre, so
misty, too.   The sun has not yet thought of rising;
the dew is thick upon the young grass.   How quiet
and calm and still is all around.   The very trees
look asleep; no breeze stirs a leaf on the branches.
The horses stand stock-still in the pastures, with
drooping heads.   Not even the fowls have moved from
their roosts, not a bird has twittered on the spray.
But familiar feet have climbed the she-oak hill, and
the old fallen tree at the summit is again Marian's
chosen seat.

She could not sleep.   That day was to commence a
new epoch in her existence.   She wanted to be away
for a time from all human objects—she wanted to be
alone with her God.   For this she left her bed at very
peep of dawn, and wrapping herself up warmly,
away she crept from the house—away—away to

her old prayer station, her favourite she-oak hill.

All nature lay in repose beneath. The sky was still one entire grey: but over the lake there was a bright streak,—a promise of beauty and loveliness. She clasped her hands as she gazed, it was as if there was portrayed the earnest of future happiness and joy to her. But all *that* she could trust in a Father's hand! So much of His guidance she had experienced—so much of His goodness she had felt—so many prayers had been answered, it would have been strange could she not have trusted Him now. She felt the truth of the poet's words—

> " Sweet to lie passive in Thy hand,
> And know no will but Thine."

She knew and understood how His will was love. As for the future, she left that to Him.

Seated on that fallen tree, memory went back to her first Sabbath at the homestead. She had wandered up that she-oak hill, had seated herself in that very place, had there prayed for guidance, for direction, had prayed that her little light might shine, even though feebly, that she might not have vainly come to that place. How had it been? Had not God blessed His feeble instrument? and were there not other hearts now upraised in love to Him? Ah, she rejoiced, not in pride, but humility—with trembling. She sifted to the uttermost her internal feelings, and with tears exclaimed, " To Thee be all the glory! "

She prayed, prayed for continual guidance and

direction, prayed that earth and earthly affections might not engross her love; but that she and Allen might hereafter go forth hand-in-hand in the same sacred path, with the same love hallowing their footsteps, the same hopes influencing their actions, the same glorious end in view.

She raised her head, which had hitherto been bowed upon the old she-oak branch. As she did so, the first golden beams shot out from the horizon, and the clear silver lake became perfectly deluged in its glory. The rosy clouds came crowding forward like Hebe's attendants on the god of day. The whole eastern heaven was a flush of beauty. The tops of the trees caught the tint, and at the same instant the whole air became vocal. Forth came the merry triumphant laugh of the jackass, the sweet soul-gurgling of the magpie, and flocks of green parrots flew with their glad but discordant matin notes from the branches near her. She rose and gathered her shawl round her. Yes, there was her future home, now nestling in its bowery garden. She could see the sun glitter on the window panes of her favourite room. How soon was she to be an inhabitant, the mistress of all within it! But there was no glimpse of the Hall to be caught from where she stood. That thought recalled to her the day, and what awaited her. She turned her face from the homestead, and hurried down the hill, for the sun rose higher and higher every moment, and the cock's shrill clarion echoed on the morning breeze.

In a short time she reached the house, and hurried to her bed-room, but a few moments before the household were aroused. It was yet early, and having passed a sleepless night, she drew her window-curtains close, and throwing herself on the bed, was soon in a profound sleep.

The sun was quite high in the heavens when she again awoke. She had only left her pillow a moment or two when the door was gently opened, and her cousin Isabel stole in.

"Oh, you are up; that's right. You were so quiet, I expected to find you sleeping. Well, Mari, you have a glorious day before you, and if the old proverb may be relied on, future bliss in abundant store, for you know, 'Blessed is the bride that the sun shines on.'"

If any one had a right to know what kind of a day it was, Marian certainly had, but she kept that to herself, also her views as to the source from which all happiness and blessedness must proceed.

There was a large party at the breakfast table, for most of the neighbours round had been invited to be present at Allen's wedding. The ceremony was to be performed in the house; that had been decided on long since, and many of the guests had spent the night at the Hall.

Marian insisted on attending Julie as usual, in spite of remonstrance. She made and took up the tempting little breakfast to the gentle invalid.

Julie's kisses were mingled with tears, as she rose in bed to throw her arms round Marian's neck.

"My sister to-day," she whispered below her breath. "I am only sorry you are going away, but you will not stay long."

The little tray, temptingly arranged as it was, went back almost untouched.

Marian was perfectly calm. There was, it was true, a deep rose-bloom on her cheeks, but her eyes wore that serene expression, that trusting light, which can only proceed from peace within. In her simple morning dress, with her curls pushed back from her clear, open brow, few who knew not would have guessed her to be the bride of the day.

Once the colour deepened on her cheek. It was Alf did the mischief, as quietly stealing behind her chair, he placed a white rose among the dark curls. She raised her hand at the moment to remove it, but a hand at her side gently arrested hers, and Allen's whisper, "Leave it, dearest," was sufficient. The white rose was permitted to grace its wearer.

Marian had no cause to regret her stolen hour of prayer that morning. Breakfast over, and she became the property of her friends. She was almost bodily carried off by her troop of young bridemaids, all pleading for the honour of arranging her costume.

One thing only gave her anxiety, it was the thin face of her chief bridemaid, her lovely young sister Julie. She trembled at the deep hectic, that made her look so lovely, at the liquid blueness of her eyes, at the pearly fairness of her skin, and tears were almost gemming her bridal robe as she thought— "Not long indeed for this earth art thou, sweet Julie."

Yet even with this thought, came the remembrance of a brighter, a fairer, a heavenly home in waiting, and it brought consolation, it restored happiness. There were no tears in Marian's dark, glowing eyes, as they led her forth to the side of him who was hereafter to share her path through this world below, to journey with her to that above.

No silk, no satin, clad in pure, snowy, transparent muslin, bride and bridemaids were all alike, and only the delicate veil that swept nearly to her feet distinguished her from the rest.

What a group was there! The proud father of a happy son; the mother, with eyes glistening through joyous tears; Alf, with his curly head tossed on one side, scarcely able to solemnize his face for the occasion; and that fair group of bridemaids, conspicuously among whom beamed Julie's lovely face and the merry little bush-sylph, Bessie.

But the clergyman in his robes has arrived. The young couple slowly advance; a few words, solemn, quiet words, and all is over, the tie is cemented. Allen leads forward his bride.

The spell is broken now; smiles and gaiety and laughter are rife. Amidst it all, the happy Allen lifts his young wife into the chaise at the door, and before any one is fully aware of it, they are gone

CHAPTER XLIV.

THE RETURN.

"To-day!   Yes, they come home to-day," was Julie's low, joyous exclamation as she opened her eyes one morning, a fortnight after the events of the last chapter.

"Is the sun shining, Maggie?" she asked the girl who brought her little breakfast-tray to the bedside, a few moments after.

"Indeed and it is, miss," replied Maggie, cheerfully; "the bride will have sunshine, sure enough, to welcome her back;" and she walked to the window, and drew aside the curtain, letting a full bar of golden light fall all across the carpet, even to Julie's pillow.

"Beautiful! beautiful!" murmured Julie, looking up from her breakfast-tray with sparkling eyes. "O Maggie, I shall not lie in bed long to-day; I must get up.   I am glad I feel so much better."

Maggie looked at her. Was she better? Certainly the vivid flush gave almost the appearance of health, and the brilliant light of her blue eyes was almost too much for the gaze. But Maggie was not deceived; she looked and trembled, for a young sister of her own, long since in the cold grave, had worn just the same deceitful aspect.

Julie did get up, as she said she should, at a much earlier hour than usual. She startled her mother exceedingly as she entered the sitting-room leaning on Maggie.

"It was so beautiful, mother, I could not lie in bed," she exclaimed, sinking back in the chair, rather exhausted after her unusual exertions. "And *they* are coming back to-day," she added, the colour deepening in her cheek.

"But, my precious child, the rawness of the morning has not yet gone off. I am afraid for you," said Mrs. Burton, hurrying about, securing windows and doors, and putting the wood together in the fire-place, till the flames shot up cheerfully and warmly.

"Oh, but I feel better to-day, dear mother, so much better; better than I have felt for a long time. They are coming home, perhaps that's one thing, and this beautiful sunshine. I must go with you this afternoon, mother, when you go down to Allen's place, to see if all is right."

"My dear child, you will not be able."

"Oh yes, mother. I want so much to go. I can ride poor little Dapple, I am sure I can, I feel strong to-day."

"*She does* look better," thought the happy mother. "After all, doctors don't know everything, and there is a great deal in the native air;" and she went about her employment with a lighter heart than she had carried for many a day.

For a long while Julie sat looking out of window at the green trees and flowers in the garden, or clustering round the verandah. Once she opened the window and pulled a white half-blown rose-bud; placing it on the table at her side, she sat fondly regarding it, but her thoughts quickly went from its fair leaves to a higher subject—to the land where flowers never fade; where no blight nor frost can approach the delicate leaves, where there are no scorching sunbeams, no wild storms, but all is beautiful peace and serenity.

She presently crossed the room for her portfolio, the same one that had formerly been so ruthlessly rifled by Alf, and unlocking it, she took out pen, ink, and paper, and began writing with trembling though rapid fingers. She kept the rose-bud before her as she wrote, often glancing at it, and now and then taking it in her hand. After a little she laid it with her writing, then carefully sealed it, and closed the portfolio.

Her Bible lay on the table near her seat; as she slowly walked back, she took it up, and then reclining in the large easy-chair, was soon absorbed in its pages. As she read, her soft eye brightened with joyous tears, and her thin cheek deepened its flush. She was bending over a description of the country towards which she herself was rapidly tending. Its streets of gold, its pearly gates, its deep flowing river, the banks of which were enamelled by never-fading flowers, and over-shadowed by the healing branches of the tree of life. These were congenial subjects to her; she felt them deep down in her heart. Tired at last by the excess of feeling, she fell into a tranquil sleep. In her dreams she entered that lovely country, and stood in the presence of the "Lamb who is the light thereof."

It was indeed a beautiful day, such a day as we often see in our fair southern clime at the commencement of the winter months. Here and there a cloud of snowy whiteness floated like a little island, amidst a vast sea of blue; but none obscured the brilliancy of the sun. He shone in undiminished glory.

The trees had renewed their rich foliage since the first rains, and the grass was now growing in luxuriance. It was a glorious afternoon for the return of the bride, and Mrs. Burton could see no harm in Julie's accompanying her to the homestead.

Pretty Dapple! patient Dapple! How he tossed his graceful head, and uttered a pleasant little neigh as his young mistress was once more lifted to her saddle. In the gaiety and gladness of his heart, he would have cantered off bravely with his fairy-like burden, had not Frank's hand restrained him, for Julie was too weak to bear anything but the most gentle motion.

How fondly Julie looked at the old familiar walls! for, spite of the changes within and without, they had not lost their dear home-like appearance. It was many a day since she had been there, and only once since her return home. Now the garden extended all round the house, and at the entrance was a very pretty park-like gate. The "ugly stock-yard" was gone. It had been placed behind a thick clump of wattles some distance from the house, and on its old site were the rising walls of a little chapel, for Allen had not forgotten his promise. Julie's eyes watered as she looked at it, and remembered the time she had asked him to build one. She remembered his answer too : " When the homestead has another inmate, ask me again." She had no occasion to ask him again. It was by his free will, owing to his sense of want, his anxiety for the good of his neighbours, that the little chapel was being erected. It made her very glad.

The dear old rooms ! Yet not quite the same— not quite. They spoke loudly of that " other inmate." The furniture was all new-looking ; Julie scarcely recognized the old sitting-room or bed-rooms. But her pleasure was at the highest when at last she summoned courage, and opening the door, walked into what had once been their music-room. How many happy hours had been spent there !

"Dear Allen ! how happy he would be now with her, in that beautiful room !" She walked gently up and down the soft carpet, admiring everything she saw. Now standing with the great Bible out-stretched before her, Allen's family Bible, and try-ing to imagine she could see him conducting the worship there, as he told her he should do, imme-diately on his return. Now lovingly handling the well-remembered books, so endeared because they were Marian's. Now leaning back in the comfortable blue-covered chairs, with eyes closed in half-sorrowful happiness.

She walked over to the piano, and, opening it, commenced a simple air. But the tones in that large room made her feel lonely, and she soon turned away from it. Something else attracted her attention. Something to be done for the dear ones, something her mother had quite forgotten, or did not esteem necessary. The vases—and there were several—were all empty, and in the garden there was a wealth of flowers. She took up a basket, one she and Marian had often used for the purpose, and opening the glass door, sauntered slowly into the garden. Roses, red and white, were glancing at her everywhere, but it was the rose-walk she sought. The choicest specimens were there.

She selected only two colours, pink and white, and roses alone, but those she gathered in profusion—chiefly half-opened buds, and of these mostly white. There was a sad feeling creeping over her as she filled the basket, and tears at last fell like dew upon the roses. It was as if something whispered, "*The last time!*" as if she were taking a last farewell of all she loved. These were natural tears, and that whisper "*The last time,*" was hard to bear.

But there came another inward whisper to cheer and comfort her—"In my Father's house are many mansions: if *it were not so,* I would have told you. I go to prepare a place for you."

She thought of these mansions, thought of the meeting there would be hereafter, and was comforted. She walked slowly back to the house, and wearily filled the vases. It was after all a labour of love, and it was sweet to be able to do it even *once* more. She grew fatigued towards the last, and there was still a heap of rose-buds remaining in the basket when Mrs. Burton suddenly appeared at the door.

"Julie, my child, where are you? They are coming. Frank declares he hears Allen's whistle, and is off to the slip-panel."

No more putting flowers into vases now. The basket, with its remaining blossoms, was hurriedly placed upon the floor, and Julie, pale and almost gasping with excitement, stood leaning on her mother at the front door, her blue eyes dilated to the utmost with the intensity of her gaze down the road.

"I thought you said they would not come till evening, mother," said Julie faintly.

"I thought so. But Allen must have come farther on his journey than he expected; and I see he prefers bringing his young wife to his own home first. I must leave you an instant, dear, just to see if Maggie is preparing tea. I dare say they will want it badly enough;" and away bustled the kind-hearted mother, anxious to see that nothing was omitted for the comfort of the young couple.

Yes; there they came down the old road, the horses prancing gaily. Allen caught a sight of Julie standing in the doorway, and waved his hat to her. It was too much for her excited feelings; she turned away, and ran to hide herself in the music-room. Another moment, and Allen entered, with his young wife leaning upon his arm. She was at home now. Mrs. Burton took her in her arms, and kissed her repeatedly, bidding her welcome as the mistress of the homestead.

"Her home!" Marian looked around it with a smile on her lips, but with swimming eyes.

Allen saw both smile and tears; he put his arm gently round her, and drew down her head to his shoulder. Mrs. Burton had gone out to superintend the tea.

"Your home now, my dearest!" he softly whispered. "Your cousin once prognosticated that you would be 'the light of some one's home,' but I little thought then that home would be mine."

"A poor, feeble little light, Allen," said Marian, smiling.

"No, darling—a pure, calm, sweet light, burning steadfastly from *within*. You will indeed be the light of *my* home. How happy am I in being that 'some one'!" he added, with a smile.

"Where is our Julie? Let us go and find her, dear Allen." And in a few moments after, what tears Julie had to shed were shed in the arms of her brother and sister.

CHAPTER XLV.

" As if she scarcely felt, but feign'd a sleep,
And made it almost mockery to weep."

" You look happy, my child, to-night," said Mrs
Burton, fondly, as she assisted in preparing Julie for
her bed.

They had returned home late that evening, leaving
Allen and Marian in full possession. Julie had turned
to take a last glimpse of them, as they stood together
at the door, in full light of the sitting-room, and a
glad feeling came rushing to her heart as she thought,
" All travelling one way—all seeking one kingdom—
all to meet in heaven ! "

" Yes, mother, I am happy, very, very happy," said
Julie, in answer to her mother's remark, and she
twined her thin arms round her neck, and tenderly
kissed her.

" I was thinking," she added, after a moment's
pause, " I was thinking how much I have to make me
happy. Allen and Marian, and *you*, dear mother,
all going with me to heaven, I know *you* all are.
Poor father, and Alf, and the rest !—but I feel that

will all be right, some day. I feel sure I shall meet you all again. That makes me happy, mother."

"It makes me happy, too, dear," said her mother, with tears in her eyes; "but I hope we shall yet be permitted to spend some time on earth together."

"And if *not*, mother—if not, you must try to feel that it is because *He* knows best—because all *He* does is in love;" and Julie looked wistfully at her mother as she spoke.

Mrs. Burton did not quite comprehend her; she only replied,—

"You are much better to-night, darling."

"Yes, I *feel* much better—only tired, very tired. I shall soon sleep—but kiss me first, mother."

Again and again the kiss was given and returned. How in after days that kiss and those words were remembered!

Softly the mother wandered about the room, hanging up dresses and folding away clothes. She placed the little table, with its cooling drink, between her own and Julie's bedside, drew the curtains to exclude the cold air, and shaded the night-lamp, lest it should disturb the repose of her child. When she again looked at her before seeking her own bed, she was calmly sleeping, her hands meekly folded upon the white counterpane—themselves almost as white.

"At midnight there was a cry made, Behold the bridegroom cometh!" But Julie was one of the wise virgins—there was oil brightly burning in her little lamp: for to *her* that cry referred.

At midnight that hitherto quiet chamber was the scene of lamentation and tears.

Julie had left them! Had left them in her sleep, left them without a sigh, without a struggle—a smile yet lingering round her lips. The white hands still lay folded upon the counterpane, the soft, fair hair, escaping beneath her little cap, was still pressed under the thin cheek, but *life* was gone! The pulse had ceased its motion, the heart had ceased to beat, the spirit was beyond the clouds.

It was the singularity of her sleeping so long that led to the discovery. Mrs. Burton at length, astonished by her long silence, left her bed, and hurriedly put back the curtains, stooping down to her child, and placing her hand on her white brow. Cold! cold! With a heart almost stopped in its action by a vague fear, she rushed to the lamp, and threw its broad light over the fair face.

With a wild cry she sank to the ground. The truth in that one glance was too apparent.

They carried her away from the room, and laid her in a distant chamber, far from the quiet sleeper. They gave her opiates to deaden her sorrow, but the memory of that moment never left her through the years of after-life.

Grief seldom kills; and she learnt eventually to look upon the Hand that took her child as the hand of love.

Sweet sleeper! No more sorrows for her, no more tears. The fair land was reached; her dreams were more than realized. Those whom she left behind sorrowed not " even as others which have no hope "— they looked forward to a happy re-union.

They laid her in her quiet bed at last, amidst the flowers she loved. At one end of the rose-walk, beneath a drooping willow, the little stone was erected. It was always a favourite resort of Allen and Marian in after-years. The simple headstone bore as simple an inscription—

To the Memory

OF

JULIE.

The grave itself was a bed of violets. These spoke more of love and affection than a volume of elaborate praise.

What more, gentle reader, have we to add? Our tale is told. If but one heart through its quiet teachings has learnt to discern a beauty in holiness; if one sinking spirit has been revived and strengthened in the Christian path; if one young friend has found that the paths of obedience are those of happiness, through the humble medium of the author's pen,—her highest ambition is more than satisfied.

THE END.

www.ingramcontent.com/pod-product-compliance
Lightning Source LLC
Chambersburg PA
CBHW032016120726
47902CB00013B/978